Praise for the Davis Way Crime Caper Series

"Funny and wonderful and human. It gets the Stephanie Plum seal of approval."

— Janet Evanovich

"Archer navigates a satisfyingly complex plot and injects plenty of humor as she goes. This madcap debut is a winning hand for fans of Janet Evanovich and Deborah Coonts."

— *Library Journal*

"Filled with humor and fresh, endearing characters. It's that rarest of books: a beautifully written page-turner. It's a winner!"

— Michael Lee West,
Author of *Gone With a Handsomer Man*

"As impressive as the amount of sheer fun and humor involved are the details concerning casino security, counterfeiting, and cons. The author never fails to entertain with the amount of laughs, action, and intrigue she loads into this immensely fun series."

— *Kings River Life Magazine*

"Davis's smarts, her mad computer skills, and a plucky crew of fellow hostages drive a story full of humor and action, interspersed with moments of surprising emotional depth."

— *Publishers Weekly*

"Archer's bright and silly humor makes this a pleasure to read. Fans of Janet Evanovich's Stephanie Plum will absolutely adore Davis Way and her many mishaps."

— *RT Book Reviews*

"Snappy, wise-cracking, and fast-paced."

— *New York Journal of Books*

DOUBLE WHAMMY

The Davis Way Crime Caper Series
by Gretchen Archer

Novels

Coming Soon

Bellissimo Casino Crime Caper Short Stories

DOUBLE WHAMMY

A DAVIS WAY CRIME CAPER

Gretchen Archer

DOUBLE WHAMMY
A Davis Way Crime Caper

Second Edition | June 2018

Gretchen Archer
www.gretchenarcher.com

Copyright © 2018 by Gretchen Archer
Cover design by The Creative Wrap
Author photograph by Garrett Nudd

Paperback ISBN-13: 9781983162244
Kindle ASIN: B07DQS3ZC1

Printed in the United States of America

For my husband, who's still running this show.

ACKNOWLEDGMENTS

I'd like to thank my tribe: Annette, Cynthia, Julie, Meredith, and Wendy. I love you girls.

Thank you, Bellissimo Players Club, for all the Pine Apples. And a special thanks to Amy, Cynthia, Christine, Linda, Lisa, Marilyn, Melanie, Shannon, and Tonette for your recipe contributions.

Thank you, Deke Castelman, for correcting my lightening to lightning so many times I finally learned it. Thank you, Stephany Evans, for sticking with me through thick and thin. Thank you, Susan Boyer, for the hydrangeas. Thank you, Julie Mulhern, for the coffee talks. Thank you, Larissa Reinhart, because they just don't come any better than you. Lastly, and mostly, thank you, Erin George, so very much.

ONE

A little unemployment goes a long, long way, and after more than a year of it, applying for every available position in L.A. (Lower Alabama), I took a right and tried Mississippi. At the end of the road I found Biloxi, where instead of applying for fifty different jobs, I applied for the same job fifty different times.

My final interview, like the dozen before it, began in a posh corporate office with an executive assistant at the Bellissimo Resort and Casino, Natalie Middleton. From there, the others had gone in several different directions. There'd been a marksmanship test with long-range pop-ups (I aced it), ink-blob and dot-to-dot psychiatric profiles (not sure how I did on those), and an extensive photo shoot with costume changes, tinted contact lenses, and wigs. I couldn't wait to hear what my last interview act would be.

"You'll be meeting with Richard Sanders," Natalie said, "our president and CEO. The final decision is his, and it will go quickly."

I'd applied for the job six weeks earlier. It was two hundred miles from where I lived. Most of the interviews had been all-day ordeals. It had already not gone quickly.

Richard Sanders' office had museum qualities: everything was quiet, valuable, and illuminated. Natalie directed me to a leather chair. "He'll be right in."

Right in, for the record, was almost an hour later.

I'd just helped myself to a fifth Red Hot cinnamon candy from the crystal bowl on Mr. Sanders' desk when a hidden door on the right side of the room slid open and a man stepped through, then froze, staring at me as if I was a ghost. I wondered who he was expecting. From the look on his face, not me.

He cleared his throat, then cautiously crossed the room with a guarded smile, hand outstretched. "Richard Sanders."

I skipped around the candy. "Davith Wathe."

He took his seat behind his desk and reached for the folder in front of him. I could see the right angles of a stack of photographs. Of me. The dress-up interview.

I sat up straighter, looking for somewhere to lose the candy. I gave him the once-over while he looked at the photographs, the whole time discreetly working the candy at top speed, the roof of my mouth on fire. Mr. Sanders was in his early forties, six-two, strikingly fit, blond, and either perpetually tan or just back from the Bahamas, since it was the dead of winter and he had a late-July glow about him.

He looked up. Baby blues. "Davis?"

The cinnamon disk burned going down. "Family name."

"Davis Way," he tried it on. "And you're from Pine—?"

"Apple." The hot candy brick was stuck sideways in my throat. "Two words?"

"Ach." I discreetly pounded my chest. "Garkle."

"Are you okay?" he asked.

I was anything but.

He pushed a button on his phone. Two seconds later Natalie returned. She gently patted me on the back, then landed one between my shoulder blades that almost knocked me into the next week. She poured me a glass of water while he slid the candy dish out of my reach. As soon as it appeared I would live, Natalie said, "Well then," and disappeared, leaving me alone with Richard Sanders again.

"Why don't we start over, Davis?"

"That'd be great."

"Where is Pine Apple, Alabama?"

"South of Montgomery."

Other than the Red Hots, the real-live Monet on the wall, and the expensive Oriental rug under my feet, I was in very familiar job-interview territory. I'd applied for everything with a heartbeat, and the resulting interviews had all had common elements. First, my name threw people off. In my thirty-two years it had been pointed out to me thirty-two thousand times that Davis Way sounded more like a destination than a person. After that, potential employers liked to suggest that I'd written down my hometown incorrectly. My resume clearly stated my credentials, including two college degrees, one in Criminal Justice and the other in Computer and Information Science. As such, would I really forget where I lived? Next, he would bring up my size, because I was considered undersized in general, but especially so for the line of work I was in. (I'm five foot two.) (And a half.)

He surprised me when he asked instead, "How large is the police force in Pine Apple?"

"There are two of us." There were two of us. Surely he'd read that far.

"Is there a lot of crime in Pine Apple, Alabama?" He leaned back, elbows to armrests, his hands meeting mid-chest. He rolled a thin platinum wedding band round and round his left ring finger.

"The usual," I said. "Domestic, vehicular, theft. We double as fire too."

"So you've had EMT training?"

"Yes."

"And you write computer programming?"

"I'm not sure I'd go that far," I said. "Pine Apple's a small country town, not exactly a hotbed of criminal activity. I had a lot of time on my hands and spent most of it on the computer."

"It says here you rewrote the program for incident reporting nationwide."

I hadn't put that on my resume. What else did it say there? "Not so much, Mr. Sanders. I only eliminated the inefficiencies of the old program and it went viral."

"Why do you want to leave Pine Apple, Davis?"

Oh, boy.

"You know what?" He looked at his watch. "Let's save that for later."

Yes. Let's.

He started up with the wedding band again. "I'm going to say something that could be construed as politically incorrect." He made direct eye contact. "With your permission, of course."

"Sure."

"I have a thirteen-year-old son who has at least five inches and fifty pounds on you."

There it was. "Is he my competition?"

Richard Sanders unexpectedly laughed. "Not hardly. Maybe if we were looking for someone to play Xbox."

"For all I know, Mr. Sanders, you *are* looking for someone to play Xbox." I surrendered. "I've been interviewing for this position for six weeks now, and I still don't know what it is."

"I don't either."

Could we get someone in there who did?

"Did Paul and Jeremy not go over it with you?" he asked.

"Who?"

"Paul and Jeremy," he said. "My security team."

I had nothing.

"Big guys," Mr. Sanders said.

Ah. Those guys. I remembered. The two mammoth men from my tenth interview I'd been trying hard to forget. One had no hair and the other had the biggest, brightest teeth I'd ever seen in my life. The bald one wore strange neckties and the one with the teeth dressed monochromatically—everything, tip to toe, the same color. Natalie introduced them as if I had no idea who they were. As if they hadn't been following me around since my first interview. I'd spotted one, the other, or both giants every time I'd been there. They'd jumped on elevators with me, the bald one had been at the shooting range, and the one with the teeth had actually followed me all the way home once. But on the day I officially met them, I played along. Nice to meet you, large total security strangers.

Then they drilled me for three solid hours on subjects far from security. My waitressing skills, or rather my lack thereof, had been heavily discussed. How did I feel about gambling? (I felt like you shouldn't do it with other people's money.) Would I care to explain that? (No, thank you.) How did I feel about hundreds of pounds of dirty linens? (Opposed.) How about scrubbing shower stalls? (Again, opposed.) Did I know or had I ever known or had I ever seen photographs of someone named Bianca? (No. Wasn't that a breath mint?) How many times had I been married? (None of your business.) Could I type? (How many fingers were we talking about?) Had I always been a redhead? (I wasn't one of those pale, freckled, flaming-red redheads. My hair was a coppery-caramel color, and my eyes were the same color, only darker.) Had I ever been convicted of or committed a felony? (Which one? Convicted or committed?) Either. Both. (There's a big difference.) Let's hear it. (I'd like to use a lifeline.) Did I have culinary skills? (Could I cook Pop Tarts? Yes. Do I know what to do with a dead chicken? No.) Had I ever held a customer service position? (Not specifically. More no than yes. Okay, no.) The hairless one asked me if I could operate an industrial vacuum cleaner. I didn't know such a thing existed.

If I thought I knew what the job was before those two, I sure didn't know after. And there I sat in my final interview with the president, and *he* didn't know.

I picked up my purse.

"Wait," Richard Sanders said.

I put down my purse.

"It's a new position, Davis, and a highly classified one. If I knew exactly what you'd be doing on a day-to-day basis, I'd tell you."

Finally, some bottom line.

"You'll be working undercover throughout the casino and hotel, and if you want to know more than that," he said, "you'll have to agree to the terms."

"Are you offering me the job, Mr. Sanders?"

"Do you want the job, Davis?"

I wasn't sure I wanted it. I was very sure I needed it. "The terms," I said, "what are they?"

"In a word? Discretion." He steepled his fingers, then used them as a pointer. "Your job is to be discreet."

"And?"

"Use discretion," he said.

Use discretion while being discreet?

"Don't talk to anyone on or off this property about your job," he said. "And don't reveal your identity under any circumstances."

"When do I start?"

"How soon can you start?"

"I'm good to go, Mr. Sanders. You say when."

"Today's as good a time as any." His hand went for the phone. "You can start now."

My eyebrows shot up. I didn't mean that very minute. I was thinking Monday. Or the Monday after that.

"Do you need time to think about it?" His hand hovered over the phone. "Because the iron is hot now."

Wait a minute. No one had said a word about ironing.

"Davis? Do you need a little time?"

Yes. "No."

"Good." He smiled. "Welcome to the Bellissimo."

And with that, I was well on my way to prison.

TWO

Natalie Middleton's office was adjacent to, and just as nice as, Mr. Sanders'. She had the Junior Suite. His smelled like cinnamon, hers smelled like roses.

Natalie was within a year, one way or the other, of my age. She was, as first line of defense to the president of a place like the Bellissimo would be, Cover Girl pretty, and always impeccably dressed. She wore very little makeup, and much of her medium-length, medium-brown hair escaped a silver clasp at her neck. Designer eyeglasses completed her sexy librarian look.

"First, Davis, I want you to know that your new job was my idea."

So she would know where the industrial vacuum cleaner fit in.

"Therefore, it's of utmost importance to me that you're successful. Whatever you need, come to me first. When you have information, bring it here. If you have questions," she said, "ask me."

"Start at the beginning," I said, though I should have been more specific. I meant the beginning of my new job requirements. She started with the Big Bang.

She gave me the corporate orientation speech, at length, to include Mississippi state gaming laws, barge permits, net revenues, the three movies filmed here, Hurricane Katrina, and had a lot to say about Cher. Then she told me about herself. Single, graduate degree in marketing, and she'd been Mr. Sanders' personal assistant for seven years. She told me who I could speak to: Mr. Sanders, herself, Jeremy Covey (the bald one) and Paul Bergman (the one with the big teeth). Then she talked about the resident royals: Mr. Sanders (very complimentary), Mrs. Sanders (not so much), their son Thomas (typical teenager), and in all of that, the word vacuum didn't come up.

"She's a Casimiro."

"Who is?" I asked.

"Mrs. Sanders."

"What's a Casimiro?"

She paused. "Really? You don't know?"

I shrugged.

"Her family owns half the Las Vegas Strip."

"Wow."

"Right. Avoid her at all costs," Natalie advised. "It won't be hard. When Mrs. Sanders is here, you won't be."

"Why is that?"

"She's hardly ever here, Davis." Natalie dodged the question. "It won't be that big a deal."

Either I wasn't asking the right questions, or she was deliberately giving me the wrong answers. I wanted some go here, go there. Shoot this, shoot that. "Natalie?" I asked. "What is my job other than avoiding Mrs. Sanders?"

"You're our new super-secret weapon." She stood. "Come with me."

I hopped up.

"Leave your things," she said, "we're not going far."

I dropped my purse in the chair, then followed her across the room at a clip. Natalie, if the espresso maker on her credenza was any indication, consumed large amounts of caffeine. Which might have been what her big rush was about. We were headed straight for a wall when she stopped so fast I all but ran into her.

"Get dressed." She pushed, and a seamlessly hidden door opened. "Then we'll talk more."

The door closed quietly behind me and left me alone in a lounge, but a lounge larger than my living room at Pine Apple Luxury Living Condos. If I had Natalie's job, I'd do it in there. It was library quiet, magazine beautiful, and who didn't love a secret chamber? And the clothes waiting for me were nicer than any stitch of clothing Alabama, the whole state of, sold. Ten minutes later, nine of them poking myself in the eye, I stared at a stranger in the mirror. The stranger, dressed in designer everything, had thick, dark, shoulder-length hair and envy green eyes. The only thing left of me were my shoes, because the boots Natalie had for me were too small. (Technically, the only thing left of me were my sister's shoes. I'd accidentally borrowed them.)

"I guessed you at a six," Natalie said when I braved her office again, a chocolate leather boot in each hand.

"Seven," I said.

"Now we know."

I stood there. Blinking my green eyes.

"You look great," she said.

I looked like someone else, which was, I suppose, the point.

"Have a seat."

I had a seat, trying not to move my head, on which I was wearing someone else's hair.

"Relax, Davis." Then she passed me a fat stack of paper. "Sign here, here, and here."

I signed there, there, and there.

She whisked away the paper and replaced it with a Marc Jacobs messenger bag. "Your room keys are in here, a little cash to get you going, a new cell phone, and an ID."

I had no idea what I'd just signed, but the wardrobe and accessories for my new job were great.

"You're already checked into your room, and everything you'll need for the next few days is there."

And still, I sat on the edge of the chair.

"Right." Natalie clapped her hands. "You need to know what to do."

Finally.

"As our new in-house investigator, Davis, your first assignment is to play video poker."

In-house what? I thought it was a security job. And how might one go about investigating video games?

"Double Whammy Deuces Wild." She stood and walked around her desk. "Got it? Go straight through the middle of the casino, then take a left for the Whammys. You can't miss them." She waited to speak again until she was sure she had my undivided attention. "Play it, learn it, come back and tell me how it's won."

Was that all?

"Good luck, Davis."

I swallowed hard.

"I hope you win."

THREE

Guest room 20027 was like everything else I'd seen of the Bellissimo, perfect. It was a showroom of luxuries and amenities, including a full ocean view, a fifty-inch LED television, and a bed too pretty to sleep in. The armoire held at least five days' worth of clothes, all my size, ranging in style from designer jeans to a peacock blue cocktail dress so pretty I was tempted to put it on right then. In the drawers I found silk pajamas, a Bellissimo t-shirt, and three more cashmere sweaters. It would seem that Bellissimo in-house investigators dressed to kill, and that might be the saving grace of my new job. Well, the expensive clothes and the gorgeous hotel room. Well, the expensive clothes, the gorgeous hotel room, and the paycheck. But in-house investigator? Police officer-to-investigator was the same as executive chef-to-fry cook. An in-house investigator was nothing but a private investigator who stayed put. Their cousins were mall cops and parking lot attendants. Investigative services were a thing of the past, when you couldn't find everything you never wanted to know about a person on social media. Facebook and Twitter were good for three things: meatloaf recipes, skip tracing, and proof of insurance fraud. These days, PIs were down to taking photos of cheating spouses, because it still took hard evidence in divorce court, especially when the stakes were high. (I knew all this firsthand.) And I seriously doubted the Bellissimo hiring me had anything to do with evidence against cheating spouses when they had, even I knew, better surveillance than NASA.

Why did these people hire me?

I dumped out the contents of the new Marc Jacobs bag onto the king-sized bed. Maybe the answer was in it. I found a cell phone and a wallet. Inside the wallet, I learned I was no longer Davis Way. My new name was Marci Dunlow, and I was from San Antonio, Texas—my photoshopped likeness on the driver's license was a dead ringer for my new look—and Marci had a thousand dollars in cash so fresh off the press I had trouble separating the bills to count them. Marci was tempted to put on the blue dress, take her thousand dollars, and head for the hills.

I opened my own purse, a beat-up Louis Vuitton knockoff, and dug for the noisy, bulky mass that hid the key to my black Volkswagen Beetle. First things first, I checked the room with my radio-frequency detector I never left home without. I found two signals: one emitting from the smoke alarm in the center of the ceiling (clever—who'd look there?) and one from Marci's cell phone on the bed.

What did they think they were going to hear in my hotel room?

Thankfully, there were no cameras—I'd have hit the road—and there were no bugs in the bathroom, which was always a good thing. It was spacious, decorated like the bedroom in a sort of antique French Riviera, with a recessed makeup table that would serve me well as a desk, so I deemed it headquarters. I sat on the wide edge of the bathtub with the two cell phones, my own and Marci's. Marci had the smartest phone I'd ever seen, borderline brilliant, with features I'd heard of and features I hadn't. I picked up my own phone, feeling sorry for it, and wondered why it smelled like a rose. I popped off the back, and found a new memory chip that Natalie had slipped in. ("Leave your things. I need to plant a bug.")

For the record, I didn't particularly trust them either.

It was time to go shopping.

* * *

No doubt someone was busy installing a tracking device on the car I'd parked in the seven-level garage adjacent to the main building. I didn't want to interrupt, so I decided to grab a cab.

The glitzy street entrance of the Bellissimo was packed with people—coming, going, working—and more cars than people, including limos, taxis, rideshares, and hopper buses. I could easily have gotten a ride there. But another more discreet entrance on the east side of the building had caught my eye. Almost every time I'd been there—interviews four, seven, eleven, and earlier that day—I'd seen the same dirty white taxi tucked a half a block from the doors, almost hidden behind thick landscaping, and I took off in that direction, heading east through the lobby. I thought I'd reached a dead end when I noticed gold lettering on dark-glass double doors to my right: VIP.

I took a deep breath and pushed through. This would be where the rich people checked in and out. I crossed the quiet room and stepped outside, where I was met by a blast of winter. January only looked like June on the Mississippi coastline. The difference was the icy wet wind whipping off the Gulf, and that entrance to the Bellissimo was two feet from it.

Three limo drivers perked up. Spotting the taxi I was looking for, I waved them off.

I woke the driver, a black man well into his sixties, with a knuckle on the window. He seemed none too happy to see me.

"Unavailable," he said without looking at me. "Off duty."

"Really?" I didn't want to put in another mile walking back to the main entrance. I dug out one of the hundred-dollar bills and slapped it against the glass. That got me a huge sound of disgust from the old man, then the door locks clicked open.

"Could you turn on the heat, please?" It was ten degrees colder inside the cab than out. He pushed a button on the dash, then the car filled with burning dirt.

"Do you want to go somewhere or not?"

I batted at the cloud of singed dust with both hands. Maybe not.

He drove me to a big box store several miles down a busy road. Each time I looked up, I caught the old guy staring at me in the rearview mirror instead of watching the road. I unearthed the seat belt and buckled up. No one had been in that cab in a decade, and I certainly didn't intend to get in it again if I managed to get out of it that time with life and limb. The only thing in it that wasn't an antique, including the driver, was a custom-installed satellite radio scanner. Odd, considering the scanner was worth more than the cab. I forgot all about it when he slammed to a stop so fast I added neck brace to my shopping list.

"I need you to wait on me."

"Then you'd better hurry," he said.

I purchased a pre-charged burner phone, had someone at the customer service desk break into it with a chainsaw, then made my way to the deserted automotive department, where I dialed my parents' phone number as slowly as humanly possible.

My mother could answer a telephone in the most hostile way imaginable. She said "hello" but it came out "WHAT?"

I steeled myself. And there it was.

"Mother, it's me."

A giant pause. "Well, Davis, so good of you to call. Make it quick; I'm in no mood to talk. In fact, talk to your sister."

(See?)

"Hey," my sister, Meredith, said, and thankfully her voice wasn't dripping hostility like Mother's. But then she ruined it. "Where are you? What are you doing? What's going on? Start talking."

"Give the phone back to Mother."

"I will not," Meredith—my rock, my shield, my salvation from Mother and my only sibling—was turning into our mother. "Davis? Why do you keep disappearing? We turn around and you're gone. Again."

I fingered the packages of windshield wiper blades that hung on hooks in front of me, getting them all swinging and bouncing off one another.

"I got a job in Biloxi."

I heard the back door squeak on Mer's end. "You did not."

"I did."

"Why?" Meredith demanded.

"Because I need a job."

"Why there, Davis?"

"You're the one who told me to get out of town."

"That's not what I said. And even if, there are a million other towns. Why Biloxi? How can anything good come of following him down there? You know if it was anyone but Daddy, you'd have restraining orders on you that would put you on a different planet from Eddie. You can't go sit in his lap. You'll be in jail by the end of the week."

Eddie. My rat ex-ex-husband, Eddie Crawford, formerly of Pine Apple, had been scratching his raging gambling itch in Biloxi for years. Yes, I married him twice. And yes, it would be a nightmare if Eddie and I crossed paths, because I had a $150,000 bone to pick with him, and he wanted me locked up.

I'd taken our second divorce pretty hard, if burning down his double-wide bachelor pad (he started it, I just didn't put it out), taking cheap shots at him with my service revolver (grazing his girlfriend Danielle once), and giving him salmonella poisoning constituted taking it hard. And that was just in the months leading up to the divorce. As a result of all that misbehaving, I lost my job, then got nailed in divorce court, which irritated me even more, often at three in the morning when it was just me and my laptop. Eddie found himself badly burned by identity theft, had a credit report that would prevent him from borrowing a wooden nickel for the rest of his miserable life, and one night I was so mad, I plastered him all over the National Sex Offender List. Eddie had the nerve to take me back to court, where Pine Apple's one and only judge—a friend of both our families—said that what I'd done to him was no worse than what he'd done to me, and he told us to stay far, far away from each other. For as long as we both shall live. Taking a job in the city where I knew he was wasn't exactly staying far, far away. I was well aware, and I didn't need my sister reminding me.

"This isn't Pine Apple," I said. "Fifty thousand people live here and fifty thousand more visit the casinos every day. It's not like I'm going to run into Eddie on the street corner. Besides," I scratched the itchy wig, "even if I did, he won't know me."

"He'd know you a mile into a dark cave, Davis, because you'd be the one shooting at him."

"You know Daddy took my gun. How am I going to shoot anyone?"

I could see my sister on the back porch, shivering in the January chill, a mirror of my mother thirty years ago, looking out over the seven acres that made up the family homestead.

"I finally found a job," I told my sister. "And I'm not getting anywhere near Eddie, because I don't want to lose it before I even get paid. You're the one who keeps saying I need to get my fresh start on."

"You're not going to get your fresh start on in the same city Eddie's in, Davis, and you know it. Job or no job."

Speaking of my new job, I needed to wind it up. A blue-vested boy who'd been hanging on my every word and peeking at me from between containers of transmission fluid and pine tree air fresheners had worked up the nerve to approach me directly. Not to mention I had a new purse full of my new employer's new money and should probably get back to my new job with it. "Cross your fingers for me, smooth things over with Mother, and don't tell Daddy anything. Let me handle that."

"Be careful, Davis."

"Meredith," I said, "you worry too much."

"Wait! Don't hang up! First of all, I want my shoes back."

Shoot.

"And second of all, where are you working? What will you be doing?"

"I'm not sure."

"You're not sure? Which part? Where or what?"

I heard the squeak of the back door. Meredith either went back into the kitchen or she was standing there with the door open to aggravate Mother by letting out all the heat. Wait. That would be me.

"When you figure it out," my sister said, "let us know."

"I will."

"Love you."

"You too." I blew her a kiss.

*   *   *

On the ride back to the hotel, Grumpy at the wheel, I stared out at the gray afternoon, wondering how the highlights—some might say lowlights—of my life had escaped an organization as seemingly shrewd as the Bellissimo. True, there was no hard documentation of my end-of-marriage misdeeds, but only because my father hadn't arrested me for them, and I knew how to get on and off a computer without anyone knowing. But truer than that was that our divorce played itself out on the sidewalks of Pine Apple, in the produce section of the grocery store, at the Gas and Go on Banana Street, and everywhere else Eddie and I happened upon each other. Every resident of Wilcox County, Alabama, knew every detail. How had the Bellissimo missed it?

I had a leg out the door, ready to be away from the surly cab driver, when I glanced up and caught him watching me again in the rearview mirror.

"Surely you don't expect a tip."

He continued to stare. I reached up to pat my head; maybe the wig was on fire.

"I'm going to give you some advice," he said. "First time and last time."

He pivoted slowly to face me directly. He had the eyes of a thousand-year-old-man, and they cut straight through. I pressed myself into the backseat.

He enunciating every word. "Get in your car and go back where you came from."

I probably shouldn't have slammed the car door that hard, but I didn't want advice from a total stranger. I had enough to last a lifetime from people who knew me.

FOUR

Twenty minutes later, with one last look in the mirror, it was a sure bet my own mother wouldn't know me.

I made my way from my hotel room to the casino (four miles, at least), a noisy, bright, and busy destination. Seven of my five senses overloaded. Other than the perfume of it all—liquor, cigarettes, desperation—it reminded me of Chuck E. Cheese's. Chuck E. Cheese's for grownups. There were flashing machines as far as the eye could see. Row after row after row. I was going to need a treasure map to find the Whammy game I was supposed to play.

Shoulders back, wig held high, I made my way through the middle of the casino. I had three cell phones riding inside leather on my right hip; their weight and placement reminded me, as my sister had earlier on the phone, of my pistol-packing days. Meredith had grown up at Mother's knee, learning how to knead dough. I cut my teeth on my father's lap, learning how to keep a gun oiled. And it was a good thing the bag was full of AT&T and not Smith & Wesson, because one of them went off. I stopped short and dug through the collection for the alarming one. "Davis Way."

"No, you're not."

Natalie Middleton.

"Take a right. The Double Whammys are on your right." I glanced up at the three thousand camera orbs dotting the ceiling. So my new employer had a listening device in my room, had bugged my phone, and was watching me. What had I gotten myself into? "Good luck." She hung up.

I looked right and saw a rotating neon sign announcing my

wandering days were over: Double Whammy Deuces Wild. Beneath that, a scrolling number was whizzing through the mid-seven thousands. That was it? They had me in witness protection over seven thousand dollars? They'd spent that much on the wardrobe and smartphone.

Nine gambling machines sat under the scrolling number marquee. Four lined one side, four backed up to them facing the other way, and one end was capped with a Double Whammy machine. Two elderly women were poking the display screens on my right.

I skipped the third seat and parked myself in the fourth.

I wasn't sure what I was supposed to do next.

The women cut their eyes my way. One half-smiled, then they both went back to their poking. I had the distinct feeling I'd invaded their territory.

Digging one of the crispy hundred-dollar bills from the cell phone collection, I inserted it into an opening on the front of the machine that seemingly wanted it. It had a blinking backlit graphic depiction of George Washington, strategically placed so you couldn't miss it. The machine gobbled up the money so quickly, I jerked my hand back.

A counter rolled up credits. I had one hundred. The touchscreen offered lots of options, and the shelf below it held buttons with the same offerings. I could deal, I could bet max, I could double, I could whammy (what?), I could hold. What in the world? I pushed bet max, because it was the one blinking.

Oversized video likenesses of playing cards turned over in five spots on the screen, each with a pleasant plinking noise. I stared at the screen a little longer. An entirely new set of options were offered as the machine began singing an impatient song.

"You got a whole fleet!"

I turned to my right. One of the elderly women was speaking to me. She repeated the odd phrase.

"Excuse me?"

"You got sailboats, honey."

"Fours," her friend said. "Fours look like sailboats. You got four fours. That's a whole fleet."

Oh dear. I looked from them to the screen, then back to them. "What do I do now?" My new hair swung back and forth with my head. All the fours, or the sailboats as it were, had a word flashing across their hulls: HOLD.

"Take the money and run," the first woman said.

"Shouldn't I try to get *five* fours?" Clearly, the machine had malfunctioned, because it was also advising me to hold the red two, occupying the middle slip between all the boats. And it didn't match.

The two women exchanged a look. The one closest to me leaned in, "Honey, there aren't five fours in a deck of cards."

And that wasn't a deck of cards.

"And besides, you *have* five fours," the other said. "Your deuce is wild!"

Were these women speaking a different language?

"You could Whammy," the first one said, "but I wouldn't—"

Too late. I pushed the big red blinking Whammy button before she had the warning out, if for no other reason than to shut up the edgy machine. Then, as if I wasn't confused enough, the machine put larger cards in front of me, but only two. Where'd my boats go?

"Pick," one of the women said. "You have to pick a card."

Easy enough. I tapped the one on the left. It flipped over and revealed a four of the suit that looks like a paw print. Clubs, I believe. And they said the machine didn't have any more fours.

Both of the women sucked in a breath. Before I could ask if I'd done something wrong or try to scoot the new four in with the absent old fours, of its own free will, the machine turned over the other card: a three of hearts.

"Well, I'll be dipped," one of the ladies said.

"Holy Moses," the other said.

"Double Whammy," they said in unison, shaking their heads.

"Did I win?" I asked. The machine was screaming.

"Sixteen hundred dollars, honey. On your first spin," one said.

"I've never seen anyone whammy on a four," from the other.

I could get used to this.

And I did.

* * *

On my second afternoon of gainful employment, I woke the same grouchy cab driver by slapping a different hundred-dollar bill against the window, one I'd earned. Sorta. I wasn't really clear as to whose money the gambling winnings were, so I thought it best not to wire any of it to my bank in Alabama, but spending a little on necessities, cabs and such, seemed permissible. I had the surly driver—as happy to see me that day as he'd been the day before—take me to the closest electronics superstore, almost forty minutes away with him at the wheel, because he stopped at all traffic lights and waited for them to turn red.

"You know," I said, "it's dangerous to stop at yellow lights. You're going to get hit."

He threw it in park. Right in the middle of the intersection. "Do you want to drive?"

This would be my last clandestine mission; I'd had enough of him.

He parked as far away from the door as he could and pulled a black knit cap over his face.

I sat there a second. "Would you mind dropping me at the door?" It was cold.

He lifted the cap to reveal one bloodshot eye. "You got legs. Use 'em."

I'd been in the casino since nine that morning, ending my gambling shift after eight straight hours, when four lovely ladies lined up in a row: queen, queen, queen, queen! I whammied, my ten beating the machine's eight, and my new friends, the sisters Maxine and Mary who, it turned out, were locals, retired school teachers, and came to the casino every day except Sunday (the Lord's Day), celebrated with me. They called four queens a hen party, which I thought was funny. The game was entertaining, the elderly women great company, the drinks kept coming. When I remembered, with a jolt, that I was supposed to be working, I calmed myself with the certainty that if Natalie Middleton wanted me to stop, she'd let me know.

As jobs went, I may have hit the jackpot.

Inside the store, I purchased the world's smallest laptop computer. I would have happily used the laptop delivered to my room while I was downstairs lining up snowmen (eights) and cowboys (kings), instead of taking it for granted I could spend the gambling winnings that weren't technically mine, but I didn't want Natalie, or anyone else, tracking my cyber steps. If they'd bugged my room and phone, they'd certainly cloned the computer. I needed my own secure computer for my bathroom office.

Not soon enough, we were back at the Bellissimo.

"Are you the only cab driver on this side of the building?"

"Who wants to know?"

"Never mind."

Thankfully, he had no advice for me today.

The computer, only slightly larger than a hardback book, easy to hide, cost a little more than two hundred dollars and couldn't do much, which was fine; I wasn't trying to hack into government databases or write a dissertation in a hotel bathroom. The scrambling software I downloaded onto it cost quite a bit more.

Back in my room, sans itchy wig, it took ten minutes at my vanity desk to learn the game the sisters and I were playing reached a positive expectation point for the players when the jackpot climbed past seven thousand eight hundred dollars, which it was closing in on. It was simple math calculated after a quick computer search yielded a complicated website called Winner Winner Chicken Dinner Video Poker Calculator. I plugged in the numbers it asked for, which took donning the wig again for a midnight trip downstairs to memorize the machine's payout schedule. The chicken calculator came back at me with this advice: Play the game after the big number goes past seven thousand eight hundred. At which point, so said the chicken, the player's chances of winning the big pot by being dealt a royal flush—a ten, jack, queen, king, and ace of the same suit—were optimal.

That would be the hot iron Mr. Sanders mentioned.

* * *

Feeling froggy on the third morning of my new lease on life, I took my time getting ready for work, which was to say I flipped the pillow to the cold side and slept until ten. When my toes finally found the thick carpet, I emptied aromatherapy bath salts into the lap pool of a bathtub across from my vanity desk and stayed there aromatherapying myself so long I had to take a shower to recover from taking a bath. Thirty minutes later, I was in front of the mirror admiring myself in yet another new outfit, and anxious to join my new friends Maxine and Mary at the poker game.

Five hours into my workday, I was stuffing my winnings into my bra, because my purse couldn't hold any more money.

Six hours after that, I was back in my room, standing at the same window-wall, this time counting the stars. I climbed into bed with a goofy grin on my face, which might have been about the three glasses of wine I'd had for dinner, but I didn't think so. My warm glow was a result of having landed the World's Greatest Job.

The next day, I quit.

FIVE

Morning Four of the World's Greatest Job began peacefully enough.

"How do you know all this?" I asked the sisters. I'd just taken my seat, and before I could even prime the video poker machine with cold, hard cash, Mary and Maxine began telling me what I'd missed so far. Their shift started at eight o'clock sharp; my shift started after I talked myself into the wig.

"We taught school for forty years, Marci. We see everything," Maxine said.

"We can spot troublemakers from a mile away," Mary added. "We know a prankster when we see one."

From Maxine and Mary's sixty-hour-a-week perches, they watched the comings and goings in the casino, and were very well-versed in all things Bellissimo.

"So this man is having an affair with two women, and they're both here today?" I asked.

"I think there's going to be a cat fight before the day's over," Mary said.

"He's the pit boss," Maxine said of the two-timer. "And both the girlfriends are blackjack dealers."

"And get this, Marci." Mary leaned in. "He's *married*."

"Nooooo!" I threw my condemnation in there too.

So the guy was a three-timer. That couldn't be good for the pit he was boss of. I took a pause to watch the sisters, who expertly played the games in front of them, all the while keeping tabs on the dramas unfolding at the blackjack tables and beyond. It wasn't necessarily the video poker that brought the sisters there every day;

it was the soap opera of it. All My Addictions.

We played until noon with the sisters giving me the dirt on almost everyone passing by—their fellow regulars, the barely-dressed girls passing out cocktails, and the purple-jacketed people who made up the casino floor security team.

"Those security people are just here for show," Maxine said. "They're good for nothing unless your machine jams up. Not a one of 'em could catch a cold."

Not necessarily welcome news.

"Now, that bartender?" Mary tipped her head. "He clocks in then sleeps till noon. He gets between those whiskey bottles and acts like he's doing paperwork, but he's sawing logs."

I nodded along. "Why doesn't the other bartender say something?"

"Because when the one is sleeping, the other one isn't ringing up drinks," Maxine explained. "He's getting out of the way of the cameras and pocketing the cash."

"And that one there?" Maxine gave a nod to a passing server carrying a tray loaded with liquor at nine in the morning. "She's pregnant again but doesn't want anyone to know just yet."

"She had a little girl last October," Mary said. "Seven pounds, eleven ounces."

Maxine leaned in. "Named her Devon. Isn't that cute? Devon?"

I hit two straights in a row, whammying the second time. After several false starts, I worked up the nerve to ask the question Natalie Middleton wanted answered. "Ladies," I cleared my throat, "how do you win that?" I pointed to the dazzling marquee above our heads.

"The jackpot?" Mary asked. "You don't."

"We don't, anyway," Maxine added. "It will hit tonight about midnight."

"Really?" I asked. "How do you know?"

"Because it's time."

The three of us looked up. $7,883.60. $7,883.97. $7,884.22. The Chicken website and the Sisters were in agreement.

"And we've watched them do it," Mary said.

"Watched who do what?"

The sisters communicated silently, debating. Maxine gave Mary the go-ahead nod, then Mary motioned me into the sister circle. We huddled. They wore the whispers of the beauties they'd been back in the day, and they wore bright red lipstick that was sneaking away from their thin lips.

"There's a man who works here who has teeth so white they'll blind you," Mary said. "He's a big ole guy, Dapper Dan type, and he has great big white teeth."

I knew who they were talking about.

"He comes by late," she said, "when there's not a soul in sight, and I don't know what he does, but the game flashes."

"It what?" I asked.

"It just bleeps." Maxine clapped her hands. "He walks by, doesn't even really slow down, but when he's ten feet gone," she said, "the whole game goes black for a second, then it pulls right back up. It's real quick."

"And you've seen this?" I asked.

"Four times," Maxine said.

Mary held up four crooked fingers.

I nodded. Go on.

"The big guy leaves, then about twenty minutes later," Mary said, "a really good-looking young man comes and wins it."

"Every time?" I asked. "Same two guys every single time?"

"About every three weeks," Mary said, "like clockwork. We leave in the evening and the total is seven thousand eight hundred and change. We come back the next morning and its reset back down to five thousand."

"We just can't stay up that late," Maxine said.

"Does the good-looking young man work here too?" I asked.

"No," Maxine said. "He's from a little city in Alabama."

"Pine something," Mary said.

Then on the same beat, "His name is Eddie."

* * *

Natalie Middleton was nowhere to be found, so I quit my new job in writing on a sheet of paper I tore off her monogrammed notepad. I told her I'd wait in my room until I heard from her. I left it taped to her espresso machine.

She asked me to play the game (check), learn it (check, check), and figure out who was winning it (check, check, check). That was where and why I quit. I couldn't turn Eddie Crawford in. If I pointed one finger at Eddie Crawford, he'd point all ten of his at me. (Or would that be eight?) It wouldn't get ugly; it would come out of the gate ugly. They wouldn't hold Eddie ten minutes after he started spilling my secrets, then they'd be slapping the cuffs on *me*. And my father had no jurisdiction in Mississippi. At the very least, I'd be out on the street. Finding a new job after I'd been fired from my last one had taken more than a year. Finding a new job after being fired from two would take, what? Ten years? Thirty?

I couldn't believe it was happening.

It wasn't that I didn't want my sister to be right (again), (which I didn't), about this town not being big enough to hold both me and rotten, rotten, snake-in-the-grass Eddie Crawford. And it wasn't that I was so thoroughly exhausted with Eddie Crawford tripping me up at every single turn. (For two decades.) (Which I was.) It wasn't even the combination of the two. The problem was, and the reason I quit my new job was, it smelled like a trap. I only knew one thing about my new job: my new employers wanted me to figure out the whammy-whammy game, and that could only mean they already knew something wasn't right with it. If the something wrong was my ex-ex-husband, I had a way bigger problem on my hands than being out of work again. Because taking him down wouldn't just be the end of him. It would also be the end of *me*.

There wasn't even a remote possibility that Eddie Crawford had set up the Whammy sting. Eddie Crawford couldn't set up breakfast. That meant it was either a nightmare of a coincidence (I didn't even believe in coincidence) or someone at the Bellissimo was playing me.

Best, all things considered, to never know.

So much for my new start on life. I could find another job playing dress up and casino games (luxury accommodations included), that passed out cash and was on the beach.

In about a million years.

* * *

After some liquid courage from the minibar in my hotel room, I decided Natalie wasn't going to call and the best thing to do was leave. She'd figure it out. During this decision-making process, though, I accidentally took a little nap. I napped through the night, and I'd have probably napped until noon if bells and alarms hadn't started blaring. The sirens were coming at me from all directions: the phone in my purse, another on my vanity desk in the next room, and beside the bed.

I batted for the closest one.

"Davis, be in my office in an hour."

I protested vehemently, but only after Natalie hung up. It was then that I remembered the previous day's events and the fact that I'd quit my new job.

I reached up and gently examined my head to see if it might have railroad spikes sticking out of it. I tried to recall the events of the previous evening, and the only thing that stood out was the minibar. I looked around without moving my head and located the fridge.

Yep. Wide open and almost empty.

I lobbed one limb at a time off the bed and didn't get anywhere near upright when I attempted to stand. It was all I could do to walk across the floor, because it was a landmine of teeny wine bottles. I drank three gallons of water straight from the tap, then washed down a Migraine Unlimited with a fourth.

* * *

Natalie Middleton's office always smelled like there were a dozen roses in it, but it wasn't my best day, so the bouquet of Natalie almost knocked me down. She dropped her sexy glasses in the middle of her desk, sat back, crossed her arms, and waited for me to sit.

I glanced at Mr. Sanders' closed door.

"He's in Dubai."

Do what?

"How are you this morning, Davis?"

I gave her the blankest of blank looks. "Did you not get my note?"

"I did." She waved it. "Did you not get a copy of the employment agreement you signed?"

She was talking about the stack of papers I'd signed there, there, and there.

"You agreed to work here for a minimum of ninety days or reimburse us the cost of hiring you. So your choices are to write me a check or fulfill your commitment." She crushed my resignation letter into a gumdrop-sized ball. "Up to you, Davis."

Not good.

"It's a simple breach of contract," she explained, "just as lying on your application, withholding pertinent information, or misrepresenting yourself during any of your interviews would be breach of contract."

Worse.

"How much money are we talking about?"

"Oh, I don't know." Natalie pushed the resignation gumdrop around. "Somewhere in the starter-home range."

"It cost a starter home to hire me?"

"Your background checks took an unusual amount of resources, Davis."

The very worst.

"I asked you to play the game, learn it, and tell me how it's won," she said.

All of which I'd done, before I hit the Eddie wall.

The room grew quiet.

It was hard to tell if I knew something she needed to know or if she knew something I needed to know.

Probably both.

"Natalie, if you think someone is cheating the Whammy game, if someone is stealing the jackpot, why can't you just arrest him?"

"Him?"

"Or her! Or it!"

"No, Davis. We can't just arrest *him* for winning. I want to know *how* he wins it. That was your assignment."

"Can't you ask the man with the big teeth?" I was trying to come up with Teeth's name. I grabbed for my phone and pulled up the contact list. "Jeremy?"

"Jeremy?"

"Is he the bald-headed one?" I asked.

"Yes."

"Then the other one," I said. "The one with the really white teeth."

"Paul," Natalie supplied.

"Right."

"Why would I ask Paul?"

Something in the tone of her voice let me know we'd changed lanes. I had no idea why, nor did I want to know. "I thought I saw him," I said.

Natalie's fingers tapped out a tune on her desk. "He works here, Davis. You'll see both Paul and Jeremy often." She rose, poured two cups of espresso, then returned.

I thanked her, then burned my mouth.

"I'll give you the chance to make this right in a few weeks when the jackpot climbs back up. You can try again." She picked up the gumball that was my resignation, then let it drop on her desk. "And I'm going to ignore this." She leaned in, taking me into her confidence. She spoke slowly. "I don't know if you saw a ghost, or if someone offended you, or if you simply don't like the food here."

"Oh, I love the food."

"Good to know, Davis." She rolled her eyes. "Good." She sat back and crossed her arms. "You're welcome to go if you want to," she gave the door a nod, "but you've made a ninety-day commitment, and I'll need a check from you before you leave."

I was brokity-broke-broke-broke. And then some.

"I went to bat for you, Davis."

I saw a little mean streak in her I hadn't met before.

"And I don't want to talk to Mr. Sanders and have him ask me how it's going with you, then have to tell him this." She tapped the resignation ball.

I slinked around in the chair.

She passed me a teal-blue canvas duffel with caramel leather trim. "Take the weekend, Davis, and be back here Monday morning at eight. Your assignment won't be in the casino."

I couldn't think of a thing to say, but opened my mouth and spoke anyway. Mostly vowels.

"That'll be all, Davis."

* * *

Welcome to Pine Apple, Alabama. Population 447.

We thought of ourselves as larger, counting every beating heart, including livestock, but the fact remained, Pine Apple was too small for me to sneak home and my mother not know. There were twenty miles of AL-10 to cover between I-65 (civilization) and Pine Apple (back, back woods), and on my way home that day, my mother's phone must have rung every other mile marker. "Davis just zipped by here, Caroline."

At each and every family gathering a story was told. Somehow, someway, at some point, someone sneaked it in. My mother, a maverick of her day, went to college. She swapped her mortarboard for a white veil and married my father the afternoon of the same day she graduated. There was where the bottom dropped out for

Caroline Annette Davis Way—she immediately became pregnant with me.

The obstetrician asked her if she wanted to hold her baby. "No," she said. "Give her to her father."

Daddy and I had been inseparable since. I worshiped the ground he walked on, meanwhile my hair stands on end at the very thought of Mother.

One lazy Alabama afternoon when my sister, Meredith, was pregnant with her daughter, Riley, I sat at one end of the porch swing with Meredith, propped on pillows and stretched across, resting her swollen feet in my lap. We were drinking the kind of lemonade that's nine parts sugar and one part lemon, swatting mosquitoes and praying for her labor to begin. "What if my baby and I end up like you and Mother, Davis? What if the baby and I just don't like each other?"

My phone rang.

It was my mother.

I didn't answer. She wouldn't kill the messenger who told her I was moving to Biloxi. I needed a messenger.

* * *

I drove straight to the police station.

"There's my girl!"

I collapsed into my safe place without speaking. My safe place wrapped his arms around me.

"Where have you been, Sweet Pea?"

"Daddy," I took the perp seat beside his desk, "I got a job."

"It's a good thing, because your landlord's threatening to evict you."

"Mother's so full of hot air." I dropped my purse to the concrete floor. "If she evicts me, she'll have to move all my things home."

"She claims she's going to have the Goodwill pick up your things."

"Isn't the property in your name too? Can't you control your own wife?"

"I'm much better at controlling her than I am you."

I took a swat at him.

"Your mother is looking for you, by the way."

"I know. Is she the only one? Has anyone else been nosing around about me?"

"Let's have a cup of coffee," he said, "then we'll talk."

It made the back of my knees cave to see my father aging. He was the best man in the world. He was the greatest gift I'd ever been given, the smartest and bravest person I would ever know, all the way around, my hero. And my hero, who I truly believe hung the moon in the sky, now rose from his chair with an unconscious groan, and when he sat back down, placing a cup of coffee in front of me, he did it on a deep sigh.

"Oh, these old bones," he said.

"I love you, Daddy."

He smiled, and the gullies around his eyes deepened. "Now what have you gotten yourself into, young lady?"

I squirmed, wondering what I could and what I should say. "It's security work."

"That much I gathered."

"With one of the casinos in Mississippi."

"In Biloxi," he said.

Meredith ratted me out.

"Don't blame your sister."

Daddy read my mind.

"Blame Blanche."

Someone needed to go down for this. Might as well be Blanche, one of Pine Apple's two bank tellers.

"She called several weeks ago because your debit card was being swiped in Biloxi, and since then, by my count, you've been there seven more times." He crossed his arms and leaned back. "I'm relieved to hear you say this is about a job, and not about Eddie." He smiled. "Congratulations."

World's Greatest Father.

"Now, what can I do to help, Davis?"

Universe's Greatest Father.

* * *

On Sunday, I cleaned house—closets, drawers, and cabinets—then attempted to put it back in a more orderly fashion. I didn't intend to give up my apartment just yet, but should Mother make good on her threat to give away my worldly possessions just because my rent was a few dozen months late, I could have Meredith intervene. It would be easier for my sister if she didn't have to decide what to do with the baton collection leftover from my high school fire-twirling days. Anything that in any way reminded me of my marriage went into black lawn-and-garden bags.

It was time.

Throwing away stack after stack of four-year-old magazines, restraining orders (so unnecessary), and eviction notices (from my own mother) gave me time to think. My head finally clear of the minibar party for one I'd had the night before, it occurred to me that Natalie Middleton hadn't asked me to tell her who won the Double Whammy game at all; she wanted to know *how* it was won. I had eighty-something work days to figure out how the game was won and avoid Eddie the Ass while I was at it. The further I went down the I-screwed-up road, the hotter my face felt. Natalie Middleton probably thought I was crazy. I blamed it on the clock: gambling round the clock, liquor available round the clock, and clocks in general, because time healed all divorces, and I was tired of waiting on it.

The clock struck three when I threw out the last of my old life, and with that done, I mentally wiped my new job slate clean. I'd show Natalie Middleton I could be trusted to stay on my rocker, I was grateful to her for giving me a second chance, and I couldn't wait to check back into my hotel room. The Bellissimo was a big place and Eddie Crawford didn't know Marci Dunlow. He wouldn't know it was me if I walked up and slapped him. I turned to see

Daddy's patrol car winding down the long drive.

We sat at the kitchen table, a football game on television providing background music.

"I wish I had something to offer you, Daddy, but tap water's it."

"I'm fine."

"There's no reason for me to fill this place up with groceries." I gestured wide. "I'm leaving for Biloxi in a couple of hours."

"About Biloxi," my father said, then landed a case file between us.

It turned out Richard Sanders, President and CEO of the Bellissimo Resort and Casino, began his career at the age of sixteen as a part-time bellman at Glitz, a 4,500-room hotel and casino on the Las Vegas Strip. He remained employed by Glitz through college, then UNLV's graduate program. A few short years later he was the casino manager, and engaged to marry the owner's youngest, Bianca Casimiro. Fifteen additional years brought us to today. The Sanders had one child, Thomas, the Xbox gamer who was twice my size. The move to Biloxi happened seven years earlier, the same month I was dragging my feet down the aisle for the second time, when the Casimiros, already the owners of eight resorts in Las Vegas proper and two in New Jersey, acquired additional properties in Indiana, Louisiana, and Mississippi. All cash deals.

"Who has billions in cash sitting around?" I asked.

"Casinos."

Right.

"This," my father pushed a photograph my way, "is the man who had lunch at Mel's."

"Teeth."

Daddy rotated the picture and took another look. "He does have a mouthful."

"If he mentioned my name at Mel's, you know he got an earful." They didn't serve anything at Mel's but cholesterol, heartburn, and the We Hate Davis special. Mel, of Mel's Diner, a run-down greasy spoon and permanent resident on the Health Department's disaster list, was my former father-in-law. My former mother-in-law, Bea, ran the cash register and her mouth.

"This fella," Daddy slid another mug shot my way, "is the one Meredith met."

"No Hair."

Meredith owned a curiosity shop one block east of the police station, on the first floor of the three-story antebellum my father grew up in. The main parlor was where she sold toys, doodads, antique toys, and antique doodads. The former library was also the current library, where Meredith kept the rare and collectible books, mostly mysteries, packed in the old floor-to-ceiling wall shelves and displayed in antique curio cabinets. People came from everywhere for those dusty old books—go figure—but never stayed. Which was how she met Riley's father, who didn't stay either. The library (where Riley was conceived, not something Meredith broadcasted) led to the old sitting room she kept stuffed with racks and trunks of vintage clothing, and she'd converted the kitchen to accommodate an old-fashioned soda-fountain lunch counter, with huge glass jars full of old-fashioned candy, like licorice jujubes, bubblegum cigars, and Razzles. She served homemade vegetable beef soup and grilled-cheese sandwiches she prepared with three slices of buttered Texas toast and a pound of cheese. It was a heart attack on a plate, and my father ate one every single day. You needed a crane to pick it up and a nap immediately after.

Meredith had it going on. Not only did Mother and Daddy both like her, she was a wonderful mother, had an endless supply of energy and imagination, she was crafty, clever, and six inches taller than me. It was a wonder we spoke.

"He told her he was just passing through," my father said.

"Sure he was. To where?"

Daddy drummed his fingers on the table. Everyone knew Pine Apple didn't lead to anywhere else.

"What did she tell him about me?"

"She didn't. He didn't ask. He poked around, had a chocolate malted, bought three books, a handful of old neckties, then left."

I wasn't surprised about the ties.

"And this last guy," my father pushed an index card my way, then tapped it. "George Morgan? Nothing, Sweet Pea. I couldn't pull up a current residence, a full Social, or even a library card. I couldn't find where he's ever purchased a piece of property, borrowed a dime, been in the Big House or the military. All I could find was a vehicle registration and license, and you gave me those. Who is this guy?"

"He's my driver."

"Your driver might be living in his car."

I suspected as much.

"How is he in play, Davis?"

"I think he's been on the job."

"Is that so. And?"

I shrugged. "Makes you wonder." Which it didn't. We both knew why a former law enforcement officer might fall off the grid, and it wasn't pretty.

"Watch your back, Davis."

"Always, Daddy."

I watched from the window until his taillights disappeared. The sun would set all too soon, and I had three hours of road to cover.

I'd savored the surprise of what great getup Natalie had in store for me until then, only glancing at the duffel bag expectantly. Not peeking. The dress-up aspect of my new job was the best part—it made me feel anonymous, and I loved the clothes. I unzipped the bag slowly, tooth by tooth, like opening a present. Natalie Middleton had missed her calling; she should have been a personal shopper instead of a personal assistant.

Inside the duffel, I found a sealed envelope with my name handwritten across the front. In it, I found a short page of instructions, a car key on a round silver ring, and a tarnished metal key on a green plastic fob, number thirty-four and EconoLodge stamped in flaking gold ink. Under the envelope was a maid's uniform, plus flesh-colored support hose, a dark brown ponytail wig, and thick-soled white industrial shoes. Size seven.

SIX

The EconoLodge was horrible. The housekeeping job even worse. Two weeks into both, I was sleep deprived, my hands were raw and blistered, my back broken, my feet blown up to small pillows, and I didn't have a clue who was stealing money from guest-room safes. More than that, I barely cared.

The good news was I'd all but forgotten the bad taste my first Bellissimo assignment had left me with, and the drudgery of this new assignment only had a bad odor. My ninety-day commitment was down to the high sixties.

A heap of junk that Natalie insisted was a rental car was parked outside room thirty-four at the EconoLodge the first night. "Housekeeping personnel don't drive brand new shiny cars, Davis. Drive the rental back and forth to work."

That pile of scrap metal reeked, died twice at red lights, and the radio only hissed. I decided quickly that my first commute in it would also be my last. I'd rather take the bus. I'd rather hitchhike. I'd rather crawl. I parked it in the employee parking garage, which, as it turned out, was in a totally different zip code than the Bellissimo. As I switched off the ignition the engine backfired, the amplified bomb blast bouncing off the concrete walls, taking ten good years off my life. I left that rattletrap there for good. I left the keys in it, very tempted to leave it running. I could walk to work and back in thirty minutes. It wouldn't kill me.

Eight hours later I was so near death that walking to the EconoLodge would have been the last straw. At the end of my first day with Guest Services, I felt like I'd pulled a log truck uphill by the bit between my teeth all day. I'd been screamed at in rapid-fire Spanish often and at length. I'd been forced to hover over an endless succession of toilets. I'd inhaled toxic chemicals all day. I'd manhandled mountains of suspicious bed sheets. I'd picked up a thousand gooey bars of soap, and, possibly the worst, I shattered a mirror into a million shiny slivers.

As I stood in line to punch out, everyone else jabbering cheerily as if they'd spent the day poolside, the very effort of inhaling and exhaling was about all I could manage and walking to the hellhole EconoLodge was no longer an option. The thought of meeting up with the clunker I'd already said goodbye and good riddance to almost brought me to tears, and then I remembered my friendly cabbie.

I couldn't very well whistle through VIP in my maid getup and hail myself a taxi, so I left through the employee service entrance and circled around the property on foot, which was about six miles cross country; I could have walked to the EconoLodge just as easily. George was right where I left him, and he was asleep. I found a nice big magnolia tree to hide behind and lobbed cherry LifeSavers, one at a time, onto the hood of the dirty white car.

The LifeSavers came from a guest room I'd all but licked clean, at the bottom of a basket of goodies the room's last occupant had walked off and left, along with a rancid water glass full of drowned cigarette butts on a non-smoking floor. The rule seemed to be if the guest was still a guest, leave everything as close to where I found it as possible. If the guest had checked out, anything they left behind was fair game. All explained to me in pantomime.

I eyed the basket.

Finder's keepers—the only, single, solitary perk of this job.

There were only two LifeSavers left when George finally stirred, craned in my direction, and beckoned me with no energy and no recognition.

I ducked my head and made a run for the backseat.

He let out a huge sigh. He didn't turn when he said, "You make a better redhead."

I froze. I stared at the back of his head until he turned around and acknowledged me. We locked eyes. "Shut up, George, and drive."

He cranked her up. "Where to?"

"The EconoLodge."

I swear I heard him snicker.

We pulled into the parking lot, and he drove straight to my Volkswagen. I knew I was right about him; he'd been on one side or the other of the law. Otherwise, he'd have had no idea what I drove. Or what color hair was under the wigs.

"What time do you want me to pick you up in the morning?"

(See?)

I huffed. "Six forty-five." I passed him a plastic bag full of loose change I'd collected off nightstands and dressers. He shook the bag, then looked at me.

"What? I can't pay you a hundred dollars every time you drive me three blocks!" I got out, slammed the door, and braced myself for my next chore—surviving the EconoLodge a second night.

* * *

"It couldn't be *that* bad," Natalie said. "There's very little turnover in housekeeping."

"That's because they're raking in the dough on that job. The housekeepers are filling up ten bags a day each with loot from the rooms."

At the end of my second week, Natalie and I were having a sit-down at the casino next door, the Gold Mine, hidden amongst gigantic slot machines.

"Why are we here?" I'd asked.

"I love their coffee," she'd replied.

"The job is nasty, Natalie," I told her. "The hotel guests are just *gross*. And they steal everything that isn't nailed down. Today? Today I had a room with a lamp missing. I cleaned the same room yesterday and the lamp was there."

"What about the safes?"

Each guest room had a ten-inch recessed wall safe inside the closet. It was there to tease the guests: *Go to the casino and get a pile of money to put in me.* When the guests checked in the little vault was wide open, the instructions loud and clear: leave this as you found it. If the guests had any reason to use the safe, they program their own top-secret four-digit code that allowed access to whatever valuables they'd placed in the safe, and if they happened to check out without opening it, the housekeeper had to stand there and try four-digit number combinations until they guessed the correct one.

Just kidding.

Ninety-nine percent of the time the wall safes, like the two sheets of Bellissimo stationery in the desk, weren't touched. Here's an interesting fact: the Gideon organization doesn't put Bibles in casino hotel rooms. Did that make any sense? You'd think they'd put two in every room.

"Everyone seems to follow procedure," I told her. "If we get to an unoccupied room where the guest left the safe locked, we call the supervisor. She brings the master key and opens it."

"Have you run across that?"

"Once," I told her.

"What was inside?"

"French fries."

Natalie's head jerked. "What?"

"Congealed French fries. I swear." I flashed her the Scout's Honor salute. Or maybe it was the Witches' Honor. "They were swimming in so much ketchup I thought someone had locked up a body part, like a kidney or a big nose."

"What did you do?"

"I had to pick up the nasty things, then scrub out the safe."

Natalie recoiled.

"See? I told you."

* * *

The room safes were being broken into randomly; the common denominator eluded me other than baby powder, because traces of it were found all four times. All I really knew was that I hated cleaning hotel rooms and that the thief was wearing Pampers.

I had *Jeopardy!* turned low on the television to muffle the noise of my neighbors, who'd had screaming sex twice already, once during the news and then again during *Wheel of Fortune*, with the four incident files and a take-out pizza spread out on the EconoLodge's version of a bedspread: it was made of plastic, didn't provide a single blanket element other than covering the cardboard sheets, and it smelled like feet.

I'd studied the files for two weeks and couldn't get a pattern to emerge. Truth be told, I only glanced at the stack of files the first week, unable to hold anything as heavy as a sheet of paper after my grueling day shifts, but began digging through them in earnest that weekend. Two things dawned on me while staring at the stain patterns on the thirty-seven EconoLodge ceiling tiles: one, the Bellissimo had higher sanitation standards than the EconoLodge, and two, the reward for catching the thief would be a different assignment, something that didn't involve removing gooey things from the bottom of hotel garbage cans during the day or having pervy neighbors at night.

The security footage was the same. I ran all four clips a dozen times on my teeny computer, backed them up, and watched them a dozen more. A dark-haired man, the same man each time, who knew the camera angles, because I couldn't get a full shot of his face, stood outside a guest room chatting it up with the housekeeping floor supervisor. She used her passkey to give him entrance to an occupied room where he went on to relieve the room safe of its pesky contents. Only, as it turned out all four times, he wasn't the registered guest.

The timeline was erratic, the first theft occurring in August of last year on the twenty-eighth floor, the second in November on sixteen, and the last two during the same week in December, the first on the twentieth floor and the follow-up break-in on floor thirteen. The victims claimed losses that totaled forty-nine thousand in cash, with the third incident on the sixteenth floor including jewelry, bringing the grand total up to almost sixty-thousand dollars the man had made off with.

For his late-summer heist, he was decked out in golf attire, lugging a bag of clubs. The next one, he wore tennis whites, a racquet tucked under one arm, hands full of Bellissimo Café take-out. The third—this was cute—he wore a spa robe and slippers. For his final act, only two days after his lucrative spa adventure, he seemed to have run out of energy. He was dressed in nondescript street clothes: khaki pants, a V-neck sweater over a button-down, and leather loafers.

How did he know there was anything in the safes worth stealing and how, once in the room, was he getting into them?

* * *

It was noon on a bright sunny Monday, my third on the housekeeping assignment, and I knew it was his room the second I entered it. You don't marry someone twice and not know a bed they've slept in.

Sixteen hundred and twenty guest rooms, more than five hundred people issued the same black, tan, and white uniform I was wearing, and somehow I was the lucky one who knuckled the door ("Housekeeping!"), card-swiped the lock, strategically blocked the door with my cleaning cart, and entered my ex-ex-husband's hotel room. I fell against my cart, sending a hundred tiny shampoo bottles flying off the other side.

"Okay? Okay?" Santiago, my coworker, cleaning the even-numbered rooms to my odd, raced across the hall to lasso the shampoos. "Okay?"

"I'm fine, Santiago," I panted. I squeezed my eyes shut, pinched the bridge of my nose, and tried to concentrate on standing upright.

"Bad stinks?"

That would work, so I nodded.

"You me do?"

I shook my head. "I'm fine, Santiago. I'm going to close this door so no one walking by gets a whiff of this." I waved my hand in front of my face.

Santiago gave me his I-have-no-idea-what-you-said smile and asked again, "You me do?" this time, pointing to me, then himself. He drew his toilet-brush sword. He tilted his head back, sniffing the air.

"No, Santiago, but thanks." I closed the door to an urgent string of speedy Spanish. An interpreter would have come in handy just then, because what Santiago was trying to tell me was that we weren't allowed behind closed doors in a guest room. We used two card keys: one to enter and clean the room, the other to exit and let all interested parties—our boss, the front desk, and, as it turned out, Natalie Middleton, should she want to know—the room was ready. If the door closed between the two swipes, warning bells sounded all over the building: Someone on the housekeeping staff was locked up in a guest room. Hello, lawsuit.

Santiago was on the other side of the door hollering about piñatas, enchiladas, and conquistadors. The housekeeping supervisor was thumping down the hall, slinging Spanish curses right and left. Natalie Middleton was in action, sending an emissary to both save me and read me the riot act.

I was locked in Eddie's room, so I didn't know.

I fingered his hanging shirts and poked around in his shaving kit. No surprises. I grabbed my clipboard and flipped through, wondering how I'd missed this. We were issued our marching orders at the beginning of every shift. It almost always gave us the surname of the guest in the room and if not, it gave clues. VIPs were highlighted with a pale green stripe, which most of the floor was, and Casino Marketing guests were listed as just that—no name, just Casino Marketing Guest. There was no additional information about the room's occupant other than they were there on the casino's dime. So Eddie Crawford was a Casino Marketing guest. Which was exactly when it hit me. Buried deep in the incident files, behind the reports, profiles, photographs, claim forms, and interview transcripts, were the single-sheet housekeeping assignment charts for the day of each robbery. All four room-safe thefts had occurred in Casino Marketing guest rooms.

An urgent pounding on the door scared the very life out of me. It was most certainly Eddie.

I dropped my clipboard, clapped my hand over my mouth to muffle my screams, and wondered, wildly pacing a small circle, what to do. My eyes were drawn to the Gulf of Mexico, out the window and nineteen floors down. Suicide? That early in the morning?

He knocked again.

I jumped a mile and screamed into my hand.

"Everything okay in there?"

It wasn't Eddie.

I stretched to the peephole and saw a perfect set of glow-in-the-dark choppers. Their owner could have chewed through the door. Accompanying the teeth, a great big man dressed in head-to-toe white. He looked like Dr. Death.

SEVEN

"Is this it?" George shook a can of mixed nuts.

"It can't be Christmas every day." In the two weeks George had been shuttling me back and forth from the lovely EconoLodge, I'd loaded him down with things I found in the guest rooms: food, candy, wine, soft drinks, bottled water, flowers, t-shirts, coffee mugs, four hundred little jars of condiments, visors, golf balls, hand lotion, and enough cell phone chargers to open his own kiosk at the mall. The first few days I simply left the loot in the car. The day he almost got us killed because he was craning in the rearview mirror to see what I'd be leaving instead of watching the road was the day I began passing the boodle to him when I got in. For reasons I might never know, old George loved the flowers the best, although he'd be driving the governor's limo before he'd let on. The most I ever got out of him was a grunt. The three times I'd climbed in and passed him flowers, though, he'd been speechless, which was to say he didn't grunt. So old George did have a soft spot.

He shook the can again. "Peanuts?"

"I only cleaned two guest rooms, George. And unfortunately for you, I didn't find a pot of gold in either." I rubbed my temples.

"You spent all day cleaning two rooms?" He waited until there wasn't a car within five miles of us in either direction before pulling out onto Beach Boulevard. "Must have been some big rooms."

I didn't have the energy.

"And is that the new maid's getup?"

I didn't owe George a wardrobe explanation.

"You don't strike me as the kind who'd take the time to be good at that sort of thing."

Was George baiting me?

"I probably would have let you go two weeks ago."

I shot up in the seat, my energy miraculously returned. "I didn't get *fired*, George. I'll have you know I stared at a computer screen all day."

George made a noise he was so good at, I think he invented it. It said, *uh-huh, sure you did,* in just one guttural syllable.

I came *this* close to bailing out of a moving vehicle, because breaking a leg or two would have been the best part of my day.

Three blocks later he asked, "What'd you find?"

"I'm not speaking to you again, George. Ever, ever."

"Fine."

"Nothing," I caved. "Nothing."

We were at a red light. He twisted in his seat. "Did you have a bad day?"

I started bawling.

Teeth had yanked me out of Eddie Crawford's hotel room by the ear, then pulled me kicking and screaming into a stairwell where he chewed me out good. I thought he was going to bite my head off. I'd been on the receiving end of many protocol and procedure lectures before (the circumventing of), but never across from those kind of teeth. He gave no indication I'd been in the wrong guest room, or that there was any connection between me and that particular guest room, he gave me down the road in general about being in *any* guest room alone with the door locked. "Were you *looking* for something?" When he'd had his say, his parting words were, "Go see Natalie."

I wasn't about to tell Teeth or Natalie it was the collection of my ex-ex-husband's personal effects that had prompted the breaking of all those cardinal rules (which I knew absolutely nothing about beforehand), so bracing myself for another lashing, avoiding both the guest and employee elevators (something they had bothered to make me aware of), I made my way to the Executive Offices. I put a toe in the door.

"Davis, come in. The coast is clear." She was refilling Mr. Sanders' cinnamon candy bowl from a ten-pound bag of the offensive stuff, the sight of which made me dizzy. Natalie was crisp, cool, calm, and didn't appear to be the least bit upset with me. She offered me a cup of coffee; she didn't offer me a cinnamon candy.

"Now, Davis." Natalie smiled. "What can I do for you?"

I scratched at the wig. I thought she had asked to see me for round two of Let Davis Have It. "I need a computer," I said, "and a desk."

"Okay," she said. "Why don't you step in the back and change out of your uniform."

Gladly. If she'd suggested I step in the back and change out of my life, I'd have taken her up on that too.

After setting me up in street clothes, Natalie set me up in an empty cubicle in the print shop, located several miles under the Bellissimo basement. "Keep your head down," she said. "You won't run into anyone because the print shop employees only work graveyard. But if for some reason you do, keep quiet."

Aye, aye, Captain.

"And don't ever do that again."

She said it to my back as I was making my escape. I barely turned, one foot already out the door. "Sorry." Hand in the cookie jar. "I won't."

"Is there anything else, Davis?" She tapped a pen. "Anything we need to talk about?" Her expression was as blank as a Bellissimo bed sheet.

I fell against the doorjamb for support, because with her words, a ghost had snuck up from behind and knocked my knees. Then laughed. "Not that I know of, Natalie."

I got out of there as fast as I could.

* * *

Not many people went into police work for the money. The ones who did weren't protecting and serving the public, they were protecting and serving the dark side. The most I'd ever earned in my life was peanuts, and I hadn't saved a one of them, because at the time, I had a nest egg. Today, at age early thirties, I had no nest egg, I had no roof over my head, and I'd never work directly in law enforcement again. I could get a job as a computer programmer, but I'd probably blow my brains out by the third day.

My new job had shocked me stupid three times. The whammy-whammy game had slapped me so hard I actually quit. The severe tongue-lashings, both directly and not so directly, I'd received that day set me back again. But both of those events and their bright red Eddie flags paled in comparison to the shock I received when I checked my bank balance.

The Bellissimo was paying me a brain surgeon astronaut's wages.

In all the interviews, the subject of salary had never come up. Not once. I never asked; they never offered. I emailed Natalie my banking information after opening a local account, and she replied my paycheck would be directly deposited every Friday, and instead of wondering how much it would be, I consulted a calendar, counting the number of Fridays in ninety days. (My interest was more on Visa's behalf than my own. And I owed my sister a little. My grandmother too. My father had loaned me the money for my car, something my mother didn't know.)

It took every dime I had to divorce that rat-bastard Eddie Crawford, immediately followed by extreme unemployment. My finances had gone from sad to tragic until I began receiving Bellissimo paychecks. Things were looking up in my financial department; Visa and I were both very happy about it. My ninety-day commitment was nearing the four-week mark, but they were paying me so much I caught myself thinking if I could stick it out six months, I could be debt-free both inside and outside of my family. If I could hold out an additional six months, I'd have the makings of a savings account.

I looked at myself in the reflection of the elevator doors on my way to the print shop, and gave myself this advice: "Make this work,

Davis."

* * *

I was certain the same Casino Marketing person booked the four guest victims, but ten minutes after I settled in to solve the room-safe-theft caper, I hit a wall. Four different casino hosts had been assigned to the four injured parties.

If it wasn't a casino-host culprit, who was it?

I had no choice but to hack into the Bellissimo mainframe, which raised my blood pressure through the roof. Years ago, out of boredom, I wrote a program that would shut down a system the millisecond it was compromised. The only reason I hadn't tried to sell it to Microsoft or the iPod people was because I hadn't had time to develop Part Two, a sprinkler system device in the monitor that blasted the hacker with tear gas. Hack *that*, buddy. (The real reason I hadn't pursued it was because if it did fly, my hacking hobby would be over.)

Boom. Gotcha. I was in.

I examined the four guest portfolios from their inceptions. After three hours and a headache, I found nothing but typos. No one had altered anything.

It had been a long, long day. I'd been traumatized, terrified, told off, and I'd struck out. Tears were in order.

George waited patiently until I stopped leaking. "What were you looking for?"

We were stuck at a railroad crossing while an endless succession of gang-graffitied railcars rolled by, so I let my head fall back and closed my eyes. "I'm looking into this casino host business, how it works."

"Nothing to it."

"How's that, George?" My head snapped up. "What? Are you a casino expert now? I haven't seen you in the casino rubbing elbows with the hosts."

"That doesn't mean I don't know how they work." He turned and made the rare eye contact again, but I didn't cry this time.

"I'm listening." I crossed my arms.

"It's a sweet gig."

"In what way?"

"It's the easiest job in the building."

"That couldn't be true," I said. "It looks to me like they take care of the whims and fancies of a thousand people each." Clicking on the client list link of a casino host's profile, a Rhode Island roster ensued. Page after page, thousands of guests, were assigned to each of the fourteen hosts.

"The hosts have assistants who do all the grunt work," he said. "They spend their time in the restaurants and on the golf course."

Thirty minutes later, ignoring my next-door neighbors' headboard trying to beat its way into my room again, nose to computer screen, I had my mark: Miss Heidi Dupree, Executive Assistant to the casino hosts. She was one of eight executive assistants, but hers were the only administrative initials on the portfolios, a zillion computer screens back, for the four rooms that had been broken into. I recognized her from her employee profile too; I'd seen her entering a guest room to deliver flowers.

* * *

The next day, I cleaned seventeen guest rooms. Three were barely touched, only one corner of the bed turned back, and a single pillow had a head dent. I'd learned quickly that not all the guests were there for the glorious guest rooms, extra glorious to me now that I knew EconoLodge squalor firsthand. A good portion of Bellissimo guests checked in, threw their bags inside the door, then hit the casino never to return.

I'd had one room for three consecutive days, nineteen thirty-seven, where the guest had yet to get near the bathroom sink, tub, shower, or, for all I could tell, their suitcase. Down the hall, I had adjoining rooms that made up for that one; the occupants and the preschool they brought with them had moved in. Stuffed animals, gummy worms, hills and mountains of discarded clothing, bowl after bowl of liquefied ice cream, bathtubs used as toy storage, and half-full juice boxes on every flat surface. In another room, it had rained shiny black condom wrappers, and in yet another guest room, the ravenous occupants had ordered one of everything on the room service menu, taking a single bite out of each dish, leaving all the uneaten food and enough tableware to set a table for ten for me to deal with. The room safes today, like almost every day, hadn't been touched. The best part? Eddie Crawford had checked out of his room. A guy named Millard Martin had checked in it. I had no beef with Millard.

My coworkers didn't take lunch breaks so much as they took extended smoke breaks. As the clock inched toward noon, and I said job-well-done to myself about guest room nineteen thirteen, Santiago, my work buddy, exiting nineteen fourteen and in the throes of severe nicotine withdrawal, asked, "We lunch?"

"Sure." I couldn't see him through the king-sized bed roll of laundry I was hefting. I tipped it into my bin. The muffled music of broken glass filled the space between us. It sounded like I'd dropped a chandelier.

"Oh!" Santiago's eyes were saucers.

We both cut our eyes up and down the hall, and seeing no one, I shrugged. Santiago shrugged. Whatever I'd just rolled up in the dirty sheets was now Coast Laundry Services' problem.

I had the small break room behind our supply room all to myself; everyone else had made their way to the employee smoking patio on the sixth floor.

I dialed the Casino Host's office extension. "Heidi Dupree, please." I studied my ravaged cuticles and listened for the door. I remembered I'd forgotten to look under beds all morning. No telling what I'd missed.

"Casino Marketing," a soft voice said. "This is Heidi."

She didn't sound like a safe cracker.

"Hello," I said. "I'm in housekeeping and one of the guests is complaining she didn't get a fruit basket."

"Who is this?"

"Housekeeping."

"We order the amenities," Heidi said, soft voice gone. "Room service fills the orders. Call them." Then she hung up on me.

* * *

"I need a hardware store, George." I dropped the day's treasures over the seat: two paperback books, a three-pack of disposable razors, and four Snickers bars, one smashed flat.

"No, you don't."

I reached over the seat, took the loot back, lowered the window, and tossed it to the traffic.

(No, I didn't.)

"What makes you think you know what I need and what I don't?" I demanded.

"I just do. Because you can't get in those safes with a tool."

My jaw unhinged. How in the *world* did George know what I was doing?

"Those are S700 Protectaguards," he went on, "and you can't break in them. You have to have the code or the electronic passkey. That's the only way. Whoever you're looking for has the code or the passkey."

"I'll tell you what, George. You take me to a hardware store and we'll talk about it some other time." This guy got on my last nerve. More than that, he was just about to scare me.

"It's your money."

Soon enough he was backing into the loneliest parking space Center City Hardware offered.

"George," I whined, "come on. It's raining. It's raining ice. Let me off at the door."

He ripped into one of the candy bars. "If you're going to waste your time and mine, you can waste some of it walking."

I could reach up and smack the back of his head so easily.

"And don't get a jackhammer," he said through chocolate. "If you're going to get something, get a multi-tool, like a Gerber."

Gibberish. "What?"

He swallowed and caught my eye in the mirror. "You think you're going to break into the safe, right?"

I blinked.

"Don't think they're going to let you lug a power tool into a hotel room. Get a multi-tool, like a Swiss Army knife, that you can slip in your pocket. But it won't work. All you're going to do is tear it up."

I had one angry foot out in the rain, and I quickly pulled it back in. "How do you know that, George? How do you know any of this?"

He shrugged one shoulder.

I got out, slammed the door as hard as I could, and ran through the biting rain.

* * *

Twenty minutes later, we pulled up to the entrance of the Silver Moon Resort and Casino, a shrunken Bellissimo, and the only other show in town that bragged on their website about the foolproof S700 Protectaguards. A bellman craned his neck our way. George waved him off, because, of course, he didn't need any help with his bags. "Are you going to get out or are you going to sit in my car all night?"

My new goal in life was to slam the car door so hard that it fell off. Of course, if I were successful, it would probably land on my feet.

The bed begged me to get in, the thick white comforter screaming, "I'm soft! And I smell good!" and I complied, for two dreamless hours I don't remember a second of. The rest of the time I tried to break into the S700 Protectaguard safe with no luck whatsoever. None of the ninety-three tools that jutted out from the eight-pound thing I'd purchased at the hardware store, including the two-tine fork, fazed the safe. The only thing I managed to do was scratch the hell out of it and ruin most of the appendages on the tool.

"So?" George asked the next morning.

"I'm late, George. Drive."

The next night, I dialed the Silver Moon operator after an hour-long blistering shower. "My safe won't open." She transferred me to the security office.

"Have you forgotten your code?" a man asked.

"No," I lied. "It just won't open. It's stuck."

"What's in it? You might have jammed the door."

At which point my mind began racing. The safe was empty. I had a little more than forty dollars in cash, which wouldn't impress them much.

"We'll be there in ten minutes," he said.

I looked across the room to my purse. My wedding rings were somewhere in the bottom keeping company with lint, year-old peppermints, and loose change.

EIGHT

There's a framed photograph of my first birthday celebration at my parents' house, on the shelf of a bookcase in the upstairs hallway, right outside of Meredith's old room. In it, I'm barely balanced on roly-poly legs in the middle of the dining room table at ground zero of a cake and frosting explosion. It looked like fun, and I wished I could climb on a table and eat birthday cake with both hands again, although I wouldn't smear it in my hair this time. On one side of me were my parents, my father beaming, my mother glazed over. On the other side was my mother's childhood friend, Bea Crawford, her eighteen-month-old son Eddie in her lap. So I never actually met Eddie, he just always was. Eventually he became, out of small-town boredom, my boyfriend, and I was sort of dating him when it was announced I was pregnant (again, out of small-town boredom) at the ripe old age of sixteen. It was my mother, the keeper of the inventory of feminine hygiene products, who broke the news to our family at breakfast one morning, and none too gently. I was as stunned and slack-jawed as my father and sister were. In retort, I threw up everywhere, providing my mother with the proof she sought.

"See?" my mother demanded.

No one wanted to see.

"I knew it," she spat.

My mother was thrilled at this new development—her being the goose to my gander—insisting all our lives that her four years of higher education were just a waste of time and money (cutting her eyes at me), and Meredith and I might as well skip it and go straight to the real deal: dirty diapers, pot roasts, and laundry.

Mother wasted no time telling Eddie's parents, turning their breakfast into a celebration. His dad probably wrestled him into a bear hug and gave him noogies. "Way to go, son!" Mel and Bea Crawford were beside themselves with glee, because we were as close to royalty as it got in Pine Apple. They envisioned a future of no parking tickets, the end of those annoying restaurant report card failures, and they probably thought sharing a grandchild with the Chief of Police/Mayor of Pine Apple would make them exempt from federal taxes too.

Why, after all those years and heartache for everyone involved, I still lugged around my wedding rings was anyone's guess. They weren't worth hocking should I need the cash, the combined weight of the diamond chips maybe totaling an eighth of a carat. They had no history; it's not like they were Crawford Estate jewels retrieved from a vault hidden behind a portrait of great granddaddy. They weren't even pretty; they had been on clearance at Sears, the rock of the Westside Mall in Montgomery.

There were two reasons I kept them handy: they reminded me of what could happen if you lived a big, fat lie, and they were proof that no matter how hard you tried, some points weren't worth making. There was a distant third reason; I secretly longed for the opportunity to give them back to Eddie in a fashion that would require subsequent surgical removal from his person. With long, pointy tongs. And no anesthesia.

They sounded like two pennies going into the safe as the knock came on the door.

"Security," I heard.

I closed the safe door, pressed in the code I'd assigned the night before, pushed the star button to lock it, tied my robe tighter, and let the crew in.

Same drill as the Bellissimo: to get into the room safe of an occupied guest room, it took one housekeeping supervisor passkey swipe, one security passkey swipe, and two other employee witnesses, one from housekeeping, the other from security. Everyone, including me, had to sign on the dotted line before and after.

They all peered at the pathetic wedding rings. They all turned to me.

Really?

I smiled.

* * *

I had Natalie Middleton's blessing to stay at the Silver Moon as long as I was working. So I could justify the two glorious nights, but I couldn't justify a third on the Bellissimo's dime, because I now knew there was no entering the safe without an authorized break-in crew, two passkeys, the code, an act of Congress, or a bulldozer. Did I give George the satisfaction of hearing those words pass these lips? No, I did not. But I didn't have to. He figured it out when I pushed through the doors the next morning with all my earthly belongings in tow. It was Thursday. I'd been on the room-safe-theft assignment for two and a half weeks, and no doubt, I was headed back to the EconoLodge after my housekeeping shift that day.

My workday started, like every other workday, with Maria, the housekeeping supervisor, complaining about the shoddy job we'd all done the day before. It was a total waste of time, the purpose of which was to give Maria's pets time to drag into work. The second they staggered through the door, Maria announced, "Dat all. Geet to de work." I sat through the ten-minute pep talk every morning wondering how Maria managed to maintain her perfect manicure. Her fingernails were blood red, out to there, and her ring fingers had geometrical designs in white. At the end of the lecture, I gave Maria a big hug when she passed me a clipboard full of room assignments. She pulled away from me and looked at me as if I'd lost my mind. I pulled away from her with a passkey to every room on the floor.

At eleven that morning, six guest rooms spicked and spanned, Santiago knuckled the door frame of the room I was cleaning, lucky number seven, and in his heavy accent called, "Anna? Anna?"

I rose to my knees. I'd been between the queen-sized beds spot cleaning red wine off the carpet. At least I hoped it was red wine. "Do you need me, Santiago?"

He blabbered in his native tongue. I didn't catch a word of it. Then Miss Heidi Dupree's lovely frame stepped into the open doorway beside Santiago's. In her arms she held a basket. I could see the top half of two dark bottles of wine pointed in opposite directions.

"I need in a guest room," she said. "And this guy can't hear a word I'm saying."

"He hears you." I stood, smoothing my uniform. "He doesn't speak fluent English."

"Then he shouldn't work here." She shifted the weight of the basket to her hip. "I'm in a hurry. Come open this door for me."

Protocol was crystal clear: never let anyone in a guest room for any reason, that's the supervisor's call. I'm sure, though, somewhere in small print, it says temporary residents of the EconoLodge wearing hot, itchy wigs were exempt.

"Which room?" I asked.

She took off.

I followed.

"Here you go." I used the passkey I'd stolen from Maria to open the door of room nineteen twenty-two. She and her basket breezed by me, then spun.

"I've got it from here."

I smiled and stepped back an inch.

"Really." Miss Dupree was becoming impatient with me. "I'll only be a minute." Then she slammed the door in my face.

I sprang into action, using Maria's key again, to slip into the room directly across the hall where I could watch from the peephole. I wish I had knocked first.

"Nelson?" A wild-haired woman sat straight up in the bed, saw me, and screamed out a lung. *Who are you?* The part of her I could see was completely naked. She grabbed for the covers. "Get *out*! Get *out* of my room!" She flailed an arm at the door, showing me the way.

"Oh!" I screamed. "Pardon! Pardon!" I used my best Tex-Mex voice. "Excuse! Excuse!"

Heidi Dupree and I spilled into the hallway on the same click of the second hand, and she looked at me as if I were crazy, which, at the moment, I was. I fell against the wall to catch my breath and Heidi Dupree took off, but only after throwing me a parting glare. She had one hand balled into a fist, like she was holding something. As soon as she turned the corner to the elevator, I took off after her, my orthopedic shoes thumping. I slowed and waited until the elevator doors opened, then closed, peeked around the corner and saw a wad of wet tissue, still grooved from her grip, in the ashtray between the elevator doors that I'd just cleaned and stamped a perfect script "B" for Bellissimo into not an hour earlier. I really didn't like this girl.

I ran back down the hall and stopped outside of naked wild-haired woman's room. If she was on the phone tattling on me, I'd probably be able to hear her muffled outrage, and if that were the case, I planned on hiding. I couldn't hear a thing over my accelerated heartbeat from all the running; hopefully naked woman had gone back to sleep. I counted to twenty, then pulled a new set of latex cleaning gloves from the pocket of my apron, tugged them on, and used Maria's key again to enter the room Heidi Dupree had done her business in.

The gift basket containing the wine was on a table in front of the Gulf-view window. A small card was tented in front of the basket.

Congratulations! Present this for a Couple's Massage at four o'clock this afternoon at the Bellissimo spa as our honored guests.

It was signed Mark Fredrickson, a name I recognized from the Casino Host roster. I walked to the closet. Pulling the doors open, I was greeted by the unmistakable tang of hairspray.

* * *

From the housekeeping break room, which I had all to myself again, I called Natalie. "I need a quiet place, a computer, and street clothes."

"For how long?"

"At least a few hours."

"Give me ten," she said.

Hours? This thing would be said and done in ten hours.

"And I'll need computer clearance again for restricted files, Natalie." I could almost hear her raising one perfect eyebrow.

"Which ones?" she asked. "Internal or client?"

"Both."

I tracked down Maria, fifteen tissues to my face, blowing my nose with gusto.

She put all ten of her red fingernails straight out, hands splayed. "Stay over," she warned me.

I stayed over.

She eyed me, up and down. "I take guess. You feel no good?" She blinked a hundred times.

I coughed for her.

"Aye, aye, aye." She shooed me away.

Natalie set me up in an unoccupied guest room on the fourth floor, which was—I hated to complain—not as spiffy as the rest of the place. The higher the floor, the nicer the room, all the way to the penthouse, which was rumored to be one massive breathtaking suite fit for Elvis. Hotel floors four, five, and six were the junket floors, where busload after busload of retirees were temporarily housed. Don't get me wrong, my new room beat my EconoLodge room to death. And I was happy, happy, happy to be in it without a cleaning cart.

A chocolate-brown Nike warm-up suit in a clingy knit blend, strappy tank in the trim color, a bright teal, and Airs with a bright teal stripe were on one of the beds. Dropping my ponytail wig to the floor, I got out of my housekeeping uniform and into my tennis star outfit as fast as I could, shaking my hair out and loving Natalie.

A laptop computer was on the desk. I fired it up. I would watch my steps while romping through Bellissimo's cyber world, just in case someone was following me. I didn't really need to know Richard Sanders' exact age or see his Las Vegas wife's photo. There was a time and place for everything. That wasn't it.

The registered guest in room nineteen twenty-two was Robert Edding, and I supposed his wife, Gracie, was with him, because the hair-sprayed closet had several women's blouses hanging in it. The Eddings were from Corpus Christi, Texas, and the computer told me they'd visited four times the previous year, staying three nights each time. I pulled up Robert Edding's play history. He was a slot player, and his casino activity rated him a five, meaning, after a ton of calculating on the casino's part, he could be counted on to leave five thousand dollars there, more or less, each visit. In the big picture, that made him a decent, steady player. Put him in the company of a hundred thousand others who came four times a year and dropped off five thousand each and that would be a nice bottom line. And fives were the least of it; the Eddings were small casino potatoes.

That being said, Robert Edding lucked up. He found himself at the right place at the right time that morning. His electronic portfolio showed him charging two buffet breakfasts plus a six-dollar tip to his room at 9:38, and at ten fifteen, hitting a slot jackpot of $22,500 on machine 238007. Way to go, Robert.

And that was how Miss Dupree knew there'd be something in the safe. And she knew when they'd be out of the room too, because she'd booked the spa herself.

Two questions remained: who was her partner, and how was he getting into the safe? A third question loomed. If I ordered room service for lunch, would Natalie have a cow?

* * *

I held my fake Louis Vuitton hobo wide open over the bed, flipped it, and set the vast collection free. I gave it a good shake to dislodge the stuck-on stuff and twice as much fell out. Goodness gracious. I waved through the toxic cloud and vowed to clean out my purse more than once a year. I needed the three cell phones, my three pounds of keys, and should probably keep the seventeen or so paperclips, but as far as I could see, everything else could go. I found a ten-dollar bill in the mix, freed a penlight from my keychain, and pushed the rest of it into a small mountain for later.

Downstairs, hugging the walls, head down, I ducked into the gift shop, the twenty-four-hour kind that sold beef jerky, toothpaste, and souvenir dice. I stood in line to purchase an ounce and a half of hairspray for five dollars, and a miniature plastic container of baby powder for four. Surely there wasn't a baby butt out there that needed to smell that fresh; save your money and just put the kid in the tub. I thought of my sister, Meredith, after Riley was born, telling me until I had a child of my own, my nuggets of parenting wisdom weren't welcome.

Back in my room on the fourth floor, the first thing I did was remove a pillowcase from one of the bed pillows. Not the same thread count as on the higher floors. I pulled open the closet doors. The florescent interior light came on automatically. It was half the size of the upstairs closets.

Next I stepped into the bathroom and pulled a handful of tissues from the box on the vanity. I passed them under a slow stream of water, then swiped back and forth across the keypad of the wall safe. I blew the keypad dry, then gave it two good squirts of hairspray, put the pillowcase over my head, and plopped down on the floor to wait. I hummed to pass the time. After two stanzas of "We Wish You a Merry Christmas," I stood, felt around, and found the edges of the safe. I stabbed in the general direction of the keypad quickly, four times, before I could seriously orient myself to the ten-digit keypad, and even so, I'm pretty sure I pushed one, three, seven, and nine. I yanked the pillowcase off my head, dug the flashlight out of my pocket, and pointed it directly on the keypad.

Nothing.

I angled the beam. More nothing.

I squeezed a perfect circle-dot pattern of the baby powder into the palm of my hand, then blew it onto the keypad like fairy dust. While it clung, sort of, I still couldn't see anything noteworthy, even with the flashlight. I stepped in, pulled the doors closed to eliminate the overhead light, and tried the flashlight again.

Bingo.

In the ambient darkness, the thin illumination revealed three smudges in the light powder film: numbers four, five, and six. Wait a sec. I'd pushed four buttons.

The World Wide Web told me that there were twenty-four possible combinations of four different digits, but because I liked to make things as hard on myself as humanly possible, I'd pushed one of the numbers twice, which bumped the possible combinations up to thirty-six. Even so, a ten-year-old could sit down with a pen and paper and come up with the thirty-six possibilities in a flash. Me being far past ten, it took almost fifteen minutes. And another twelve minutes testing them. I hit pay dirt about halfway down the list: five, six, four, five sprung the safe open. On my sixth go-around, I popped it in less than four minutes, probably because I skipped the pillowcase part and just squeezed my eyes closed until I could see dancing dots. By then it was almost three o'clock and I was choking on hairspray and baby powder.

Showtime.

With a weary sigh, I dug through my cell phone collection for the brilliant one. It was time to do what I'd managed to avoid for a month: make direct contact with No Hair and Teeth.

* * *

The grainy overhead-perspective surveillance video of the previous four room thefts had masked how young Heidi's partner in crime was. When I finally got a good look at him, he appeared to be late twenties, early thirties, and my best guess was that Heidi was both splitting the take and spending quality alone time with him. They would miss each other when they went to prison for ten to twenty.

It was four fifteen. We took our places as Robert and Gracie

Edding checked into the spa.

I was in the closet, mostly in the dark, wedged into the opposite corner from the safe behind two hanging Bellissimo robes and Mrs. Edding's blouses. The top of my head just cleared the hanging bar. I watched the live feed coming from the hall on a three-inch handheld. My breath was coming at a slow, steady pace, with adrenaline pumping through me that was more about never seeing the EconoLodge again than anything else. I'd been in tight positions many times through the years, with opponents far more armed and dangerous than the man I was expecting. Speaking of armed, I was packing again. Pepper spray and handcuffs, but, hey, it was a start.

The teeny camera feeding me video was tucked between potted hydrangeas on a flower cart driven by—this was hilarious—No Hair. Teeth was waiting downstairs outside of Heidi Dupree's office so he could give her the good news. We'd met in Natalie's office a half hour earlier, and the two men flipped a coin for the assignments. No Hair, sporting a tie with a sleeping Garfield the Cat on it, lost.

"Two out of three," he said.

"No way, man. We don't have time for that." Teeth took his win and ran with it.

Natalie drummed her fingers on her desk impatiently. "It doesn't matter. Get going, one of you."

"I can't fit in a closet." No Hair, a.k.a. Jeremy Covey, said to Teeth, a.k.a. Paul Bergman. "Are you out of your mind?"

I'd only seen these guys in I'd-like-to-rip-your-head-off mode, and it was nice to know they were, indeed, humans, as opposed to straight-up killing machines. They were each the size, shape, and weight of refrigerators, and having spent half of the afternoon inside a guest room closet, I agreed: No way No Hair could hide in the closet, even the ones upstairs that would hold a twin-size bed. Not that Teeth could.

"Clearly—" They turned to me like *who are you again?* "Neither one of you is going in the closet. I'll do the closet. You wait outside the room in the hall."

No Hair said, "No offense, little lady, but you couldn't take down a bunny rabbit."

"You'll be right behind her," Teeth said.

"I can do my job, thank you," I assured them.

"And what am I supposed to do in the hall?" No Hair demanded. "You think the guy's going to blow me a kiss then go load up the cash?"

He had a point. Those two could clear a church of nuns; a thief would most certainly tuck and run.

Natalie reached for her phone. "This is Natalie Middleton from Mr. Sanders' office. I need a room service uniform in size..." She looked up at No Hair. He let his meaty cheeks fill with air, then let it out slowly. If I'd been wearing a hat, I'd have been chasing it.

"Fifty-two." We barely heard him.

"What?" Teeth asked on a laugh. "Fifty-*what*?"

"Shut up."

"Well, what about housekeeping?" Natalie asked. "Do you have a fifty-two in a housekeeping uniform?" We all waited. "Send it up," she said. No Hair threw his hands in the air. Natalie dialed another number. "I need a horticulture cart," she said. "I don't care. Whatever you have. And right now."

So No Hair, in a forest green jumpsuit, was pushing a cart full of pretty potted flowers when our mark strolled down the hall in one of his previous disguises, the spa robe and slippers. On the tiny screen it looked like he was running, so No Hair must have had the cart on the move, going about his blossom business in the opposite direction. And just in case I was in the closet doing my nails, No Hair's voice boomed through my earpiece, "Coming your way."

"Right," I said, just as I was attacked by serious vertigo. No Hair must have swung the cart around, and there was our mark's backside.

"I forgot my inhaler," he explained to the second-shift supervisor, who I hadn't had the pleasure of meeting and who, incidentally, spoke perfect English. "And my wife has our room key," he added.

"I need some identification, Mr. Edding."

He showed off his spa wear. "I don't have any! It's in the spa locker." He looked down the long hall. "Do I need to go get it?" Right about then, he sucked in a huge gulp of air. "I need in," he squeaked, pointing at the door.

"Okay, hold on, hold on. Let me make a call."

I measured him against the door and got a feel for how much space he would take up in the closet, choosing the spot and angle he'd most likely work from based on his size. No Hair and I continued to eavesdrop as the housekeeping supervisor called the spa. She asked if there was a Mr. Edding checked in. "And what's his room number?" She said thank you and snapped the phone closed. She whipped out her passkey and granted him entry. "Have a nice day, Mr. Edding. Hope you feel better soon."

I drew a huge breath when I heard, and felt up and down my spine, the door to the room close. I switched the handheld off and dropped it into the pocket of a robe.

His padded footsteps grew closer, then the closet doors burst open. He didn't pat around behind the robes for anyone hiding. First hurdle jumped. Almost immediately he pulled the doors closed behind him, plunging us into total darkness. He clicked a flashlight on; I could see the glow. The whole time he made a quick and quiet clucking noise with his tongue.

It took him four hours to get the safe open; you'd think he'd never done this before. I listened to my heart beating in time to his clucking and talked myself out of screaming and running for what felt like forever but turned out to be only three minutes.

When he finally got the safe open, I took my shot straight to the back of his knees with a quick kick, both shocking the holy stew out of him and sending him flying out of the doors and down to his knees. The bright lights popped on, and I let him get half of his bearings before I knocked his legs out from beneath him. He went down in an angry, fighting pile.

"Come on!" I screamed into my piece and heard my own echo.

No Hair was right beside me. He planted a foot in the guy's

back, surely rearranging his vertebrae, and sending his curses and cries straight into the carpet. No Hair bent to calf rope him, and as he did, a tearing noise ripped through the air. The seams of No Hair's flower-boy jumpsuit gave completely away, and it fell off him in shreds, like a monster green banana being peeled.

The worst of the entire assignment, EconoLodge included, was finding out that No Hair actually had a lot of hair.

* * *

Heidi Dupree and her brother, Mike, via separate service elevators, were thrown in an interrogation room together ten minutes later. Teeth and I watched through a two-way. I was still panting. Heidi Dupree took one look at her brother, then went for the garbage can, sticking her whole head in it—an almost foolproof admission of guilt.

"Where's Jeremy?" Teeth asked me.

"Getting dressed." Thank goodness. Speaking of dressed, Teeth was, tip to toe, wearing dark camel, including accessories: belt, tie, socks, and shoes. As much as I hated to admit it, it was a snappy look.

No one else at the Bellissimo had a clue as to what had gone down, and the Eddings' room had already been put back together; they would never know what almost happened. We still had the red tape to deal with, but overall it was a quick and quiet takedown.

All of a sudden, though, it was anything but quiet. The Dupree siblings were trying to kill each other.

"I'd better get in there," Teeth said.

"Wait a sec." I held up a finger. "Wait and see what they say to each other."

"Why? We have them."

I turned to Teeth. "Do you really think they could have pulled this off alone?" I asked. "Look at them."

Heidi had launched herself onto her brother's back, beating him about the head, and he was riding her around the room trying to sling her off. The metal table was on its side, four metal chairs were on everything but their legs, and, gross, the garbage can was upside down. The soundtrack was deafening, the language atrocious.

Teeth pushed an intercom button. "You two settle down."

The Duprees froze and both looked up as if God had fussed at them, then went right back at it.

"Neither of them is the mastermind," I told Teeth. "There's no way they acted alone."

He looked at me a long minute. He had huge pores. "We've done this job for years without you." He hiked his pants up. "We've got our guys." With a nod in the Dupree's direction, he said, "I'm going in. You can sit this one out."

Almost immediately, Richard Sanders stepped in and replaced Teeth. He took a look at the Duprees. "Those two are going to kill each other." As Mr. Sanders spoke, the room filled with the spicy scent of cinnamon. I fanned my face.

We recoiled as Teeth accidentally took one on the chin that was meant for the brother, at which point, he'd had enough, and the family feud ended as Teeth promised them both they'd leave on stretchers if either of them moved another muscle or opened their mouths again without permission. He could have put it this way: "Either of you move and I'll bite you." That would have done it.

Mr. Sanders turned to me. "Great job, Davis."

I said thanks, and then gave all the credit away.

"That's very gracious of you, but I've worked with Paul and Jeremy for years, and I don't believe they could've done it without you."

I was too tired to explain to Mr. Sanders it wasn't that I was particularly good at my job, so much as I was, at times, particularly lucky. And luck, as everyone there knew, eventually ran out.

"How do you screen potential employees for this type of behavior?" I asked the boss.

"There's no way to." He shifted his weight. "You see, Davis, I have a small percentage of honest employees, and I have an equally small percentage of dishonest employees."

"And the rest?"

"Are just like these two." He tapped a knuckle on the glass that separated us from the siblings. "They're the middle ground," he said. "They could go either way. And if a situation like this isn't handled with discretion," he paused, "and becomes a hot topic in the employee cafeteria, five hundred in the iffy category would figure out a way to do it bigger and better."

His words hung in the cinnamon air, and it felt like there was something he wasn't saying. I looked up.

"You're my discretion, Davis."

He put so much emphasis on the words that a goose walked over my grave. This man was putting too much faith in me, because I wasn't exactly an expert in discretion. I had no idea what to say and thought it best to let the moment pass without blubbering. When I was tired, I said too much. So I summoned the most serious look of acknowledgement I could, then turned to watch the rest of the show.

Heidi and Mike Dupree were spilling their guts, confessing everything from stealing Double Bubble from the corner store to peeking at Christmas gifts, repeatedly incriminating each other for both the ancient and current crimes. Heidi was sobbing, her brother was staring at the wall, his chest rising and falling rapidly, and again, I felt certain these two weren't alone in this.

Out of the corner of my eye, I watched Mr. Sanders sneak a peek at his watch.

"I've got this from here, Mr. Sanders."

"Are you sure?" he asked.

"Positive."

"I could use some sleep."

"Go ahead. I'll stay with them until they're booked."

He stuck his hands in his pockets and began backing toward the door. "If you're sure."

"I'm sure." I tried to smile. Not sure how it came out.

He gave me a smile and a wave, then I collapsed into a chair.

The sun rose and ushered in Friday before No Hair and Teeth

finished up with the Duprees and called Metro to come get them, and not once in all that time did Teeth begin to ask if there'd been anyone else involved. He didn't even hint at it.

I tied up the loose ends, then fell into the backseat of George's cab. I hadn't slept in more than thirty hours. He'd actually shown some concern for me, so I jumped all over that.

"Where to?"

My head was back, my eyes were closed, and I pointed in the direction of the EconoLodge.

"Staying there?"

I pointed to Alabama.

Three blocks later, he stopped for a red light. "What in the world is the matter with you?"

"I was up all night."

"Well, you look like something the cat dragged in."

"Thanks a lot, George."

"You don't need to be driving to Alabama."

And there, I took my shot. "I can make it today, George, but I really need your help on Monday."

"I wasn't volunteering to drive you to Alabama."

I used my last drops of energy to roll my eyes. "I need your help on Monday, George, not right this minute."

I went on to ask him to drive me all over Biloxi looking for apartments.

"Why?" he asked.

"Why?" We were staring at the EconoLodge. "*Why*, George?"

He hemmed. He hawed. He threw in the towel.

"I'll meet you at the regular place on Monday?"

He waved me off, which was George's whatever, anything to shut you up, just get out of my car.

"See you then?" I had a weary leg out the door, the teeniest bit energized by knowing I'd never be back at the EconoLodge again. "About noon?"

He waved again.

I dragged myself the rest of the way out of the car, and was pointed toward my own car when George cracked his window.

"Good job."

I barely heard him. "What?"

"I said good bust."

I stood there, staring straight ahead, feeling George's eyes on my back. There was almost no way for him to know what had happened. No way at all. No police chatter, no Bellissimo Security breach, he'd have to have been a fly on the wall.

"By the way," George said, "their mother's a blackjack dealer."

I spun. "*What?*"

"Different last name. Kempler. Lorraine Kempler."

He had his hand on the gear shift, about to drive off.

"Wait! Wait! George!" Somehow my legs managed to close the space between us. I took a peek at his radio scanner. (Off. But probably warm.)

He stared straight ahead.

"What the hell is going on, George?"

Finally, he turned his head. There were the eyes, the thousand-year-old eyes, the eyes that had seen Evil.

From the EconoLodge parking lot, George's taillights long gone, I located the Bat phone and chose the first big guy on the list, hoping it was Teeth. I pushed Go.

"What?"

It sounded like Teeth. "A blackjack dealer named Lorraine Kempler needs to be picked up on the room-safe thefts. She's the mother of the two we just turned over to Metro."

"Who told you that?"

I hung up. Jerk.

NINE

After an equally glorious and nightmarish weekend—which was to say after time spent with one's immediate family—I saw my twin. They say everyone has a twin, but I always thought it meant someone on the other side of the world. Like Iowa. I found mine in Biloxi, practically my own backyard. She was me, plus a billion dollars.

Natalie put me on the road after the Duprees were behind bars with the only clue to my next assignment being nose into a marriage. (Marriage, my specialty. I couldn't wait.)

"And let's look at Wednesday morning, okay, Davis?"

"Sure."

"Take a long weekend. You earned it."

I hadn't had any decent sleep in so long, I'd've agreed to take off until May.

"Also, Davis," Natalie pushed a set of keys and a brochure across her desk, "I want you in the executive apartments for your next assignment. I'm sure you're tired of living out of a suitcase."

Not so much. I loved living at the Bellissimo.

She caught my look. "Don't worry. I promise you'll be back in the hotel soon enough. For now though, we'll do the apartment. I'll have it set up for you by Tuesday afternoon, and I'll see you on Wednesday."

"See you then."

But at the strike of noon on Monday, not Wednesday, I parked my Bug in the garage for casino patrons, then hiked the mile to George. I had zero intention of spending my non-working hours under Bellissimo surveillance if I could help it, and since I had my own paycheck, I went back early to find my own apartment.

I was weaving in and out of the landscaping, taking the exterior shortcut to the VIP entrance, when my twin exited the building through the gold doors.

I was fifty feet away, between Southern oaks wearing thick capes of Spanish moss, about to step onto the sidewalk, when I heard someone say *Mrs. Sanders.*

My head snapped up and my feet quit working.

That was Bianca Casimiro Sanders? I caught my breath, my mouth dropped open, my heart stopped beating, and I couldn't have looked away if the trees I stood between had burst into flames. I almost passed out. There wasn't a doubt in my mind we'd been poured from the exact same mold. We were double whammies. She was me on my forty-sixth interview for this job: the blonde wig, the green contacts. I remembered Natalie taking all those pictures. I remembered Mr. Sanders looking at them when he interviewed me. They knew we looked alike.

I didn't sit down so much as I fell down on the hard cold ground. I was pretty sure I still hadn't taken a breath.

The thing about her husband, Richard Sanders, was that he was so perfectly accidental, as if no part of what made him tick was an effort. His wife, Bianca Casimiro Sanders, the woman in front of me, was the opposite. Her jaw, a perfect replica of mine, was set in stone. To compensate for her stature, which was within a whisper of my own, she was wearing eight-inch heels. They peeked out from under the pelts of several hundred small animals sacrificed, I'd bet, just for her. Her blonde twist updo was pulled back so severely it made my temples hurt.

Her entourage, a black-suited human cocoon, gave her two feet all the way around and looked straight ahead or at the ground, not at her. The ocean quieted, the air stood still, and traffic at the VIP entrance, creature and otherwise, came to a dead standstill as her team escorted her to a black stretch limo. A Louis Vuitton trunk was carefully loaded into the back, accompanied by several matching bags.

Mrs. Sanders was on the move, and so, apparently, was my driver.

Of all things, George, who I would swear hadn't gone anywhere the entire month of January except when I begged him to, took off after the limo. All kinds of questions raced through my mind. Was George some sort of covert tail on the boss's wife? Was she the reason he parked three blocks away from everything? Another huge question: How in the hell was I supposed to go apartment hunting without my driver? I could barely navigate the four roads in Pine Apple after having trod them my entire life. If left on my own there, I'd wind up in Texas by the end of the day.

I was having trouble processing it all, so I stayed on the cold hard ground watching the entourage pull out, including my ride, waiting for my heart rate to return to normal, all the while contemplating the largest curiosity of them all: was I a stunt double for the boss's wife?

"Davis."

I screamed.

Natalie's voice was cool. "I thought we said Wednesday."

I stammered a few syllables that came out, "Ya, ya, daaa."

"Get your things," she said. "Come with me."

* * *

"Do whatever you want, Davis." Natalie wasn't very happy with me. "But don't ask for a housing allowance." She poured herself a cup of coffee. She didn't offer me one.

"It's not that I don't appreciate the executive apartment offer, Natalie," I lied, "it's that, you know," I stumbled around, "the ocean and all. I'd like to be closer in." And have a little privacy.

"It's February, Davis. Not exactly ocean weather, and we call it the Gulf. Not the 'ocean.'"

We had a stare off, the stiff-smile variety.

"If I were you," she said, "I'd think carefully before signing a lease."

Funny she hadn't had any advice for me when she'd given me three seconds to sign the encyclopedia she called an employment agreement. "I'll keep that in mind, Natalie. Thanks."

"Do that." She drummed her fingers on her desk with one hand and reached for her coffee with the other. "As long as you're here," she said, "you might as well get to work." She pulled a file from somewhere behind her desk, opened it, and a photograph of a man appeared. "The husband, Hank, is a slot tech."

She seemed rattled, jumpy, not her usual perky self, and that was in addition to being irritated at me. I think she hadn't wanted me to know just yet that I was a dead ringer for the boss's wife.

"What's a slot tech?"

"Technician. He repairs and maintains slot machines."

"And the wife?" I asked.

"She's a casino host. Beth Dunn. She was here first. He came onboard five or six months later. They were married a year later. And now we're six years down the road."

"What's the problem?"

Natalie reached up and pushed hair out of her eyes. "Her clients win too much money."

"How much?"

"A better way to put it might be that an unusually high percentage of her clients never lose."

"Gotcha," I said. "What else do you already know?"

"Well, just like with the room safes, we looked into it. We assigned surveillance to the Dunns, but that's tricky. When we shadow one of our own, they figure it out or the person next to them does, which gives them time to stop whatever they're doing and cover their tracks on anything they've already done. We wasted a hundred security hours on the Dunns and came up empty. So we put our internal auditors to work on it, and they came back agreeing that a high percentage of her clients had unusually profitable play, but nothing jumped out at them." Natalie shrugged. "Let's get you in there, Davis. See what you can dig up."

Getting me in there could go several ways. I sure hoped it didn't go the slot technician way. I could barely change a light bulb.

Reading my mind, Natalie said, "Our plan was to register you as one of Beth's players, but with Heidi Dupree's exit, there's a host assistant seat to fill at Beth's elbow."

I nodded along, catching every tenth word: auditors, technicians, elbows.

"I'll have the paperwork run through HR," she said, "and you be here at seven thirty *Wednesday* morning." She shot me a look. I crawled under the chair.

(No, I didn't.)

"Any idea where you're going live?" she asked.

"I'll find a newspaper and figure something out." I tucked the two files into my gigantic tote bag and stood.

"Let me know where you land, and I'll have your wardrobe delivered."

The most promising thing I'd heard all morning. "Oh, hey, Natalie." I turned at the door.

She looked up.

"What's the deal with Mrs. Sanders?"

One of her eyebrows rose. "What do you mean?"

"What do you mean, what do I mean? Isn't it obvious?"

The other eyebrow rose. "I'll see you Wednesday morning, Davis."

I stumbled out mentally checking box four (times this job has sent me reeling) and calculating my debt against my paycheck (still the largest reel).

I couldn't quit just yet.

* * *

I had to have somewhere to sleep. And knowing I looked just like the boss's wife, I needed something furnished, because I had no intention of sticking around long enough to find out why. There were exactly three classified ads for furnished rentals: one had to be the EconoLodge, the word kitchenette was in there, another must have been a highrise penthouse with twelve bedrooms and four butlers, and there was one in the middle, a one-bedroom terrace condo, Gulf view, available for a six-month sublease at a reasonable price. Perfect.

Pushing my laptop aside, waving the waitress away, I went for my cell phone and dialed the number.

After three rings, a female answered. "Grand Palace Casino. Mr. Cole's office."

Of course, it would be a casino. This city was Little Vegas. "I'm calling about the condo," I said.

Turned out, Bradley Cole was the lead of three in-house attorneys at Grand Palace.

"Wow." I was duly impressed. "Very cool."

"It's really pretty dry stuff," the secretary said. "Once a week, someone walks in, pulls a banana peel out of their pocket, then hits us with a slip and fall lawsuit. Otherwise, it's just contracts."

"Why would someone put a banana peel in their pocket?" I asked.

"We're in the middle of one right now," she said, "in which a patron claims he was poisoned by the landscaping."

"How?"

"He ate trumpet lilies from one of our gardens and they made him sick."

Wow.

Casinos. So full of surprises.

* * *

Like the Bellissimo, Grand Palace's parent company was in Las Vegas, and Mr. Cole, according to Chatty Cathy, was there, negotiating something or another, and the lease on the condo was a one-shot deal for six months only. Exactly what I was looking for.

The casino was easy enough to find (curses on you, George), because it was on the same strip as the Bellissimo, only several miles east and tucked back off the road. A nice place, the Palace: low-key, very little neon, no more than seven or eight stories high, but on almost as much property as the Bellissimo. Three hundred and eighty guest rooms to the Bellissimo's sixteen hundred. I'd call it a boutique gambling resort. It had an itty-bitty casino floor that catered to high-rolling table players, lots of dimly lit private gaming venues off that, and according to their website, not to mention the lobby that looked like a Pro Shop, had some major golf going on.

I followed Bradley Cole's secretary's assistant to the condo, so I didn't get lost. Her job must have been to safety-sample every morsel of food the kitchens prepared and log it for future food-poisoning claims—"It couldn't have made you sick. I ate three pounds of it and I was fine."—because she was one extra-large girl, about the size and shape of Teeth. If she hadn't had relatively small teeth, I'd swear they were siblings.

She eyed me. "You don't take up much space, do you?"

I showed her my teeth.

"I got a leg bigger than you."

One step into the quiet condo and I said, "I'll take it."

After writing a check for the first and last month's rent, I tore it off and passed it over, and with it, added six months to my ninety days.

"Your name is Davis Way?" She looked up. "Like a place?"

I flashed my teeth again.

"And there's actually a city called Pine Apple?"

I should change my permanent address. Or at least permanently change my name. Could I permanently change my name without getting married? (Again?)

TEN

I married Eddie Crawford the first time because I was pregnant.

My mother, who was driving my life anyway, had the whole thing said and done in under two weeks. The times I opened my mouth to protest, I either lost my nerve or my breakfast. I sloshed to the police station one day in monsoon rains to confess all to my daddy (who couldn't even look at me), but the note on the door—even his handwriting looked heartbroken—said he was out on a deer-in-the-Wilson's-kitchen-again call. The thought of which almost made me lose my lunch.

The problems were too numerous to list. There weren't sixteen-year-olds anywhere, under any circumstances, who had any business being married, and Eddie and I topped that list, mostly because it wasn't his baby. I, of course, knew it. He, genius that he was, suspected it—and here's how stupid he was—because we'd never had sex. He was too busy enjoying all the attention to admit that all we'd done in his dumb truck was drink Bud Light and listen to Nine Inch Nails. I really didn't like Eddie, on any level. I was only hanging out with him so no one would know who I was really hanging out with.

I married Eddie at sixteen out of raw fear. I married him ten years later out of guilt, boredom, and pheromones.

Double whammy.

Luckily, the first time around, I had an almost clear-thinking, brand new adult in whom I could confide, whom I trusted, and who had a vested interest. The vested interest part was because it was his baby.

Jason Wells, recent college graduate and the most exciting

thing that ever happened at Pine Apple High School, taught me way more than History.

"You still haven't had sex with him?" Mr. Wells took a sick day ten days into my marriage and picked me up behind Mel and Bea Crawford's double-wide, my terrifying new home. "Isn't your plan to make him think it's his baby?"

"I can't have *sex* with him," I cried. I sobbed. I wept. "He's a *freak*! I don't think I could have sex with him if someone held a *gun* to my head!" I was shrieking. "And I thought he *was* going to shoot me the other day, because I used his stupid hair brush. And then I got *sick*!"

"You're just nauseated because it's your first trimester, Davis."

"You're damn right I'm nauseated!"

With Mr. Wells' help, I ran away. ("Please stop calling me Mr. Wells, Davis.")

I didn't have to be emancipated from my parents, because that had effectively happened when my mother signed off on the marriage license. I didn't have to get a divorce; a mail-order annulment was all that was necessary, considering the marriage hadn't been consummated. I didn't have to scrape up the money to move into the Methodist Maternity Home in Birmingham, because Mr. Wells handled it. And I didn't have to meet the sweet couple from Tennessee who adopted the seven-pound six-ounce baby girl I delivered, but I wanted to. I wanted to see the people who would raise my child.

I cried. They cried. We all cried.

I was allowed an hour alone with the tiny creature who tore out of me, and I told her everything I knew. The other fifty-five minutes, I sang to her, wiping my tears off her tiny face.

Mr. Wells deposited five hundred dollars in a checking account for me. I was seventeen years old, five days postpartum, standing on the steps of the maternity home, hugging my very pregnant housemates goodbye. To my name I had a General Education Diploma, two sweatshirts, one pair of extremely tight jeans, the five hundred dollars, and a bunch of literature on birth control. As I started down the concrete steps, crying again, my daddy pulled up in his patrol car.

I found my voice. "How did you know, Daddy?"

"I got a very nice letter."

"From the nurses here?"

"No."

"Why didn't you call?"

He swallowed hard before he spoke. "You have to live with your decision for the rest of your life, Sweet Pea." My daddy's chin quivered. "I couldn't interfere."

"What about Mother?" I asked.

Daddy stared at the road.

"We're not going home, are we?"

Instead of answering, he took a right. Pine Apple, it would seem, would have been a wrong.

"Daddy," I said, "tell me something about home. Anything."

"The new teacher at the high school left." He cut his eyes at me. "Transferred. I never heard where."

We said goodbye at 1720 2nd Avenue South, where I got a degree in Criminal Justice from the University of Alabama in Birmingham. Dorm life was a shock, because no one there was pregnant. Thinking things had cooled off in Pine Apple, I made my way home, hoping to go straight to work for my father, but all I managed to do was stoke a sleeping fire. My hometown wasn't big enough for me, my mother, and Bea Crawford. Within three weeks, I was back in Birmingham, back in school, and working toward a second degree in Computer and Information Science. Two more years passed, and I dropped my bags inside the door of the police station.

"I'm back, Daddy, and I'm not leaving. This is my home too. Mother and the Crawfords are going to have to learn to live with it."

Daddy was leaning on several large boxes. "Can you help me set up this computer?"

* * *

I believed, deep down, my mother loved me. I do think she'd turn the garden hose on me if I was on fire, and just as far down, I loved her. I wished my mother nothing but good health, prosperity, and happiness. But for whatever reasons—stretch marks, maybe?—she has always refused to cut me even the smallest amount of slack, and I didn't/wouldn't/can't stop pushing her buttons. (All my life: "Mother's going to *kill* you, Davis!" Me: "She'll get over it.") On the flip side, Mother and Meredith were two peas in a pod. When Mother looked at me, she saw a pitchfork and flames, and when she looked at my sister, wings and a halo.

It was the way things were, until I moved back home and went to work for my father, at which point, things got worse. And worse. And worse. I was young; I was busy; I mostly avoided her. After my second divorce, though, there was no dodging my mother's absolute disapproval, and the situation became unbearable for everyone. When the war between us reached a crescendo, Meredith cornered me and, as our Granny Dee said, read me from the Good Book.

"You're killing Mother and Daddy, Davis."

"What, Meredith? You're so dramatic."

"No," she said, "listen to me."

She'd tracked me down—not hard to do in Pine Apple—at the coffee shop across the street from the police station where I parked myself during the day so I could keep an eye on Daddy, on a Tuesday morning several months after I'd reluctantly relinquished my badge. My niece, Riley, was having her way with a six-pack of mini powdered donuts and a tall glass of milk. After one donut, she looked like she'd been whitewashed.

"Our parents no longer speak to each other, Davis."

I sucked in some oxygen. I did feel a stab of guilt at the pitiful state of our parents' marriage, which wasn't marriagey at all; it was a hostile roommate standoff. The big gridlock was ME, of course— Daddy's "failure to allow me to suffer repercussions for any of my actions," and Mother's "lack of human compassion for her own child."

(Guess whose side I was on.) (Poor Meredith was on both sides.)

"Sunday," I said, "he asked her to pass the butter beans. They're making progress."

"What he said was, 'Caroline, do any of the rest of us get butter beans or are they all yours?' and then two seconds later, 'Powder Puff, Creamsickle, Apple Dumplin', Froot Loop, would you please pour Daddy two drops of tea?'" Meredith drummed her fingers on the cracked Formica that separated us. "That's not progress."

I hid under the table.

(No, I didn't.)

"Davis." Meredith's voice softened, and she reached out and hooked pinkie fingers with me. "Honey. I love you. Mother and Daddy love you."

"I wub you, Dabis."

Tears sprang to my eyes when my little niece threw her two cents' worth in.

"But you have to move on," Meredith said. "You're a wall between Mother and Daddy neither of them can see over anymore."

Meredith passed me a wad of napkins and waited for me to stop blubbering.

"I love it here," Meredith spoke softly. "I'm a small-town girl. I love raising Riley here, and I've never wanted anything but this. You, however, have to get out if you're ever going to be happy. I'm not suggesting you run away to the North Pole, Davie, maybe just Montgomery. Get a life," she said. "Get out from underneath Mother and Daddy, and let them *breathe*."

Riley panted like a puppy, her little chest rising and falling.

"Be brave, Davis. Do the brave thing. Get out of here, and maybe you'll find a job that's a better fit. You could, maybe, start paying a few of your bills. It'll make you feel better to not have all that hanging over your head. Maybe you'll meet someone, which, if nothing else, will keep you from marrying Eddie again."

"Eddie!" Riley banged a donut on the table. "Eddie's a ass-ho!"

"Davis!" Meredith was furious.

"*I* didn't say it!"

It took two weeks for Meredith's pep talk to sink in so far I was ready to jump off Pine Apple's only bridge, a bridge I'd burned a hundred times already, and the only thing that stopped me was a well-timed job interview. In Biloxi. At the Bellissimo. And there I was. Mother and Daddy were *breathing,* and according to Meredith, heavily. (Gross.) I had a job that was a better fit, I found somewhere to live that immediately felt like home, and for the first time in a long time, I was living my own life. I liked being busy, and I loved the thought of being debt free. Meredith was right about everything, even the meeting-someone thing. I hadn't met anyone, but I was entertaining the idea. For the first time in a long, long time.

I was on the right road. Finally.

For sure, I was in the right condo.

* * *

The knock on my new door was a Bellissimo bellman, not the pizza I'd ordered, although the pizza guy stepped off the elevator a minute later. I tipped the bellman, paid and tipped the pizza guy, then tore into the pizza and the bags Natalie sent. Both were somewhat of a disappointment: the pizza had green olives, not black, and the first bag I opened led with a hot, itchy wig.

Beneath the mousy-blonde wig (the color of dead grass) was a laptop. The first thing I did was grab another slice of pizza and pick off the green olives. The second thing I did was fire up two laptops, my old and Natalie's new, inserting a blank disk into hers. After that, I typed this command: xcopy32 c:<*.*/s/e/r/v/k/f/c/h. (Try it. You could download the Pentagon's files with that simple command at the set-up screen, but don't. It's a federal offense.) One more slice, and I'd copied the hard drive.

I loaded it onto my own computer, in the privacy of Bradley Cole's condo with no Bellissimo eyes and no Bellissimo ears, logged onto the internet, and with my IP address scrambled, went to the

Death Master File for Clark County, Nevada. I needed George answers. Specifically, how long had he been chasing the boss's wife? All the way back to Las Vegas? And how far off the grid was he? Could he be operating under the cover of dearly departed?

There were seven dead George Morgans listed, none of them my George. I needed someone born in the 1940s, or thereabouts, and the dead Georges I found were way off in both directions. It was almost a relief. Sometimes I was a total conspiracy theorist, and I was glad that wasn't one of them, because I wanted and needed George to be one of the good guys.

I stood, stretched, and admired my new digs. I eyed the wine rack. I opened and poured myself a glass of wine, holding it aloft. "Thank you, Cole Bradley, half a continent away." I took a sip. "I mean Bradley Cole."

Sometimes I amazed myself.

I ran back to the computer, my fingers flying across the keyboard. It wasn't George Morgan; it was Morgan George I was looking for. Not only had my driver been dead for many years, so had his son, Morgan George, Jr. They both died within months of Richard and Bianca Casimiro Sanders moving from Las Vegas, Nevada, to Biloxi, Mississippi. I web-searched Morgan George, Sr. and there he was—one of Las Vegas' finest. It was my George, alright.

I sank into Bradley Cole's sofa with another glass of wine, a blank stare, and a sick heart. The simple fact was that this wasn't a simple job. I'd been trying to convince myself I could handle it, and what I was netting from the job far outweighed the risks, but the scales were steadily tipping the other way. I peeked around the corner of possibilities, squinted, hated what I saw, so I dug through Bradley Cole's desk (eight million printer, PC, and phone cords, eight hundred loose keys) for a calculator. If I could keep my head down and fulfill my ninety-day obligation, I could pay off my sister and grandmother, plus make a decent impression on the collections department at Visa. There was the six-month lease I'd just signed, with a lawyer, no less, but he'd never find me, because I'd be in

Bora Bora braiding tourists' hair.

More wine. A pretty substantial panic attack that included some wallowing, some "Dammit, karma!", and the bottom of the wine bottle, which led to a tropical daydream in which Bradley Cole actually did find me in Bora Bora. And we lived happily ever after. Eventually, though, I found the bottom line: if I didn't stick this out, the end result would be personal bankruptcy, moving back in with my parents (who would immediately divorce), starting a cat collection, and gaining a hundred pounds.

The job was my shot, and I had to take it.

There was a big picture, and I probably should set about seeing it. The little assignments—hanging out in the casino, rubbing toothpaste off mirrors, figuring out how a married couple paid for his-and-hers Range Rovers—weren't the real deal. The Bellissimo hired me for something else altogether, and the only pieces of the puzzle I had were that it involved the whammy game, my ex-ex-husband, Bianca Sanders, and a cab driver from Las Vegas.

ELEVEN

"You're late." It was my new coworker and trainer in Casino Marketing, a girl named Heather McDonald, a tall, thin blonde with bright orange fingernails. She spoke Perfect Southern.

"Sorry," I said. "Paperwork," I lied. I couldn't very well tell her the truth, which included getting supremely lost en route to buy a Taser gun. And then lost again on the way back.

Beth Dunn, like the other casino hosts I met in Casino Marketing, thought the place couldn't run without her. And my new casino job teetered on boring, so boring, in fact, that I began lulling myself into a safe place. It got safer by the minute. By my fourth day, I had moments of wondering if I'd cooked it all up. These people weren't out to get me! (Number one side effect of police work? Paranoia. Everyone's a felon. Everyone's after everyone else. Everyone has an agenda. Which was true, of course, about Eddie Crawford.)

The casino host assistant assignment was like the housekeeping assignment in that I had to please my egomaniac bosses and coworkers behind door number one, plus the demanding casino patrons behind door number two. The most I could say was this job smelled better, but I missed having Santiago to show me the way. Heather was very little help. "Sit here. Answer the phone. Take care of the hosts and the clients. I'll be right back." She didn't show up again until lunch.

I thought I would see a decidedly cleaner side of the clients from behind a desk instead of from behind a cleaning cart, but it was only an hour or two into my new position that I realized the players had dirty laundry both in the guest rooms and in the casino. Some of the gamblers were just nuts. They came bursting through the double doors, scaring me to death, claiming the world was coming to an immediate end. Heather had told me, on her way out to run a quick errand (two hours), that when that happened, pull their In and Out. If they truly lost a monstrous sum (double their rating), I was to track down their host, who in turn would calm them down with surf and turf and straight shots of vodka. If that didn't work, they called the player a cab. If that didn't work, they called security.

If I hadn't had pirated Bellissimo software, I wouldn't have even known what In and Out was, much less how to "pull" it, and Heather hadn't bothered to explain. In and Out was the electronic tracking of how much money the casino was making on a given player, gathered from the little identification cards the players carried around.

A woman from Atlanta, DeLonda Pierce, sat across from me my first morning, shell-shocked and mumbling the same words over and over, while I tried to find her host, Daniel Connolly. "He's gonna kill me. He's gonna kill me."

I covered the mouthpiece of the phone with my hand. "He won't." I'd just met Mr. Connolly; he seemed like a pleasant enough fellow. "He won't be mad."

"I'm not talking about my host," she said. "I'm talking about my husbin'."

I pulled her In and Out. The woman had lost more than thirty thousand *dollars* playing slot machines that *morning*. I supposed a killing was in order.

"How can that even *happen?*" I asked Heather, who I found holding court with a jury of her equally deadbeat coworkers at the cappuccino machine.

"Well," Heather said, "a pro can get seven hundred plays an hour on a machine. She plays two ten-dollars at a time. That's," Heather looked up to the imaginary calculator on the ceiling, "that's twenty-eight thousand right there."

"Holy crap."

A half hour later, a sniffling DeLonda Pierce came out of Beth Dunn's office.

I turned to Heather, miraculously present. "I thought Daniel Connolly was her host."

"Yeah," Heather whispered, "Beth's really good with the people who've lost a truckload of money, and a whole lot of those get tossed to her."

Interesting. "And Beth doesn't mind?"

Heather shrugged. "Hey," she said. "I need to zip to the bank. Cover for me? I won't be gone long."

I don't know how much steak and lobster Beth gave DeLonda Pierce, or what price DeLonda, in turn, sold them for, but by the end of the day (Heather still at the bank), when I pulled her In and Out, DeLonda had somehow managed to break even.

Even more interesting.

My second day on the job DeLonda stopped by our office again.

"I need to drop this off." It was a sealed envelope, Beth Dunn's name on the front, handwritten in block letters and underlined twice.

DeLonda looked like someone had taken her out back and beaten the tar out of her.

"So?" I asked. "Are things better?"

DeLonda chewed on the question. "Do you really want to know?"

I did.

"I came here to relax, have some fun." Her black eyes bored into mine. "And I'm leaving here hoping I can keep my husbin' and my house."

What? She'd won all the money back. "Seriously?"

"It's not as bad as it was yesterday," she said, "but trust me, it's still bad."

I wanted to ask her a million questions, but instead I smiled at her and told her to hurry back to see us.

"Oh, it'll be a while," she assured me. "A good, long while."

I checked her numbers again. For the trip, in the end, she'd actually won four thousand dollars. Which didn't sound devastating to me. I held the envelope addressed to Beth Dunn up to the light.

* * *

Natalie, who dressed this puppet, most definitely didn't have me dolled up for my host assistant assignment. Not only did I have the mousy-blonde wig to contend with, I had oversized tortoise-shell glasses that slid down my nose seventeen times every single second. The clothes I had to choose from were either black or black turtlenecks paired with black or black long floppy skirts that didn't touch me anywhere and smelled like roses. The shoes were black flats, more like house slippers, and I had to sidestep old women carefully, because if they were to get a good look at my shoes they'd whack me over the head with their walking sticks and yank them off my feet. I was a perfect candidate for an ambush makeover. You! Mousy-blonde girl! Get out of those baggy black clothes! This isn't the library! All in all, I was as unmemorable a package as could be imagined. Which came in handy when I inevitably screwed up. "Who told you that?" And the person would answer, "I don't remember."

The week passed with three more panicked players going behind closed doors with Beth Dunn, then later, the same three players dropping off mail for Beth. Just like DeLonda, the computer said they'd made up their huge losses, but just like DeLonda, you couldn't tell it from looking at them.

"What's in this, do you think?" I shook the most recent envelope. Always Bellissimo stationery and always sealed.

Heather's computer was glued to her Facebook page and Heather was glued to her computer. "Money," she said without a glance my way. "The hosts get tipped."

"Seriously?"

"Big time," Heather said. "And I'm next in line!" She updated her Facebook status. "*I'm next!*"

"Next for what?" I asked.

"To be a host!" She turned to me. "This assistant job," her hand passed back and forth between us, "is a stepping stone to a casino host position," she explained. "They go by seniority. We just lost an assistant, and I took her spot. She was the only one who had more time than me."

"Oh, the girl, Heidi Dupree? I heard about that. What happened there?" I asked innocently.

Heather shrugged. "Some kind of family emergency." She picked up the small digital clock on her desk. "Didn't you say you had to leave early today?"

"I did say that." I had a date with Teeth. I was putting it off as long as possible. I'd stretched out my latest assignment as long as I could, but it was time to move on. That meant sending Natalie an email telling her I needed assistance, and lucky me, she sent it by way of Mr. Molars.

"Let me run get a smoothie before you go."

"Sure."

"Give me ten minutes."

In Heather Math, that meant three to four hours. With her clear plastic crossover bag strapped on, she smiled at me and slipped out the door.

"Bye." I waggled my fingers at the door. I hated to leave the safety of the casino host office, but I also hated the clothes. I slipped the envelope that was supposed to go to Beth Dunn's inbox into my purse and sent a text message to Teeth: *I'll be there in 30.* I stuck my head in the back office and called out, "Can anyone watch the front until Heather gets back?" A young man raised a finger. Poor guy.

* * *

There were several reasons I didn't want to be alone in a room with Teeth. Among them: he didn't like me a bit, I didn't trust him a bit, his teeth scared me, and he had no sense of humor whatsoever. If that wasn't enough, I felt certain Teeth and Eddie Crawford (that no-good excuse for a human) had a little Double Whammy Deuces Wild something going on, and as soon as I could squeeze out one free minute, I planned on nosing into it. Nonetheless, Teeth (Paul Bergman, but I couldn't bring myself to say it), and I enjoyed each other's company watching surveillance videos from five thirty on Friday until three o'clock the next Wednesday without a break.

Kidding, but it felt that long.

Teeth was dressed in what looked like all black, until the fabric of his suit (shirt, tie, and probably boxer shorts) caught light, at which point it took on a deep purple hue.

"Where do you buy your clothes?" I asked.

"None of your business."

I clasped my hands together to keep from going for my new Taser gun and rattling his big teeth out of his head.

It had been an incredibly long week. Starting a new job was stressful, and I'd started four in as many weeks. If I stayed at the Bellissimo long enough, my resume would get me into the White House. "Is there anything you haven't done?" I'd answer, "No." Lurking, always present, in the back of my mind was the threat of the industrial vacuum cleaner, so I didn't want to complain too much about being tossed around lest I got tossed on it.

The thing was, I had other matters to attend to: I had developed a crush on my landlord, Bradley Cole, and wanted to keep nosing through his drawers and closets. Every day that week, after sitting behind the host assistant desk reimbursing high-rollers for the cost of the fuel their private jets gobbled to get them there (that they immediately gambled away), I'd returned to my new condo to either try to find more photographs of Bradley Cole (really good-looking guy, Mr.-His-High-School type, great, normal teeth) or delve deeper into what happened to George/Morgan/my still-absent driver's son, and what Bianca Casimiro Sanders could possibly have had to do with it to the point of George dropping off the map and following her here, there, and apparently, yon. And where, exactly, did Eddie the Ass fit in?

Just as soon as I placed the tiniest piece of what promised to be a very large puzzle, I'd look at the clock and realize I had to be at my host assistant desk in four hours. Let's put it this way: I'd been pulling doubles all week long, wearing a hot itchy wig for one of the shifts. If Natalie didn't stop with the wig business, I'd walk into work one day soon with the wrong one on my head. And it would be spinning, because underneath it, my brain was so busy.

"You can't solve every crime, young lady," my father had warned me years ago. "Focus on one thing at a time."

"But what if they're all connected?"

"They probably aren't."

"But what if they *are*?"

* * *

Teeth had clearance for all things, and he had the Big Brother program up and running on his laptop in the dungeon he and No Hair called home. They needed a very fragrant candle.

I'd supplied him with the dates and times of the visits, starting with the Atlanta woman, DeLonda Pierce, which had resulted in The Envelope.

"Speaking of which." I reached into my purse.

"I didn't say anything."

"What?"

"You said, 'speaking of which.' We weren't speaking."

"What?" I asked again.

He batted the air. "Never mind."

I plopped the envelope with Beth Dunn's name on it in front of the computer.

"Where did you get that?" he asked.

"I took it."

He didn't know whether to pat me on the back or arrest me. "You've got some nerve," he said.

"Open it," I said.

"I'm not opening it. You open it."

"I stole it. Surely you can open it."

He huffed. He reached for it. A sheet of stationery was folded in thirds, and nestled inside were four slot-machine cashout tickets in amounts ranging from eight hundred dollars up to twenty-two hundred, totaling almost five thousand. Teeth and I looked at each other, shrugged, and probably reached the same conclusion: in the privacy of her office, Beth Dunn was giving desperate players money to gamble with, then taking a cut on the back end. Here was the back end. Where was the front-end money coming from? Probably not her purse. I pushed the tickets around with the eraser end of a pencil. Teeth deciphered.

"Let's see," he said. "This one's this morning; the other three are this afternoon."

"How do you know that?" I didn't see a time stamp.

"The Julian date is right here," he pointed, "and the time, military, is here."

Ah-ha.

"And here's the machine number."

I leaned in. Get this: Teeth's fingernails were professionally manicured.

"Let's watch." He was in charge of the mouse. He clicked.

I put my feet up on the desk and dug into the popcorn I'd microwaved. I slurped a Diet Coke.

"Do you mind?" Teeth asked.

"Sorry." I held the popcorn out to him.

"I meant hold down the noise," he said. "I don't eat popcorn. It gets stuck in my teeth."

Lord knows we wouldn't want that. He probably flossed with nylon rope, and no part of me wanted to bear witness. "And what about those four-pound broasted turkey legs you wolf down?" I truly did not enjoy this man's company. "Do they get stuck in your teeth?"

He inhaled sharply. I cowered. "For your information," he said, "I'm on Jenny Craig. I don't eat between meals, and if I did, it wouldn't be turkey legs." He sat back, crossing his huge arms over his purple chest. "How did you get this job?"

"Honestly?" I said through a mouthful of popcorn. "I don't know."

It took until midnight to watch the feed, because to follow Beth we had to guess where she might go, and watch several feeds until we found her. If it were as simple as assigning surveillance to follow her, we could have finished in time to watch Funniest Home Videos at our separate residences, but me being me and that being that, we had to watch Funniest Davis Videos instead. Because we were on Discretion Road, surveillance had not been following Beth Dunn's every step, so we had to track her down. The first camera angle we watched was the only surveillance camera that would pick her up leaving her office, and that camera was in the reception area outside her office, trained directly on me.

I'd've given anything to have known a camera was on me. I'd've sat there as still as a church mouse with my hands folded on top of the desk. I didn't. (Know.) (Or sit there still as a church mouse.) So Teeth watched my every single move, laughing his Jenny Craig butt off the entire time. When Heather was there with me, or a client was standing at the counter, it was boring. I worked. It was when Heather ran off for one of her seven-hour errands that I took two cat naps, head on desk, mouth wide open, took my bra off once, working the strap off my shoulder and out one sleeve, then the other, pulling it through, then dropping it in the garbage, and one time when I was alone I plucked my eyebrows, mouth wide open again. Teeth was about to wet his purple pants. The worst was Wednesday, when for some reason, I had my undies on backward. Before I figured it out and threw them away in the Ladies' room, I stood at the copier, camera zeroing in on my rear end, and adjusted. Several times.

During Funny Davis, Beth Dunn would pass the desk on her way to the casino floor, and Teeth would thankfully switch camera feeds. It took repeated attempts to follow her, the classic needle-in-a-haystack scenario, which was why we had to sit there all night, but we nailed her every time. About a half hour after the four clients left her office, she'd go straight to the slot machine they were playing. How did she know?

Teeth and I raised our eyebrows in silent question. And each time, Teeth would grab a pen and scribble something.

Finally, there was nothing left to watch. I turned to him.

He was rubbing his eyes the relieving way men who don't wear mascara do.

"What now?" I asked.

"We go back and do the same thing, only this time we follow the player. See how much money she's giving them to feed into the machines."

Oh, goody, goody. I couldn't wait.

"Then we'll do it again and see where the husband fits into the picture." He pushed back from the desk. "Get ready to do a whole lot more of what you just did."

"I wonder." I stretched and yawned. "If the machines she sends these players to are machines her husband has worked on right before."

Teeth's eyes narrowed.

"And the money she's giving the players isn't currency, but tickets he takes out of the machines he works on."

Teeth's beady eyes narrowed to slits. He didn't seem to be breathing. I knew this because the man was a mouth breather. Who complained about chewing noises.

"And the player," I babbled on with my theory, "goes to the same machine with the ticket, which puts it back where it belongs. And when they eventually win they have to give her a nice cut."

He stared at me as if I'd just said the Earth was flat.

"Get it?" I asked. "She's not giving them money, she's giving them slot machine tickets."

His nostrils flared.

"Or—" I dove in and tried to backstroke quickly. Obviously I was way off.

"That's exactly it."

He slammed a fist.

I jumped a mile.

"The tickets Beth Dunn gives the players are lifted," Teeth said. "The tickets they give back to her," he shook the envelope containing the evidence, "are legitimate. She can cash them out."

We enjoyed a stunned silence. I didn't know who was more stunned, me or Teeth.

"That's exactly what they're doing." He stood. He walked a circle. He pulled up a chair and straddled it, interrogation style. He was in my face. "What team do you play for?"

I stared into Teeth's eyes and found nothing there.

He didn't intend to move until I gave him an answer.

"Are you asking me if I'm gay?"

He jumped up and the chair went down. "I don't care if you're gay."

He picked the chair up, holding it midair, like he might throw it. Instead, he righted it and sat back down. In a lower voice he said, "I'm asking you if you're a criminal, because you think like one. All. The. Time."

* * *

I'd taken to wearing Bradley Cole's clothes. All. The. Time.

I climbed into his bed at two that morning wearing his green V-neck cotton sweater that went to my knees.

Did I think like a criminal? And was that a good thing, or a bad thing? Certainly, some (okay, all) of my post-divorce antics were outside the letter of the law. But those were special circumstances, and let's not go there. The crazy thing was, and I couldn't possibly have known it then, my next assignment at the Bellissimo would be the one that would lead to a mug shot of my very own.

The question as to whether or not I had criminal tendencies, or just how far I was willing to go, would soon be answered.

TWELVE

That weekend, while I made myself more comfortable in Bradley Cole's condo, if that were even possible, since I was using his razor to shave my legs, Teeth and No Hair went to the movies, watching surveillance feed of Hank Dunn tinkering with slot machines.

Four out of five times the problem was a paper jam in the internal printer that produced the cashout tickets. He fiddled until the paper was free, printed a test ticket, sometimes two, sometimes ten. Next he'd scribble in a notebook housed inside the machine door, look at his watch, jot down the time, lock down the machine, then feed the test tickets back in. Teeth and No Hair backed up the tape, counted the test tickets he'd printed, then counted the test tickets he fed back into the machine. The count was off by one or two tickets almost every time.

We met in Mr. Sander's office on Monday. Teeth, No Hair, and I sat in chairs in front of his desk, Natalie in a chair beside and slightly behind Mr. Sanders. She had a pad of paper in her lap, a pen in one hand, and the coffee cup that went everywhere with her in the other. Teeth and No Hair just sat there taking up space and sucking up all the oxygen. They both had such big feet it was hard not to stare. Did either of them fit in a normal bed? Car? Swimming pool?

"The test tickets are supposed to be zero value," Teeth said, "but he can override and print them for any amount without altering the machine's count." Teeth was decked out in slate gray.

"And the cash boxes are only audited on Tuesdays and Fridays," No Hair said. He was wearing a fruit salad tie: mandarin oranges, green apples, cherries, and kiwis. "If the test tickets are back in the slot machine before the audit, no one's the wiser, because as we all know, it's an automated count. The audit's only going to flag a missing ticket, not a late one."

I kept my mouth shut, too busy staring at Richard Sanders to add to the conversation. In the short amount of time I'd spent in the same room with him, I'd decided his hair was his best feature, unlike Bradley Cole, who's each and every feature was his best.

Richard Sanders, however, had great man-hair. It was so much longer than you'd expect; it was the length of a sexy construction worker's hair. If it were an inch longer, he could have worn it in a manbun. It was shiny, blond, and spilled over his collar in loose corkscrew curls.

"Davis?" Natalie asked. "Are you still with us?"

Everyone was looking at me.

"Sorry."

Great Hair cleared his throat. "How much money are we talking about?"

"He printed more than fifty last week," Teeth said. "But we can only see where they disbursed sixteen of it."

They were talking thousands of dollars; I didn't have to ask. I was catching on to the casino business.

"Okay," Mr. Sanders said, "so we can't account for the balance?"

"We don't have a clue where those tickets went," No Hair said.

"Maybe," the boss said, "the players are feeding what they don't use back into the machines."

I piped up, so everyone would know I was paying attention. "What are the chances she's selling the extra tickets for cash, for less than their printed value?"

There was a dead silence while everyone else's jaws dropped.

"What?" My hand flew to my chest. Had I said something stupid again?

"See?" Teeth asked the others. "You see what I'm saying?"

There was polite coughing, shifting in seats, and uncomfortable silence.

"We're need to catch them in the act," the boss said. "And let's make it section ten."

They all turned to me *again*. "What?" My heart was pounding. "Is this about the vacuum cleaner?"

Natalie pressed her lips together and looked away.

"Give us a minute," Mr. Sanders said.

We all stood.

"Not you, Davis. Keep your seat."

Oh, dear.

"Close the door, Natalie."

Oh, double dear.

* * *

We sat there smiling at each other for the next several hours, me, nervously, him, too cool for school. Between us, a dish full of cinnamon candy.

"How's it going, Davis?"

"Fine, Mr. Sanders."

"Is the new job working out for you?"

"Yes, sir. I really like it here."

"You're doing great. We're very pleased."

"I saw your wife." (A police trick. Deflect.)

In a blink, every muscle in his face did the opposite of what it had been doing. I'd seen the same expression on his face before, the day I met him, when he realized I looked like her. He was equally shocked today to learn that I knew. He rolled his wedding band around his finger at warp speed, then said, "Tit for tat. We need to talk about your ex-husband, Mr. Crawford."

I'm pretty sure I passed out, because I'd never heard anyone refer to Eddie Crawford as mister.

* * *

Somewhere in the Bible, it says don't leave your money to your children; leave it to your grandchildren, which is what Papa Way did when I was four years old. It wasn't all that much money by today's standards—thirty-two thousand each—but after sitting in an investment trust through the dot-com bubble, Meredith and I had some buck on our hands when the estate attorney from Montgomery let us at it. It came in handy for her, because she had single parenthood in her future; at the time, though, she used the bulk of her inheritance to open her shop, The Front Porch.

It came in handy for Eddie Crawford, too, because he stole almost every penny of mine.

The first thing I did after seven years of college and moving back home was to turn around and leave again for more education. My Basic Training was two hours away, and lasted from January until April, giving the residents of Pine Apple—namely my mother, along with Mel, Bea, and Eddie Crawford—plenty of time to get used to the idea of me being home.

I was twenty-three years old the first time I wore an officer's uniform, and the first time I ran into my ex-husband, Eddie, was my second day on the job, when I picked up him and his sidekick, Jug, for drinking and driving. While they were certainly drinking, they weren't driving so much as they were parked against the double doors of the Piggly Wiggly, our only grocery store, effectively trapping four very angry people inside. They learned after the first twenty times they'd tried it that if they didn't block the back before blocking the front, the hostages were immediately free. By the time I was on the job, they'd honed it. I'd already been warned this was a bi-weekly occurrence, and that Daddy never actually booked them.

"They don't mean any harm," Daddy said. "It's Jug's way of flirting with Danielle."

Danielle Sparks was a girl I'd gone to school with all my life, and she was a cashier at the Pig. Jug had been after her since second grade. I'd butted heads with her since first.

I had the two idiots in the back of my patrol car and called my boss. "What do I do with them now, Daddy?"

"First move the car away from the door and let everyone out."

"I did that."

"Take Eddie and Jug to the station, lock them up, and I'll be there in a minute."

"Do you want me to stay with them?"

"I'll come down, Sweet Pea."

Was this really happening? "No, Daddy, go back to bed. I'll stay."

"They know where their pillows are. Call me if you need me."

It was Mayberry, and I was Barney Fife. They were Otis and Otis.

Jug had harsh words for me during the entire process, while Eddie didn't/wouldn't make eye contact, much less speak. I nodded off to Jug's drunken diatribe, me at the desk, them behind bars, and jolted awake to find Eddie Crawford's laser gawk locked on me.

"Damn, you're pretty, Davis."

He was, too, but I wasn't about to say it.

"Who was that baby's daddy?"

It became a very boring routine, spending the night in my father's chair with them sleeping it off fifty yards away behind bars. The most I can say is that Eddie and I finally found some middle ground.

"Eddie," I told him one swelteringly hot night, "you're just bored. Why don't you find something to do with yourself?"

"I work."

"You go to your parents' diner at eleven, slap out ten plates of meatloaf, and you're gone by noon," I said. "That's not work."

Eddie stared at me and sucked something out of his front teeth. "Easy for you to say, Miss Money Bags College."

"I will not have this fight with you, Eddie."

"You know, Davis." Jug had sobered. A little. "If you'll let me out of here for ten minutes, I'll fix the air."

Everyone knows that air conditioning compressors only broke in July, and it was the tenth of. Daddy had put a call in to a repairman in Montgomery who said he'd try to get to us the next week. I was pretty sure I'd die of a heatstroke before then. I wasn't worried about my prisoners.

"You will not, Jug, and I'm not about to let you out until daylight. You'll just go wake up everyone at Danielle's. Her daddy's going to come after you with a shotgun if you don't leave them alone."

"Let him get the air on," Eddie said, fanning himself with the shirt he'd stripped out of. "He can fix anything."

"If that's true, then why don't you have a job, Jug?"

Just then, the oscillating fan on my desk popped, sparked, sizzled, and died. What would push the hot air around then? I let Jug out. And I'll be dipped if he didn't fix the air.

"Just needs rewiring," he said over his shoulder.

"Is that all?" I asked.

Six months later, I became the financial backer for their new business, E & J Electric. Eddie and Jug stopped drinking 40s for breakfast. They went to community college. They got licensed. They joined the IBEW. Jug bought a razor and learned how to use it.

Things continued down a prolific path for the former troublemakers, with them staying clear of the backseat of my patrol car. The day the two local boys proved they really could be productive was the day they finished laying underground lines throughout all four miles of Pine Apple, and we joined the twenty-first century with cable television and wireless internet. It was the biggest thing that had ever happened in Pine Apple, and it would seem the hometown boys had finished their metamorphosis from Neanderthal to civilized. By that time, I was settling into life in Pine Apple again.

One devastatingly lonely night, I settled into a bottle of José Cuervo. A very large bottle. The next thing I knew, Eddie Crawford showed up and my jeans went missing, at which point (have to give him this and *only* this) Eddie and I found some very common ground. For all he wasn't, there was one thing he was. And just that one. It took him a while to convince me to marry him again, because I knew in my heart he didn't want to be married to me any more than I wanted to be married to him. I had the nagging suspicion he simply wanted revenge for the first go-around. But you know what they say: revenge is a dish best served by a really good-looking man. So I married him again. We were twenty-five years old. Then a hurricane hit.

* * *

My landlord, Bradley Cole, for all he was, wasn't much of a cook. The kitchen was stocked with these things: salt, mustard, two cans of Little Nibbler dog food (hadn't seen a Little Nibbler around), and wine, wine, lots of wine. I was living on takeout and wine, wine, lots of wine.

After the lovely chat with Mr. Sanders, in which I was forced to say Eddie's name aloud several times, I was determined to go to the grocery store and buy comfort food, but not until after I made my daily perimeter of the building looking for my driver, George.

I knew they knew. They knew I knew they knew. Knowing they knew, and them knowing I knew they knew was quite another matter. At least I didn't have to worry about being fired if they found out. Since they already knew.

I should have known they knew.

Note to self: get in front of your scrubbed record when applying for a job, because they probably already know.

Richard Sanders was neutral about the whole thing; he didn't pass judgment.

I didn't deny anything, apologize, or make excuses. I panicked, certainly, but held my own.

He actually gave me a compliment: "You're talented with a computer, Davis," he said, "and I wouldn't want to cross you."

"There's no love lost, Mr. Sanders, I need you to know that. I'm not here to win him back."

He rolled his wedding ring around, not saying anything.

"And I'm not here to settle a score on your time."

Roll, roll, roll, the wedding ring.

"The thing is, he'll recognize me."

"No, he won't," Richard Sanders said. "He'll see my wife."

How did Eddie the Ass know what his wife looked like?

"I'm going to look at my calendar, Davis, and see when we might be able to talk about this more."

This what more? Hopefully his wife. I'd done all the talking about Eddie Crawford I cared to.

*   *   *

Natalie was poring over a gargantuan stack of reports as if it were nine in the morning instead of nine in the evening. If his lights were on, hers were too. I watched a look of relief cross her face as I staggered from Mr. Sanders' office to hers, probably because the door was the way she wanted it. Open.

"Got a minute?" I asked her.

"Sure."

I found a chair and collapsed into it. "The cat's out of the bag."

She half smiled, half shrugged, the two halves making a whole expression of understanding my plight. "It's okay," she said. "We all have skeletons."

"It's hard to explain marrying the same idiot twice."

"You don't owe anyone an explanation."

"Tell that to my mother."

I looked at the door that led to Mr. Sanders, who was on the phone. "Am I going to lose my job?" My ninety days weren't up. I hadn't made enough of a Visa dent. Plus I'd signed a big, fat condo lease.

"No, Davis, you're not going to lose your job. You've had several opportunities to gun him down if that was your intent."

I hadn't even thought of that.

"Sometimes," she said, "you have to let things go."

"He stole a lot of money from me, Natalie."

"He's stolen a lot more here, Davis."

And there it went, another piece of the puzzle.

* * *

I could barely hold my head up. I left the vendor parking lot (where I hid my Bug), then drove around to the VIP entrance to look for George one last time. And there he was. Finally. He looked up. We stared at each other for a long minute. I put it in reverse, swung a half circle, and drove off.

* * *

I was up and on the road at eight thirty Friday morning to be in New Orleans, a sixty-mile drive, by eleven. Not having any idea where I was going, I allowed myself plenty of time. Natalie had warned me: "If you're even one minute late, just turn around and drive back."

My destination was the Salon du Beau Monde on St. Joseph's, for an appointment with someone named Seattle, the proprietor and stylist to the stars.

"Are you sure about this?" I asked Natalie.

"You're the one who doesn't want to wear the wig." She pulled open a desk drawer and withdrew a crisp hundred-dollar bill.

"What's this for?"

"Seattle's tip. Be discreet."

"What does she charge for a haircut if her tip is a hundred dollars?"

"It's he. And he charges five hundred for a cut and color. And be discreet."

Five hundred dollars for a haircut? My last haircut had been fifteen dollars with a two-dollar tip. "If he's that special, how'd you get me an appointment?"

"I got people." She gave me a wink. "And one more thing, Davis, before you get the shock of your life."

No, I'd already had that when I'd been called on the carpet in

Mr. Sanders' office.

"He's Bianca Sanders' stylist. The subject might come up. Be discreet."

That was three times she'd told me to be discreet. Discretion, discreet, what was next? Dismember? I had a dangerous job.

"Theese color?" Seattle, who had the longest and most glorious hair I'd ever seen on a man, even putting Mr. Sanders' golden locks to shame, looked positively Hawaiian, spoke with an exaggerated French accent, and held the wig I'd worn for the photographs before I was hired as far away from his body as his arm would allow.

"Thesse style? The cream blonde, yes?" He let the wig drop on a rolling table full of plug-in things and straight-edge razors, then circled me, tapping his chin. He twirled the chair so I was facing the mirror and pressed his cheek against mine, our eyes meeting in the mirror. "You already look just as her, no? The hair will be the finish, yes?"

This man had no whiskers, his cheek as smooth as a baby's.

"If you had the green eyes..." Seattle's laugh was a nasally series of quick snorts. "It would be too spooky. Yes?"

* * *

Morgan George, Jr. died on March 5, seven years earlier. He was twenty-eight years old. His last known residence was Henderson, Nevada. I've never been to Vegas, but I'm pretty sure Henderson was right there.

The *Las Vegas Sun* offered so little that it screamed cover-up: Henderson man found dead at his residence; police did not suspect foul play. What did they suspect? Parkinson's? Alzheimer's?

The obituary gave me more: Morgan George, Jr. was a Magna Cum Laude graduate of UNLV's School of Math and Technology. He was there the same time the boss, Richard Sanders, was. He was employed by a software writer—Technology Systems Incorporated—in Henderson.

TSI's website listed, among its clients, Total Gaming Corporation, who manufactured slot machines, specifically video poker, their most popular game a too familiar one: Double Whammy Deuces Wild.

A coincidence?

No.

Total Gaming didn't brag about their clientele, because they claimed to have more than two hundred thousand slot machines on casino floors worldwide. I guess that list would be too long. They did, however, show off their Board of Directors. The face that stood out in the crowd was the sandy-blond-haired, green-eyed one, Salito Casimiro, who was Bianca Sanders' brother.

Let's say it together: conflict of interest.

Morgan George, Sr.'s obituary was a two-liner: Decorated Las Vegas Detective declared dead on Tuesday, June 16. Private memorial service; don't send anything. The only news I could match up with my driver's fake death was a single paragraph in the Metro section, the week after Jr. died, about an abandoned dingy floating in the middle of Lake Las Vegas. The police were searching for a body.

I could tell them where the body was. It was in a cab parked at the VIP entrance of the Bellissimo Resort and Casino in Biloxi, Mississippi.

I called my father. "Daddy, I need you to ship me my computer. All of it."

"Right away, Angel," he said. "I don't suppose you can do much damage with a computer."

I called Natalie. "Natalie, I need a slot machine at my condo."

"You bought a condo?"

My head popped up and I tried to locate a clock. I'd woken her. "No, the one I'm renting."

"Why do you need a slot machine?" she asked.

Because I smell a rat, I didn't answer.

"Never mind," she added quickly. "What kind?"

"The Double Whammy game. It's manufactured by Total

Gaming with software written by Technology Systems, Inc."

"I have three of those right here," she said.

"Really?"

She laughed. "No. Anything else?"

"That ought to do it."

I sat there a minute trying to decide if my next order of business could wait until the next day. No, it couldn't. I pulled on yoga pants to wear under Bradley Cole's Life Is Good sweatshirt, grabbed my keys, and locked the door behind me. I'd forgotten to wear shoes, and it was about thirty below and foggy. I danced across the frozen asphalt. I was ten minutes from the Bellissimo, but it was late, and there wasn't much traffic. I made it in six. The VIP entrance was deserted, except for George. I pulled alongside him facing the opposite direction, driver window to driver window.

"George, wake up." I beeped my horn.

He cut his black eyes my way. Finally, he lowered his window.

"I have a question for you," and as I said it, I wished I was farther away. It occurred to me he might not like the question.

"What?"

"Do you still have his textbooks? TSI operating manuals? Anything?"

George nodded yes without displacing one atom.

"Can you get them for me?"

He nodded again.

"What *happened*, George?"

He turned, dead on. "They killed him. They slit his throat. My baby boy. My only child."

And there it was. The evil of it all.

* * *

My father had one hesitation when he hired me—the evil.

"I love you being here with me, Davis," he said, "it's a dream come true."

"Me too, Daddy."

"With one exception."

"What's that?" I couldn't move in my new uniform. I was wearing a tie. And a concrete vest. I had twenty extra pounds strapped around my middle—my gun, two extra mags, riot baton (as if), mace, cuffs, flashlight, knife, radio—and the pants were made of fabric so thick and coarse it felt like canvas. Very unflattering.

"Listen to me." Daddy held both my hands in his big strong ones. He spoke quietly. He looked me straight in the eye. "You're going to see evil. You're going to see hatred, violence, and injustice. You're going to see blood, Davis, more than you ever imagined a human body could hold. I can't prepare you for things you're going to see, because as well as we try to do our jobs, we can't predict evil. You're joining a cleanup crew, Sweet Pea. Part of your job is to help me clean up after evil's had his way. And from the moment you were born, all I've tried to do, all any parent tries to do, is keep you as far away from evil as possible."

"Here?" I asked. "In Pine Apple? Daddy, nothing's going to happen."

"It will," he said. "It will."

It did.

Obviously, I got the fluff jobs. One was standing in the middle of our only true intersection between seven forty-five and eight fifteen in the morning, then again between two forty-five and three fifteen in the afternoon every single school day of the calendar year, ushering all sizes and shapes of children to and fro. In all those years, there were maybe ten days of nice weather.

There was a little boy, Tanner Pruett, who tugged on my heartstrings from day one, and it never occurred to me that my father would be anything but supportive. He never was.

"Sweet Pea?" I was off to the school crossing in pouring rain. "Where are you going with those groceries?"

"Oh." I was lost somewhere inside a rain poncho. Finally, I found the opening. "I like to slip a little something-something to the Pruetts for the weekend. You know," I found my arms, "so they can actually eat between now and when the school cafeteria opens again on Monday."

My father's chair scraped across the floor so fast it startled me. He grabbed the bag of peanut butter, lunch meat, bread, bananas, and Yoo-Hoos off my desk. "No," he said.

"Daddy!" I was shocked.

Tanner was the oldest child of Christine Pruett, an ongoing Pine Apple headache/heartache. She was two years older than me, and I'd known her all my life. She'd been a cheerleader at Pine Apple High, rah-rah. Christine had exactly what the rest of us had— loving parents, a nice, warm home, a state-funded education, and all her faculties. Somehow, Christine slipped through the cracks. She'd gotten pregnant with Tanner when she was in eleventh grade. (Big whoop. Unplanned teen pregnancies were a rite of passage in Pine Apple.) Christine, though, seemed helpless to stop it, and she slipped up five more times with, those with eyeballs had to assume, five different men from five different ethnic origins. Between her third and fourth child, she met her true love, methamphetamine, at which point she began cranking herself into oblivion.

Eventually, Christine didn't have a tooth in her head and stopped leaving her trailer. We'd done every single thing we could possibly do for Christine through the years. We locked her up. We cleaned her trailer. We had interventions. We scattered her children around to foster homes. We held vigils. We did everything except cook her smack for her. She was, truly, a hopeless case.

But her firstborn, Tanner, wasn't. He was an old soul, and why wouldn't he be? He'd seen it all. He was a smart boy, a straight-A student. And he worked hard; he tried his best to take care of his mother. He mowed yards, he did odd jobs, he learned how to heat up ravioli and ration it out.

Daddy had a tight grip on the grocery bag. An uncommon and unnerving silence fell between us.

"Daddy," I whispered.

"Sit down, Davis."

I sounded like a plastic tarp going into the chair.

"You can't get involved. It's not your job. Don't get anywhere near those children without backup."

I couldn't believe the words coming out of my father's mouth. More than that, I couldn't believe the seriousness with which they were delivered. He wasn't giving me advice, there weren't options; he was giving me a direct order. "You have no business with the Pruetts, and if I get wind of you around them, I'll fire you on the spot."

It was the first and last time I deliberately disobeyed my father. I continued to sneak things to Tanner: groceries, school supplies, and winter coats. When Christmas rolled around, I slipped him five twenty-dollar bills.

"Spend it wisely, Tanner," I said.

On Christmas Eve, both mine and Daddy's radios squawked when we were passing the potatoes. My mother said, "Whatever it is, Samuel, let Davis take care of it. I don't want you to miss Christmas dinner."

"It's the Pruetts." My father stood. "I'm sure it'll take both of us."

He killed his mother first, with a close shot between the eyes. He lined up his siblings, execution style, killing four of them instantly. The fifth bullet had unmercifully missed, but by the time we got there, he was in the middle of smothering that sister.

She died.

"Where did you get the gun, Tanner?" my father asked.

"I bought it."

"Where did you get the money to buy a gun?"

He pointed.

Evil was out there. I'd seen it up close and personal. There's no guessing what form it might come in. There were times when it was impossible to know.

I leaned hard on José Cuervo for support. Unfortunately, he brought his friend Eddie along.

* * *

That night after visiting George, I was leaning on Jack Daniels and Bradley Cole. Surely a better combination.

I'd taken to chatting with an eight-by-ten framed photograph of Bradley taken on a ski trip with his buddies. I kept it beside the bed, so Bradley's face was the last thing I saw before I fell asleep and the first thing I saw when I woke up. In the privacy of my/his condo, I used it as a magic eight ball of sorts. (Maybe I should get a cat or a guinea pig. Or a magic eight ball.)

I asked him, before I turned out the light, if he thought there was enough good left in the world for us to bother. His answer: without a doubt. Did he like my new blonde hair? Definitely. I asked him if he minded me redecorating his dining room with a slot machine. He didn't. I asked him if he thought my theory was right: there was some dirty, dirty business going on all around the Double Whammy game that had somehow, someway, began with the murder of Morgan George, Jr. He said ask again later. And one last question: Did he think I could figure it out and avoid my ex-ex-husband at the same time? His sources said no.

THIRTEEN

His sources were right.

One-tenth of the casino floor was devoted to the irresponsible gambler. It was called High Limits, where the table game minimums were weekly grocery-store budgets and the slot machines could eat a mortgage payment in fifteen minutes. It was elevated, smack-dab in the middle of the casino, cordoned off by brass rails, and all aisles led to it so that everyone eventually got a wistful glance and wished they had the mojo to play there with the rich people. But off the main casino floor, in the northeast corner, away from all other venues and behind a backlit waterfall, was a Ridiculously High Limit room. It was invitation only, and it was the most brutal gaming east of Vegas. The draw was the anonymous geography; it was the reason so many private hangars were built for so many private jets ten miles from the Bellissino. In Private Gaming, school teacher salaries were tips and the sticker price of luxury yachts was won and lost in seconds.

A different breed of gambler played in Private Gaming, the one they called a whale. Whales were one of these: famous, a professional athlete, a politician, or so inherently wealthy their portfolio had its own summer house in France. I would've guessed self-made millionaires kept the room busy too, but Natalie—sending me to Private Gaming for my next assignment—said not to bother looking for self-made millionaires in Private Gaming. She said people who earned their fortunes didn't give it to casinos. "They gamble," she explained. "But you'll find them playing one hand at the five-dollar tables, not two hands at the five-thousand-dollar tables. The only other players in Private Gaming have something else entirely going on." She sat back and crossed her arms. "That'll be you, Davis. You're going to Private Gaming for something else entirely."

"What?" I asked. "What something else?"

"Your ex-husband."

"Excuse me?"

"You heard me."

I couldn't have. I only had one ex-husband. He wasn't famous, or an athlete, or any manner of politician. For sure he wasn't inherently wealthy. "Why would my ex-husband be in Private Gaming?" I asked. "I can assure you, Natalie, he's never set foot in the rich room."

"He has, he does, and he wins," she said. "He won big four months ago."

"How big?"

"One point two."

"One point two what?"

"Million."

My hand slapped my own chest so hard I'm sure it left a mark. "*What?*" I shot up from the chair.

"Settle down, Davis."

Settle down? Eddie Crawford won a million dollars and he hadn't bothered to pay me the money he owed me?

"How?" I asked. "How did he win? The dice game? The wheel game? Did someone draw his name out of a hat?"

"Double Whammy."

"Seriously? How does he keep winning the same game?"

Natalie leaned in. "That's exactly what I want to know."

I took my seat, quietly seething, as she picked up where she'd left off: markers, tuxedos, women who were paid to be pretty. The Bellissimo Word of the Day—discretion—found its way in there several times.

"And you want *me* to be in the same room with *him*? He'll take one look at me and World War Three will break out."

"No, Davis, it won't, because he won't see you."

"We met at the hospital when we were born, then I married him twice. How will he not see me?"

"He won't see you. He'll see Bianca."

"Mrs. *Sanders*?" The same thing Mr. Sanders had said. "How does he know what she looks like?"

"They're partners, Davis, and he's her third."

"Her third what?" I was having trouble breathing.

"Partner," she said. "The two before him are dead."

"How dead?"

"How many kinds of dead are there?"

"No. I meant how did the two before him die?"

She didn't answer.

"Natalie," I started.

She waited.

"Natalie, what manner of partnership do Eddie and Bianca Sanders have?"

"That's what I want you to tell me."

"How can I tell you if I don't know?"

"He knows," she said. "Let him tell you."

Did she just say what I thought she said?

"You're going in as Bianca Sanders," Natalie said. "Pretend you're her, spend time with him, assess the nature of their relationship, then report back to me."

"No." And I didn't mince the word. In case she missed it, I added, "No, no, and no."

The room grew still.

So still, for so long, I couldn't take it.

"Okay, Natalie. Let's say I'm a good enough actress to convince him I'm Bianca. Which I'm not. Is Bianca supposed to have amnesia?" I asked. "Are you suggesting I saddle up to him and say, 'Eddie, you ass. Let's go over the details of how we know each other, why we know each other, and exactly what it is we're up to'?"

"I'd leave out the name calling," she said.

"Natalie, even he's not stupid enough to fall for that."

"I hear he drinks."

She'd heard right. And Eddie went way past stupid when he drank.

"Davis, you can do this."

Maybe. But beside the point.

"Is this about Eddie and Bianca Sanders or the Double Whammy game?" I asked.

She didn't answer.

So both.

"If there was any other way, you wouldn't have a job. And if you refuse to even try, you *won't* have a job. Take a breath," she said. "Give it some thought." She picked up her phone. "That'll be all."

I gave it some thought, a long hallway of thought, when I had an idea, and not just any idea, an absolutely brilliant idea. I couldn't care less what was or wasn't going on between Eddie Crawford, Bianca Sanders, or the Double Whammy game. But I cared a lot about the money Eddie owed me. I retraced my steps to Natalie's office. She looked over her glasses.

"I'll do it, Natalie, but not as Bianca Sanders. Send me in as someone else. Someone he won't know."

* * *

Of the hours I'd logged on the job so far, only the first few days had been in the casino. During my three weeks of housekeeping, I'd forgotten it was even there. The casino-host office gig had been casino adjacent, but accessed from the other side. It all came flying back when I hit the red and gold carpet.

It was nine o'clock on Wednesday night, just the right time for a cocktail. I was Marci Dunlow from San Antonio, Texas again, this time blonde. I didn't look like myself, but I didn't look like Bianca Sanders either. Before I left Bradley's place I did two things: I called my sister and described every detail of my outfit, and I checked the Bellissimo guest list and casino activity on the computer. No Eddie Crawford.

Marci was dressed in black capri pencil pants, an oversized pearly cashmere sweater over a white silk tank, and she was prancing around in four-inch Jimmy Choos of a dark metal color. My blonde hair was half up and half down. My eyes were Caribbean blue.

I wore Coco Chanel shades through the casino.

When I reached the backlit waterfall that greeted the big fish, I took off the sunglasses and dropped them into my Fendi hobo like they were a pack of Juicy Fruit. Natalie had added jewelry to the mix by way of three-carat princess-cut diamond solitaire earrings, a David Yurman diamond cuff bracelet on my right arm, and a platinum and diamond Rolex on my left.

"It's all about the shoes and the accessories, Davis," she told me. "If you're wondering if someone really has money, check their shoes and accessories."

I was checking the accessories, specifically the watch. I hoped it was waterproof, because I think I was drooling on it.

I could feel all the luxury; my skin was hot beneath it. There'd never been a time in my life that I'd wanted for anything, but I had to admit that living the fab life gave me an entirely different perspective. Sixteen-hundred-dollar shoes on my feet slowed my pace. What was the big hurry? I'd already arrived.

I felt no less than twenty sets of unblinking eyes on me, and I didn't know if it was because I'd stepped into the room or if I reminded them of Bianca. A young man on loan from Hollywood walked up and gave me a slight bow. "Welcome, Miss Dunlow."

I gave him a small sigh and an even smaller nod.

The whale room was more of the same and less of the same: more opulence, less people, more gaming, less noise. One thing was noticeably absent: the air of desperation. Either the waterfall sucked out the anxiety I'd seen on so many gambling faces, or the gamblers there had so much money it simply didn't matter. The ratio of employee to gambler in the main casino was probably one to a hundred; in Private Gaming it looked to be ten tuxedoed employees per gambler. Everything in the room was cranked up a notch, or ten, and at the same time, scaled down a notch, or twenty. I felt like I was on a movie set. It was decadence at its finest.

"This way." Hollywood held his arm out, and I felt him behind me as the Jimmy Choos sank into the thick carpet. Another tuxedoed man twenty yards away gave me a bow and swept his right arm out like a ballroom dancer.

I turned the corner and found myself face-to-face with four slot machines that cost five hundred dollars per push of the button, then there they were, on my left, Double Whammy Deuces Wild. Nine of them, side by side, holding up a dark wall. A small LCD display above the three middle machines quietly announced the progressive total: $1,287,059, and climbing. They were one-hundred-dollar slot machines. Other than the stakes being incredibly higher, it was the same game I'd played weeks earlier with the sisters, Mary and Maxine. It was the same game Total Gaming manufactured, where Salito Casimiro had a seat on the board. It was the same game George's son developed the software for, and the same game I'd had delivered to Bradley Cole's condo, except the ones in front of me weren't open and in a million pieces.

"How much would you like to start with, Miss Dunlow?" Hollywood asked.

"Oh," I said to Hollywood, "ten?"

"Certainly." He backed away and returned with two tickets on a small silver tray valued at five thousand each. "Your marker balance for the evening is forty thousand. Good luck."

I wanted to say, "Hollywood, save your luck for Eddie Crawford. Because he's going to need it."

* * *

I didn't eat for four days beginning Sunday, August 28, 2005. I lived on coffee. One of those days, because my mother badgered me incessantly, I choked down three pretzels. I stayed glued to the television, then the police scanner and weather radio, then back to the television, as Hurricane Katrina sickeningly tore through the Gulf. Eighteen hundred dead, more than one hundred billion in destruction. Even in Pine Apple, almost two hundred miles inland, we were all but washed away, and spent more than twenty-four hours without power, wringing our hands by the glow of a lamp plugged into a generator at the station. Meredith and I slept in Eddie and Jug's cell, Mother and Daddy on cots between the desks. My husband of less than a year and his former partner-in-crime were in their truck doing electrical things most of that time, and when he wasn't working, Eddie was several miles away with his own parents. It was a horrifying, unimaginable, and helpless time. It got so much worse before it got any better.

"Listen, Davis," Eddie said on the Friday morning after the Storm, the television news in the background showing scene after scene of devastation and mayhem. "Me and Jug are going to head down there."

"Down where?"

"To New Orleans."

I turned down the volume on the television. "Is there a humanitarian hidden somewhere in you, Eddie? Are you going to help?"

He actually scoffed at the idea. That's what a low-life he was.

"Why do you think?" He rose from his seat at our kitchen table and poured himself more coffee. "There's so much work there, I'll be able to retire off what I make in the next six months."

"You'll never make it. The roads are closed."

"Watch me."

I was right; he didn't make it. He got as far as Biloxi, where he signed on with Coast Electrical to get the Bellissimo back up and running. After six months, I think we both forgot we were married. He never really came home until the summons to appear in divorce court finally caught up with him years later, which was around when, some say, I began behaving badly.

Eddie was right about one thing: there was round-the-clock work in the beginning. The problem was he blew his paychecks at the casinos as they reopened. For the next three years he had everyone believing he was still hard at it, showing up in Pine Apple for the occasional Thanksgiving or Fourth of July, only he failed to mention he was hard at draining my investment fund, not hard at anything that resembled work.

For my part, I knew I didn't want him back in Pine Apple, so I left well enough alone. As far as the money went, I'd never kept an eye on it, because I'd never had a reason to. The statements were delivered quarterly, electronically, and never had anything new to say, so I didn't scroll through the seventy pages, just forwarded them to my accountant in Montgomery. I even missed it on the tax returns, with E & J Electric being a C-corporation, there were three hundred pages of IRS forms to dig through, and it never occurred to me to look for the one-liner buried in there showing the taxes due on withdrawals from my investment account. After Eddie had been on the Gulf for almost three years, I accidentally downloaded and opened a statement. Out of boredom, I read it. By that time, the money was long gone.

I had an epic fit that ended with a horrible credit rating, a welcome divorce, and my father saying to me, "Turn in your badge and your gun before someone gets killed."

Eddie owed me. Big time. I'd never get my job back, but if I played my Whammy cards right, I might get my money back. And Eddie out of my life for good.

* * *

"Makers Mark. Make it a double. Neat."

I gambled in Private Gaming three nights in a row with one eye on the door and one on the game. I'd kept an eye out for him, but I hadn't been listening. So on the fourth night, when I was close to unclenching, I almost fell on the floor when I heard the biggest mistake of my life order a drink.

He turned the corner and was no more than ten feet away before I could even catch my breath. He sat down at the end of the row. There were four empty chairs between us, which wasn't nearly enough. He tossed a pack of Marlboro Reds to the side of the video poker machine.

"Thanks, darlin'," he said to the waitress as she passed him a whiskey.

"Cheers." He finally turned my way, raised his glass, then froze mid-toast.

I suppose I reminded him of someone.

There we were—Davis and Eddie—and he didn't even recognize me. Or her. What I'd dreaded for days was over. The whole thing was like having my eyebrows waxed: waiting for it was the worst part. Eddie Crawford couldn't put two and two together on his best day. Give him a whiskey, and he couldn't tell you his own name. It was borderline comical. He'd obviously had a few, so he couldn't decide if he was sitting across from his ex-wife, Bianca Sanders, or a perfect stranger.

I closed the space between us, took the glass of whiskey out of his hand, knocked it back in one swallow, took off my right Dolce & Gabbana lace platform pump, then drove the four-inch heel through his left eyeball.

(No, I didn't.)

(I wouldn't do that to a shoe.)

I did, however, take the opportunity to look at the man I hadn't seen in years from behind my blue contacts, while he knocked back the whiskey in one swallow.

He looked the same, like the cover of a really trashy romance novel (*Rake in My Garden*) and—or—Zorro. Eddie was the stray who didn't belong with the pack, or he could very well be the result of a hospital baby-swap. Mel Crawford was all gangly bones, stooped over and sunken, with a nose that took up most of his face. His wife, Bea, who could eat no lean, had little beady brown eyes set alarmingly far apart, and a mouth so small it was amazing all her trash talk escaped it. How they produced the likes of Eddie should be the Eighth Wonder of the World. And if it was a hospital faux pas, I'd hate to see the baby the Crawfords were supposed to take home. Because Eddie Crawford looked good—messy black hair, black eyes, and a five o'clock shadow ten minutes after he shaved— easily the prettiest thing to ever hail from Pine Apple. With equal airtime, he was as dumb as a rock, and his good looks had always been his downfall. He'd leaned on them so hard he hadn't bothered to develop any other human characteristics. It was all over the second he opened his mouth. Which he did.

"You look like two women I know," he said, "but not in a bad way, if you know what I mean." Then he smiled his let's-get-naked smile.

My heart pounding out of my chest, I cashed out my slot machine and got away from him as fast as I could. I had to find another way to get my money back. Because the being-in-the-same-room-with-him way wasn't going to work.

*　*　*

I was still shaking when I climbed into the backseat.

"Rough night?" George asked.

I didn't know how to answer. He pulled out, and we made the commute to Bradley Cole's in silence. He parked the car, but left it running.

"I need more stuff, George." I passed him a slip of paper.

He muttered something under his breath, probably because I'd demanded he go to the grocery store for me the day before and I had tampons on the list. I'd been working day and night, either in my pajamas pulling a slot machine apart and trying to make sense of his son's notes from years ago or dressed up like a runway model playing Whammy in Private Gaming. I'd averaged three hours of sleep a night for the week. I couldn't do it without him, and he knew it. So he could mumble all he wanted. I'd just been five feet away from my ex-ex-husband, who I loathed, and I didn't, at the moment, care.

George pulled reading glasses from his pocket and held the paper close to the glowing dash. "Who is SimonHex?"

"What, George. Not who. It's computer software," I told him.

"Is it big?"

"It'll be a disk or a slip of paper with numbers on it. Either way, it will fit in your pocket."

"What does it do?"

"It disassembles computer programs," I said. "It will let me read computer language backward."

"Why do you want to read computer language backward?"

"Because I'm done with Private Gaming."

He caught my eye in the rearview mirror. "Why?"

I didn't have the energy to explain to George that my future Double Whammy work would be conducted in the privacy of Bradley Cole's condo, where I'd never run into Eddie Crawford. And I couldn't do it without SimonHex. "Because I have a hunch."

"When?"

"When did I have the hunch?"

"No," George said. "When do you need the SimonHex?"

"Absolutely as soon as possible."

"What's your hunch?"

"My what?"

"Never mind."

The phone woke me at the ungodly hour of six the next morning. He didn't bother with hello. "They're telling me you buy it *on* the computer."

"I can't. I have to load it manually." I hung up, rolled over, and went right back to sleep. Had I stayed awake, I'd have told George that downloading the SimonHex directly onto my computer, with what I intended to do with it, would leave a trail. But I might as well have downloaded it directly. I could have taken out a personal ad: DAVIS WAY, OF PINE APPLE, ALABAMA, IS USING ENCRYPTION SOFTWARE TO CRACK THE CODE OF A SLOT MACHINE, WHICH IS TOTALLY AGAINST THE LAW. COME AND GET HER. Because George paying for the SimonHex with my debit card I'd forgotten I'd given him for Pop Tarts and peanut butter was the equivalent of taking out an ad.

The last time I'd been called to Mr. Sanders' office was when I'd accidentally hacked into the Bellissimo accounting system. Specifically, payroll. It was all very embarrassing. "Watch yourself and your cyber roaming, Davis," he'd said. "If you stumble into policy and procedure set by Gaming, you'll be in big trouble. The Gaming Board won't care what your intent was, and I can't help you if you commit a federal offense."

"I understand."

But had I?

I setup the SimonHex software load, not knowing it could be traced straight to me, but knowing full well that cracking slot machine code was felony grand theft. So federal. If caught, I'd be charged with deception and fraud, times however many Double Whammy Deuces Wilds there were in the world. While I waited to commit that cybercrime, and since I wasn't going back to Private Gaming, ever, and wouldn't be there when Eddie Crawford won again, I logged on a different computer to commit a second series of cybercrimes.

Also federal.

FOURTEEN

I hacked every account Edward Meldrick Crawford ever dreamed of having.

I couldn't find the money.

I hacked into his parents' personal accounts.

It wasn't there either.

Next, I took a hard look at the business, Mel's Diner.

Eddie wasn't hiding money at Mel's.

I ran all three Social Security numbers forward, backward, up, down, and diagonally through every database known to man.

Between the three of them, a whopping $38,575 in income was reported to the IRS for the previous year. I ran title searches, checked mortgage applications, and looked at credit card activity. I scrolled through every bank deposit, withdrawal, and processed check image going back six months. In that time, Mel and Bea bought a new washer and dryer on their MasterCard, wrote one substantial check, $2,100 to Earl and Daughters Construction, and financed a two-vehicle metal carport at Lowe's. (At 28% interest. Were they nuts?) (Yes.)

For the same six months, Eddie made small cash advances and swiped his debit card at department stores, salons, and restaurants. There wasn't a single Bellissimo hotel charge, but there were multiple charges for the Lucky Tiger, a cheesy run-down excuse of a hotel-casino somewhere nearby. How cheesy? The room charges were $22.88 per night. He had one monthly direct debit: Good Body Gym in Biloxi. $49.99. (Welcome to your thirties, Eddie.) His income was intermittent, and cash, $1,200 here, $1,700 there, no more than once a month. Which barely covered his living expenses. Nothing.

The big money Eddie won was in mayonnaise jars buried somewhere in Mel's and Bea's backyard, stuffed in a mattress, or it was never there to begin with. And I couldn't see where he had enough money to gamble, period, much less in Private Gaming. By all accounts, Eddie was barely feeding himself and didn't have two nickels to rub together.

Where was the big money?

And how was he bankrolling his Whammy habit?

I might have stumbled on the nature of Eddie's relationship with Bianca Sanders.

She had money.

And that was everything I knew about her.

*　*　*

I didn't know who my friends were; I didn't know who my enemies were. It was hard to know where to turn for dirt on Bianca, so I just turned around. And around. And around. When I was as dizzy as I could possibly be, I called my father.

"Pine Apple Police."

"Daddy, it's me. Do you still have your notes on the two big guys I'm working with?"

"I do, Sweet Pea, right here."

I knew exactly what my father was doing two hundred miles away—tapping his right temple with one finger.

"If I needed to confide in one, which one would you choose?"

"I'd pick Jeremy Covey."

I knew it. No Hair. "Why?"

"Because Bergman's a retired football player, and he has priors that have been expunged."

"I wonder what."

"You have to assume," Daddy said, "if he tackled people for a living, then went into security, it would be assault related."

"Probably," I said.

Since he clearly wanted to choke me to death so often, it wasn't too much of a stretch to think he had choked someone to death.

"The other one," Daddy said, "Covey, is local. They found him at the Mississippi Bureau of Investigation, and his record is clean as a whistle."

* * *

No Hair was off on Sundays. Teeth, Tuesdays. I called Tuesday.

"It's Davis."

I heard No Hair suck in a breath like I'd said, "It's the Devil. Come on down."

"What do you want?"

"You know this slot machine you guys brought me?"

"What about it?"

"It fell over."

"It what?"

"It fell over on the floor."

"Slot machines don't fall over."

"This one did."

"So, you want sympathy? What?"

"No. I need help getting it back up."

"Are you pinned underneath it?"

"No."

"Then why are you calling me?"

I rolled my eyes. "I changed my mind. I am pinned underneath it."

No Hair, not one for pleasantries, didn't say goodbye, or hello either, when he pounded on Bradley Cole's door twenty minutes later, scaring me to death. I needed a stepladder to look through the peephole, and not having one handy, I jerked the door open and there he was. All of him. Filling the doorway. A mouse couldn't have sneaked past him, not that it would have had the nerve to.

He surveyed. "Did a tornado run through here?"

"I resent that," I said. "I'll have you know I'm working around the clock." I turned and looked at Bradley's place through No Hair's beady little eyes, and had to admit that carrying out the garbage might not be a bad idea. Or at least corralling it. Considering I didn't really like Chinese food all that much, there were an inordinate number of take-out boxes on every available surface, and many unavailable surfaces, like the floor. And maybe just a few (hundred) discarded articles of clothing. I was having a little dust problem too, because I'd doodled Bradley Cole's name in it on the entryway table, and No Hair was trying to read it. I kind of sat on it and scooted. Then I had dust all over my butt. Embarrassing.

"Does your landlord know you live like this?" He pushed past me and kicked the door closed with one of his dinosaur feet. "Good grief." He recoiled. "Crack a window." He waved his hand in front of his face. "Didn't you just finish a housekeeping gig? Did you not learn anything?"

"Yeah." I was on his heels as he helped himself, poking his big bald head in every room. "I learned I needed a break from cleaning."

He finished his tour at the upright slot machine. The door was ajar and most of the insides out. Wires were everywhere. He looked at me. Not having eyebrows didn't keep him from raising them.

I shrugged. "Sorry. I lied."

His face contorted in a way that made me uncomfortable.

"I needed to talk to you," I explained. Privately, I didn't explain.

He huffed and turned for the kitchen. I could imagine the light fixtures in the condo below Bradley Cole's rattling in their sockets and clouds of dust and debris falling, tracing No Hair's footsteps.

He helped himself to the deep cabinet beneath the sink. He banged around and came out with two rolls of paper towels, a squirt bottle of something blue, a squirt bottle of something yellow, and two garbage bags. He carefully loosened, slid out of, then neatly rolled his Snoopy and Woodstock necktie. He put it on top of the refrigerator. "We'll talk later." He passed me a garbage bag.

Who knew? Teeth was on Jenny Craig and No Hair was on

Merry Maids.

*   *   *

I thought I'd been through every square inch of Bradley Cole's condo, but I'd missed a storage closet off the kitchen. I knew it was there; I'd peeked in, but I hadn't turned on the light, so I hadn't seen the stacked washer and dryer. Or the broom and dustpan. Or the vacuum cleaner, the non-industrial kind. It was a pleasant surprise, the bevy-of-cleanliness room, because not only were my clothes in need of a romp through the machines, so were most of Bradley Cole's.

No Hair asked for coffee as he was transferring a wet blob of bed sheets to the dryer, then loading mine and Bradley's clothes, separated by lights and darks, into the washer. He held up a pair of blue-striped boxer shorts by a fingertip and waved them through the air like a flag. "Anything you'd like to say?"

I shook my head furiously. It was all extremely humiliating.

"What about that coffee?"

"There's no coffee here."

"I bet you a hundred bucks there's coffee."

He won. There was a French press in one of the kitchen cabinets and coffee grounds in the freezer. As warm coffee smells mingled with lavender-scented laundry smells—a definite improvement—I asked No Hair what was going on at work.

"Obviously nothing." He was folding towels into perfect thirds. "Or I wouldn't be here doing your laundry."

Touché.

"Natalie's out, Richard's in New Hampshire, and that doesn't happen too often."

"I never go to New Hampshire either."

He gave me a look. "It doesn't happen often that they're both out of the office."

Right.

"What's going on in New Hampshire?"

"The Sanders' son, Thomas? He's off to boarding school."

"I thought he went to school here."

"He did. Now he doesn't."

"It's an odd time of year to switch schools, don't you think?" I asked. "Why so far away? And why did Natalie go?"

He threw down the towel he was folding. "You make my head hurt. Why can't you ask one question at a time?"

Why did I get *that* question all the time? Was it so hard to follow simple conversation? How was it my family talked that way and we understood each other?

A clean condo later, we were sitting at the unearthed bistro table in the dining alcove with three computers and the dismantled Whammy, the only mess left in the condo.

No Hair cleared his throat. "I'd like to know why you destroyed a perfectly good slot machine."

"I'd like to know about Mr. and Mrs. Sanders."

"Okay," No Hair said. "You first."

"No," I said, "you're my guest. You go first."

"Oh, no," No Hair said, "ladies first."

This went on until No Hair got tired of it.

"Okay," he said. "This is for you to know, not repeat." He looked at me like he'd kill me.

I held both hands up, surrendering, assuring him I wouldn't dare subject myself to death by him.

"How much do you know about hyenas?"

Fear gripped me. "Did you find one in here?" I jerked my feet off the floor.

He closed his eyes in a meditation sort of way. Without opening them he said, "They eat their young."

I made choking, gagging, ach noises.

"They're better mothers than Bianca Sanders," he said. "And what do you know about black widow spiders?"

"Nothing."

"They eat their mates," No Hair said about the spiders. "And they're better spouses than Bianca Sanders."

"Why would Mr. Sanders marry someone like that?"

"I'm his employee," No Hair said, "not his therapist. But my guess would be that she was a means to an end."

"People aren't that shallow," I said. "He wouldn't have married her unless he loved her."

"Funny," No Hair scoffed, "coming from you."

"You don't know a thing about me. Or why I got married."

"Whatever you say."

"You don't know a thing about marriage. Mine, theirs, or anyone else's. So don't judge."

"I've been married to the same wonderful woman for twenty-two years, thank you. And if she kept house like you, it would have been twenty-two minutes."

Well, now, that changed things. I tapped my loose lips for a second and wondered (why he didn't wear a wedding band) how to weasel out of the sticky situation I was in. I gave him a sheepish apologetic smile, while wondering what his wife's hair situation might be. He sat there daring me to say something else. I thought it best to change the subject.

"Does Mrs. Sanders know about Natalie?"

"Know what?" he asked.

"Didn't you say Mr. Sanders and Natalie were out of town?"

"I didn't say they were together," No Hair said. "What are you asking me? If Natalie and Richard are an item?"

The thought had never crossed my mind. Until just then.

"No," he said. "And if you want to keep your job, don't ever suggest it again."

"You're the one who said they were out of town."

"I didn't say they were out of town together. I have no idea where Natalie is or what she's doing. Richard is in New Hampshire moving his son. And you're nosy."

I was beginning to see why Mr. Sanders might want his son far, far away. And it was my job to be nosy.

No Hair poured himself more coffee. "Now. Your turn," he said. "What's all this?" His hands splayed open.

I sucked in a big breath. It was time to bring No Hair in on the big secret. "The big game? The one I'm playing in Private Gaming?"

He sniffed.

"It's rigged."

No Hair shifted positions. "I've got bad news for you."

"What?"

"Everyone knows that."

"Knows what?"

"That there's something going on with that game."

"Did you know she was bankrolling it?"

"She who?" No Hair asked.

"She Bianca," I said. "The black widow hyena herself."

"Yes. We knew that too."

"Is there any special reason no one bothered to tell me?"

"Everything's need-to-know, Davis. You didn't need to know. All you were asked to do was find out how the game was won. Dress up like Bianca, wait until your ex-husband has a few drinks, then say, 'Now, let's go over exactly how we win the game again.'"

I opened my mouth to speak, closed it, opened it again.

"Why can't you do that?" he asked.

I let the clock tick.

"Come on, motor mouth." No Hair tapped a big foot. "You could talk the paint off the wall. You can certainly talk to me about this."

"I could. But it would be a waste of time. He doesn't know how to win the game."

"How do you know that?"

"Because he's not winning. He may be sitting there when the game hits, but he's not winning."

"Go on," No Hair said.

"The money everyone thinks he has isn't there."

"Where is it?"

"I'd say Bianca has it. She's the brains behind the rigged game. She's the one with the key."

"How does she have it?"

"Have what?"

"How!" No Hair raised both hands to the heavens, begging for mercy. "How does Bianca have the key?"

"It goes back years," I told him, "back to Vegas, and the programmer who wrote the software. Bianca got the key from him, and the only other person who might know it is—" I clapped both of my hands over my mouth to keep the word *Teeth* in there. Something told me that if I tossed Teeth's name in the ring, No Hair would knock mine out.

"Who?"

"Not Eddie."

"Who then?"

"Who when?"

"Oh, for Pete's sake!" No Hair shot up, reached the kitchen in one big step, retrieved his tie from the top of the refrigerator, then began flipping it around in a very practiced way. "What's it going to take for you to wind this up?"

"Figuring out the software." I did *ta-da!*

"What then?"

"What when?"

"After you figure out the software. What then?"

"I'll test it."

"How?"

"By winning the game."

No Hair half laughed. "That could be dangerous. Two of the three people who've won it are dead. Your ex-husband is next in line."

And there it was, what I'd been gnawing on, and the reason I ordered Chinese food I couldn't choke down, and why I could only log two or three pillow hours in twenty-four: How far up my list should saving that rat Eddie's life be? Should saving his sorry butt even be on my list?

"You guys set me up," I said.

"You were a perfect storm for the job, and no one set you up. It's my understanding you signed a contract that covers every bit of this. If you didn't bother to read it, that's on you."

"If I'd known this job had anything to do with my ex-husband," I said, "I wouldn't be here."

"Why?" he asked. "No one's asking you to get back together with him."

I thought it best to examine my cuticles.

"Does the guy bite?"

Which made me think of Teeth again.

"Your indignation is hard to understand, Davis. You act as if you showed all your cards. You did not. You could have said, 'By the way, if I take this job, I might run into my ex-husband, and we don't play well together,' but you didn't. Maybe if you had, some of this would have been explained to you."

"By who?" I asked. "Who's running this show, No Hair?"

My hand flew to my mouth. We sat in dead silence.

Oops.

"What did you call me?"

There was a God, and he called No Hair on the phone right then, keeping him from squishing me like a bug. He listened, grunted, then stood. "I've got to get back." At the door, he turned to me. "Where does the old man fit in?"

"What old man?" I asked.

"The old guy you ride around with."

"I don't know who you're talking about."

"Give me a break," No Hair said. "Do you think the rest of us are idiots?"

I thought the I-Spy-Davis program had pretty much ended. "Do you people know when I shave my legs?"

"No one cares when you shave your legs."

Sadly enough, all too true, except Bradley Cole might care because it was his razor.

"The old man," No Hair reminded me. "I'm not leaving until you tell me."

I was ready, ready, ready for him to leave.

"His son was the first casualty in the Double Whammy war."

"The old guy's a Mississippi cab driver. What could his son possibly have to do with anything?"

"No," I said, lowering my voice. "The old guy's a former Las Vegas detective. And his son wrote the Double Whammy software. Not only that, I think he programmed the win glitch in it too."

"Where's the son?"

"He's dead."

No Hair's eyes narrowed. "Do Natalie or Richard know his detective father drives you around?"

"I don't know who knows what or what knows who."

His phone began ringing again. "Check those sheets," he said over his shoulder.

"What sheets?" I asked. Time sheets? Cookie sheets? Spreadsheets?

"The bed sheets."

FIFTEEN

No Hair's visit ate up my afternoon, most of it cleaning. I didn't go to the casino and play video poker that night to test my latest Whammy theories because Eddie Crawford was a registered guest at the Bellissimo, and I didn't want to be under the same roof with him, much less in the same room. I'd drop-kicked Eddie out of my life twice already, both at times of great personal loss, and my goal was to solve the Whammy puzzle without having to clean up after a third Eddie exit. Oddly enough, though, part of me wished he wasn't there and I was, because the quiet and opulence of Private Gaming, the expensive clothes, and a lemon drop martini would feel good.

Who was I kidding?

Quiet, opulence, and lemons aside, I wanted to play the Double Whammys. I played with the equivalent of Monopoly money, house money, Natalie called it. So when I made longshot bets and lost, the house said, "Oh, well," and printed me another $5,000 ticket. Like magic. It was more fun than I'd had in a long time. I'd played the game long enough to be challenged by it. I knew what the cards were capable of and wanted to be there when they lined up. I dreamed of hitting a royal flush and had yet to come close; the best hand I'd hit on the big-ticket Whammys was four of a kind. I was stunned by how intense the game was, to the point of losing track of the job, the luxury, and the blue contacts. It was just me and the game.

Two long blasts from a car horn in the parking lot had me raising the mini blinds an inch, then all the way. George. The software. I beckoned him up with my hand.

He blinked his lights, like, *No, you come down here.*

So I pointed at the floor beneath me, like, *No, George, you get your lazy butt up here.*

I won.

He backed the cab into an empty parking space.

"You want a cup of coffee, George?"

He was uncomfortable indoors, shifting his weight, holding his black knit cap with both hands and declining to have a seat, but I could see him admiring my spotlessly clean digs.

"I'm surprised you have coffee," he said.

"You and me both."

"You got anything stronger?" he asked.

* * *

George's eyes were black as coal, his skin a deep caramel color, his hair gray in half-moon patterns behind his ears, with a white splotch the size and shape of a postage stamp above his right eye along his receding hairline. George was roughly my father's age, but broken, where my father still had mischief and humor to spare.

"I lost Morgan's mother when he was four," George said. "It was just us all those years. I saved twenty percent of every paycheck from the day that boy was born to send him to college, and I shouldn't have bothered, because my boy was a genius, and when the time came, he had his choice of scholarships."

I refilled his short glass. I hoped George wouldn't end up sleeping on Bradley Cole's sofa. I knew all about loss, and if I were in his shoes, saying the words out loud, I'd end up on someone's sofa. Probably Dr. Someone's sofa.

"He was always smart, that one. You know that Rubik's Cube game?"

I nodded.

"He could solve it in a minute."

I was impressed.

George stared at the floor. Not another word passed between us for the next five hours. It was just five minutes, but when sitting opposite a wound that raw, believe me, it felt like five years. Finally, he looked up.

"Tell me about the Casimiros, George."

He rubbed his stubbly chin. "That bunch is barely human. More like animals."

"So I've heard."

* * *

It was me who slept on the sofa. I woke up so disoriented, my first thought was Bradley Cole had come home, and he was in the bed.

"Bradley?" I listened. "Bradley Cole?"

The details of how the night before ended wouldn't come to me immediately. I ran to the window; George's cab was gone. There were no signs of the dinner he'd cooked—George was a great cook—and he'd even carried out the garbage. I must have fallen asleep, and George let himself out.

I stretched, yawned, and logged into the Bellissimo system to find that my rotten ex-ex-husband had checked out.

Goody-goody! Let the games begin!

My inbox was full. There were emails from every website I'd ever visited, my sister, Websters-dot-com (Word of the Day), Joke-dot-com (Joke of the Day), and Natalie.

Davis, head's up. We're going to need you in Le Poisson for a few shifts starting tonight. I realize this will spread you thin, but it will only be a three-hour shift for two, maybe three, nights. Stop by my office and pick up your uniform. - Natalie

What? Le Poisson was an upscale fish restaurant in the main lobby of the Bellissimo. I'd passed it several times and had avoided passing it many more times. I didn't like anything about fish. Things that swam made me nervous. There'd been an incident when I was very young—I barely remembered it—but from that point forward, fish had never been served at my house. A few shifts? A uniform? Did I not have enough to do? I wondered if she also expected me to play video poker in Private Gaming, ask Hollywood to hold my beer while I changed into a waitress uniform, then serve dead fish. I didn't know the first thing about being a waitress. I couldn't pour myself a glass of water without sloshing most of it on the floor. Waitressing wouldn't be cute on me.

It was payback. Pure and simple. For having not solved the Whammy puzzle yet. Maybe, with the SimonHex software, which I'd been avoiding, because it was so very federal, I could get out of serving fish. I had until ten.

I rolled up my sleeves.

* * *

It was a travesty of the highest sort that an institute of higher learning would hand out a license to kill in the form of a diploma, when the recipient—me—had no more idea what I was doing than the average fourth grader. A fourth grader might have had an easier time than I was having, which was to say I was as far out of my element as I'd ever been in my life. To successfully manipulate any program or system, it has to make sense. Most did. The Double Whammy code didn't. I couldn't find the rhyme or reason. I spent more time staring at my three computer screens than anything else, and the knock on my door scared the living daylights out of me.

I jerked the door open. (I had to stop doing that.) It was the dry-cleaning delivery man. He'd picked up and delivered a handful of times since I'd moved in, and always late afternoon. He was an older guy, with a thick, ropey, protruding vein that separated one side of his forehead from the other.

The words out of my mouth were, "Do you know what time it is?"

He stared at me, took a step back, shoved the plastic-covered clothes at me, then ran.

"If you're going to come early," I shouted after him, "you could give a person a little warning."

I decided to hang up the clothes, and unfortunately passed a mirror on the way. I was wearing Bradley Cole's bathrobe over his Milk: It Does a Body Good t-shirt. Hopefully I had underwear on, but I didn't check. My new blonde hair was literally standing on end all over my head, and I'd accidentally smeared yesterday's mascara all over my face in the process of reading the backward version of the binary forms of Double Whammy's brain. I looked like scary hell. No wonder the dry-cleaning man ran. It's a wonder he hadn't screamed.

There were three computer chips soldered to the motherboard inside Whammy. Two contained the game data, and the third was a random number generator. It popped right off, and, as it turned out, wasn't so random a number generator. That made sense, because if it were completely arbitrary the casino wouldn't be able to guarantee they'd make money. Interesting, certainly, but I tossed that chip aside. I was more interested in the two that contained the game data written by Morgan George, Jr.

It took forever to get them off the motherboard. Their almost permanent adhesive was probably a security feature; otherwise savvy tech types would open slot machines, snap them off, and replace them with their own. It wasn't easy to remove them intact either. When I finally had them in my hand, I felt like I was holding kryptonite.

They were straightforward programs, both 110Gs, like found on any personal computer, and simple code, just a lot of it. After I reversed the language with SimonHex, I found a semblance of a map: $X = X$. Every blue moon, $X = Y$, and that would be when the player won a little. I was looking for $X = Z$, the jackpot, and I might have found it. I didn't stop to do the math, but my guess was the jackpot sequence occurred no more often than once every gazillion plays, because in all that, I only found it once. Just when I was about to give up, I found five places where $X = B$. B was for Bingo.

Exactly what I was looking for.

Maybe.

Decoded, the software was long strings of ones and zeroes. Thousands of long strings. Young Morgan George had, every bazillion bits of code, left half a space, five different times. I also stumbled upon five penciled-in inverted Vs, each the size of a grain of salt, in the seven-hundred-page binder he'd written to support the software, so small I needed a magnifying glass to see them. Bradley Cole didn't have a magnifying glass that I could find, so I used a clear drinking glass full of water, passing it back and forth along each page. On page 128 and then again on page 452, I accidentally dumped the glass of water all over the binder, thankfully missing everything else, but the fact remained, I shouldn't be trusted in a restaurant unless I was a patron.

The problem was that the bleeps in the program language and the pencil marks in the damp binder didn't line up. Nothing said, "Here, Davis, these two go together." The code referenced hexadecimal numbers that, when triggered, located a specific combination of five of the fifty-two card values. And that was just the first time the player pushed the deal button. It happened all over again when the player decided which cards to discard and then pushed the deal button again, bringing the second computer chip into play.

And get this: it happened five different times on both chips. Five spaces, five inverted Vs, times two chips, ten total. I took a guess because there was only one thing I could think of that could happen five times in the game: the wager. Morgan George, Jr. had written something into the program that sent the game on a different path based on the size of the bet: one, two, three, four, or five coins. It was all I could come up with short of tracking down a fourth grader to figure it out for me. After all that, was it any wonder I looked like the crazy cat lady? My brain was fried. Had I even eaten? It had to be noon. It could, I glanced out the window to see the sun in a weird place, be even later. I looked for a clock. Five thirty! In the afternoon! I raced for my cell phones. I'd missed seven calls from Natalie.

I took the world's fastest shower, pulled my wet hair back, and flew to the Bellissimo in my Bug. If my day hadn't started on the sofa, maybe it wouldn't have ended in the hospital.

SIXTEEN

Natalie hadn't quite known what to say. "Are you afraid of fish?"

"Well," I stumbled, "live fish, certainly. It would be safe to say I'm afraid of live fish. I don't even get in swimming pools."

She sat back and crossed her arms. "Davis, there aren't live fish in swimming pools."

"You never know."

I was trying to talk her into letting me serve at one of the other restaurants. I wanted to talk her into letting me off the restaurant hook altogether, but since I'd stressed her out by being MIA all day, I shot for a closer star. The No Fish star.

"It won't be a permanent position, Davis. Bianca's brother Salito is on his way to Biloxi. They always have dinner at Le Poisson, and I need you there. I need you to be a fly on the wall. The easiest way to eavesdrop on them is to serve them. If you've had no waitressing experience, you need to work a few shifts. Learn the ropes."

"Again, Natalie, I'm not opposed to waitressing. I'm just opposed to fish." As anti-fish as I was, though, her interest level in what the Casimiro siblings might discuss piqued my interest too—the brother had an understudy role in the Whammy play for sure—but not enough to spend time with fish. She had me on the fish fence.

"Just try it tonight." Natalie turned to her computer and her fingers flew across the keyboard. "They're barely booked," she said. "It will be, I promise you, a piece of cake."

Fish cake? Pass.

I rose reluctantly; there was no way out. I changed into the fish uniform, including gray tinted contact lenses, and unfortunately, another wig, one that looked closer to my actual hair than any of the others.

I wondered where Natalie shopped for wigs.

Really, I was just killing time, avoiding the fish.

"I love the transformation," she said.

I tried to smile.

"You can do this, Davis."

I took a deep breath and tried harder.

Ten minutes later, I entered the side door of Le Poisson's kitchen, and two minutes after that, they called 911. I went into anaphylactic shock. I was so highly allergic to finned fish, and there was such a large amount of it in such a small space, my respiratory system shut down. I didn't remember a bit of it, except seeing a long stainless-steel table piled high with dead salmon. The next thing I knew, I was in room 410 of Biloxi Memorial Hospital. I sat straight up in the bed and yelled, "Bradley Cole?"

My mother, in a stiff plastic chair beside the bed asked, "Who is Bradley Cole?"

* * *

"You know, Davis," my mother said, "I really thought you were on track for possibly the first time in your life. I just don't understand," she flipped through a magazine, her reading glasses on the tip of her nose, "why you'd dye your hair or tell your father that you had a security job when you were working in a restaurant."

"Mother," I tried again. "I'm not working in a restaurant." For some reason, I was slurring my words, like I'd had a whole bottle of NyQuil. And I needed sunglasses. My eyes felt like they had gravel in them.

"I know it wouldn't be easy, but you could wait tables at Mel's if that's what you want to do with your life. At least you'd be closer to your family." She let the magazine fall into her lap. "Your sister could use your help with Riley, you know. And your father would surely, at some point, forgive you and hire you back." She picked up the magazine. "You couldn't be making that much money."

I pulled a pillow over my head. There were so many things wrong with what she'd said that there wasn't even a place to start.

"Is this about Eddie?" she demanded.

I moved the pillow an inch so I could see her. "Mother." She looked up. "Do you really want me to move back home?"

The answer was in her silence.

"Mother." She looked up again. "How is Daddy?"

The answer was in her smile.

I pulled the pillow over my head again.

"Knock, knock!" I heard a muffled voice. I peeked out and saw Natalie's feet. I knew they were her feet, because I recognized the brown leather boots from my first day on the job. The gorgeous boots that didn't fit me apparently fit her. I stayed under the pillow. I listened to the boots cross the floor.

"You must be Mrs. Way."

I braced myself.

"I am! Call me Caroline! Hello!"

My mother didn't just introduce herself. She only led with an introduction, then followed it with her life story. Her whole life. Finally, she shut up, but not before telling Natalie that she had an unused college degree because of me.

Natalie made the appropriate noises while Mother droned on, and on, and when Mother finally took a breath, Natalie asked, "How's our patient?"

"Oh, goodness gracious," my mother gushed, "I'm not sure what Davis was thinking. She knows she's allergic to finned fish."

I shot out from under the pillow. "Like hell I knew. You're the one who knew."

Natalie's head jerked and she clapped a hand over her mouth.

"If you'd have bothered to mention it to me, Mother, I wouldn't be here."

I saw my mother's sly smile. I looked to Natalie's shocked face.

My mother loved me in compromising positions, and from the glint in her eye, I knew I was in one. I just didn't know which one. Was I naked? I peeked. Almost, but no. Had I grown two heads? I'd better look. I jumped out of the bed and found the mirror over the small hospital sink. I almost passed out. Two normal heads would have been a huge improvement over the one head I had. Enormous cherry-red welts covered the entire surface of my face, crept down my neck, and I could see them on my chest through the thin gown someone had half tied on me. My lips were deep, blood red, almost black, swollen, and cracked. The area between my forehead and my nose was so blown up my eyes looked like little recessed dots in the back of my head, and there was an ugly gash above the left one. For the second day in a row, my blonde hair was standing on end, like it desperately wanted away from my scalp. I was done with the shampoo from the New Orleans stylist. That stuff was toxic. It turned my hair into runaway straw.

I whimpered.

* * *

Wouldn't you know it? Bianca Sanders and her brother didn't even have dinner at Le Poisson. They were seated, got into an argument, and left before the sparkling water was even poured. I could have died a finned-fish death, and all for naught. Natalie casually dropped that bomb over the phone while I was snipping off my hospital bracelet with Bradley Cole's fingernail clippers. To make it all better, she gave me the rest of the week off. (She didn't want me at work until I could be seen in public and the public not scream and run.)

"Will your mother stay with you until you're feeling better?" she asked.

"No," I said. "She's already halfway back to Pine Apple."

Mother dropped me at the front door after snapping a picture of me with her phone. We were at a red light between Patient Discharge and Bradley's Place. "Davis. Look here." I turned. Click.

"Your father will want to see this." As if I didn't have enough to do, I added hack my mother's cell phone to the list.

The antihistamines the hospital sent me home with wouldn't let me sleep for more than ten minutes at a time. So while my immune system calmed down, I sat at my three computers in Bradley Cole's packed-out dining room, more packed-out than ever, because I was up to two slot machines. Before I was released from the hospital, No Hair and Teeth had removed all seven thousand pieces of the first Double Whammy machine and delivered two more that had, I presumed, additional code to crack because the new machines were linked together, programmed to pay a progressive jackpot. Maybe the answers I couldn't find in the single Whammy were in the programming of the double Whammys.

I wondered, not for the first time, what Bradley Cole's neighbors thought about his sublessee who, after her fish party, looked like the star of a horror flick, never had the same hair two days in a row, yelled at dry-cleaning delivery men, lived on pizza and Moo Shu pork, and had slot machines running in and out the door.

* * *

The swelling in my face went down; the swelling in my brain went up. I went to work on the slot machines, wrestling six computer chips off two motherboards, tossing the random number generators again, then running the four containing the game data through SimonHex to look at them backward.

Forty hours, one nap, and three pizzas later, between the four game chips from the progressive machines and the two from the standalone machine I'd demolished, I couldn't find a single digit reassigned. I knew there had to be a difference, other than the obvious, which was simple script at the end of the programs communicating to the Whammys on the left and right of the progressive jackpot versions. I spent an entire day and loads of Bellissimo resources looking for something I couldn't find.

Or maybe I just couldn't see.

Because if there wasn't a difference in the programming, it was an outside influence that triggered the progressive win. I hoped against hope it wasn't that, because if it was something other than computer code, I'd never find it. The possibilities were too infinite. It could be seventeen paperclips in one pocket, and three marbles in the other. Or a lunar eclipse. Or singing the machine a Broadway tune in E-flat.

There was one thing left to try, and if it didn't work, I'd be forced to try Natalie's way: digging the information out of Eddie Crawford.

* * *

I couldn't decide which one I'd rather not deal with, Teeth or No Hair, so instead of calling their individual phones, I called their office. I got Teeth.

"You need a *what*?"

"A printer," I said. "A heavy-duty printer. And about six zillion sheets of transparent paper."

"See-through paper? There's no such thing," he said. "And what constitutes a heavy-duty printer anyway?"

Why did everyone argue with me? An hour and a half later, an Office Depot delivery truck blocked the main entrance to the condo unloading two huge wooden crates followed by a rolling dolly stacked with smaller corrugated boxes. I watched through the mini blinds and raised the window an inch to listen when I suspected some unflattering chatter about me had ensued.

"It's that subleaser on three." A man, who I'd seen in the elevator, was juggling grocery bags, talking to a woman I'd seen several times in the lobby. They were shivering, trying to keep warm, waiting to get in the front door.

"You know, I thought we couldn't sublease," the woman said.

"I called him," the man said. "He was transferred back to Las Vegas for six months."

What? He tattled on me to Bradley Cole?

"He said she was his cousin."

"Right," the woman said. "And I'm his mother."

"Were you here the other day when someone delivered *slot* machines?"

"You've got to be kidding me," the woman said. "Like there aren't enough right down the road."

I slammed the window shut. They both looked up, then shrugged at each other.

"Lady!"

I spun.

"Where do you want this?"

One of the Office Depot guys had uncrated the printer. Good grief. When I told Teeth I needed a heavy-duty printer, I hadn't meant one that could print books.

In the end, we shoved Bradley Cole's bed into the corner and set up the printer in the bedroom.

"How do I get to the bed?" I asked.

"I guess you'll have to climb over the printer." He passed me a clipboard. "Sign here."

One good thing came out of being married to Eddie Crawford. Just one. I knew a little, a very little, about things electrical, probably just enough to flash fry the whole building. (And my neighbors thought standing outside for ten minutes was an inconvenience.) I spliced enough ethernet cable to network the printer to my system. It took a steak knife, duct tape, squeezing my eyes shut and praying, then dragging one of the hard drives to the hall between the dining room and the bedroom. I surveyed my handiwork. Bradley Cole's condo was officially an obstacle course.

I sat down at one of the keyboards in the dining room and typed, DAVIS LOVES BRADLEY. I hit print and heard the printer whir to life in the bedroom. Success. Then I loaded the printer's feed trays to the fill lines with ream after ream of transparencies, I printed the encoded data for the single slot machine, then for the jackpot slot machines. In the end, I had three stacks of printed transparencies on the kitchen counter that rose to the tip of my nose.

I turned from the massive stacks, opened a bottle of red wine (ignoring the dire warnings on the antihistamine prescription bottle), grabbed a Nelson DeMille paperback from Bradley Cole's shelf in the living room, made my way past the computers, climbed over the printer, and sat there staring at the bedroom walls, still hearing the buzz of the printer, sipping wine straight from the bottle. The next thing I knew it was twelve hours later. I felt like a bear just up from hibernation.

I went straight to the shower, if crawling over a huge printer was anyone's idea of straight to, and stood under the hot water until it turned cool. When the steam cleared from the mirror, I could see I'd also slept off the last of the fish. I looked just like my old self. And I was starving.

*   *   *

The coast is different from mainland America in one decided way: the deep blue sea. Another difference was the language; the coast had extra words. I'd grown up two hundred miles from the Gulf and we had a porch. Bradley Cole had a lanai, a porch with a view. After polishing off four frosted cherry Pop Tarts and three cups of coffee, I realized I had nowhere to work, because every single surface inside Bradley's condo was already designated workspace, so I bundled up in his Patagonia fleece jacket and transferred the stacks of transparencies from the kitchen counter to the lanai, then weighted the stacks against the wind with dinner plates.

I tugged out sheets one, one, and one from the three towers, tapped them together, and held them up to the winter sun in hopes of finding a variant between the three machines. I didn't. The page twos were exact matches. So were pages ninety-nine.

Nothing in the software triggered the wins.

And not only would I rather relive the fish nightmare than admit Natalie's way was the only way to solve the mystery of

Double Whammy, I truly didn't know enough about Bianca Sanders to pull it off. I'd already tried to get Bianca information from Natalie; she shut me down. No Hair compared her to vicious animals. George couldn't see past blaming her for his son's death. Who did that leave?

Her husband.

* * *

Richard Sanders probably earned an astronomical amount of money, like six figures a week. And rightly so, because he had a hellacious job, the details of which I didn't want to know. If I had his job I'd go in every day, close the door, put my head on the desk and cry. I'd yell, "Go away!" if anyone knocked.

In addition to his big job, he ran in powerhouse circles—financiers, tycoons, Democrats, celebrities. In spite of all that, I found him very approachable, and as far as I could see, treated everyone, pro golfers and librarians, with the same level of interest and respect. (Last week a little old lady librarian from Tupelo won a gigantic payday on a slot machine, the one with the wheel, and he took her out on the town to celebrate. It was all over the news.) So sidestepping Natalie and dialing Mr. Sanders' direct line to ask if we could meet only half scared me to death.

"Sure," he said. "Do you golf?"

Left field. "No. But I love the clothes."

"I'll send a car for you."

I watched at the window.

It was a hearse. A long, black hearse.

* * *

The driver, a large man in a blue uniform, didn't say boo to me. He parked the car, then followed us around the golf course from a distance.

"You've never played? Ever?" Mr. Sanders was studying his

clubs. He chose a very largish one.

"We don't have a golf course in Pine Apple. We don't even have putt-putt."

The sun was out, but so was an icy wind. I couldn't feel my nose. Mr. Sanders moved so comfortably, it could have been the middle of May. I was bundled up in everything Bradley Cole owned. Mr. Sanders was wearing a red V-neck sweater over a lemon-yellow golf shirt. And pants, of course.

"I enjoy it," he said, "it's relaxing. For the most part I only play business golf. I don't often play for fun."

Golf wasn't my idea of fun. More chit chat: he wished his son could see the benefits of the "life sport," his short game had been oddly off for months, then finally Natalie's name came up ("...an instinctive, intuitive player"), which gave me an in.

"Did you hire Natalie?" I asked.

"No," he said. "She and Paul came with the job."

Paul. That was Teeth.

"She's very good at her job," I offered.

"Which is one of the reasons I suggested we talk here," Mr. Sanders said. "She's almost too good."

He didn't want her eavesdropping on our conversation.

Interesting.

"And I wanted to talk to you anyway, Davis. If you hadn't called me, I would've called you."

"About?"

"Thomas."

Thomas—gamer/son.

He did golf business while I drew designs in the dirt path with my shoe and wished for hot chocolate. With whipped cream. Natalie was so adamant: the game, the game, the game. Find out how the game is won. Figure out the game. Mr. Sanders had me in the middle of nowhere, freezing, to point me in a different direction: his son.

There were only so many hours in the day.

We traveled a bumpy pebble path to the next golf thing that

looked just like first one. I had a feeling they all looked alike. And we were doing this eighteen times? I'd have frostbite. Mr. Sanders put his golf stuff where he wanted it, shifted his weight around, tugged at his sleeves, but before he hit the ball, he looked at me from across the grass. "Whatever happens, I want my son left out of it."

I figured as much, because he moved his son ten states away. I took a deep, cold breath. "If you could answer a few personal questions," the words rushed out of me, "it would help."

I thought the driver shadowing us had taken a shot at me for even suggesting it, but it was only Mr. Sanders smacking the ball.

"Shoot," he said.

I didn't know if he meant *ooops, you just got shot*, or, *ask away*, or, *rats, there goes my ball*.

"Sliced."

I grabbed for my neck. Maybe I'd been cut.

When I figured out I hadn't been (shot) (because you don't feel it at first), or had my throat slit (you don't feel that immediately either, because with both, there's an interminable moment of disbelief, then you have to wait on your brain to send pain signals), I managed to get a question out. "Did you know what you were getting into?"

"Did I know what I was getting into with the marriage, or the gaming industry?"

"Both."

He filled his lungs with biting winter air, focused on something in the trees beyond, pulled another golf ball from his pocket, tossed it in the air, then caught it without looking. "Yes and no."

Another shot rang out, but I recognized it this time, so I didn't drop and roll.

Mr. Sanders tilted his head, craning off into the distance. After the longest he turned to me. "I learned the business from the ground up," he said, "and studied it for years before that. So I was prepared for the work." He bent over and picked up the little stick still in the ground, then put it between his teeth. He gestured toward the golf cart, and we turned in that direction. "For the record, no one in their mid-twenties can foresee the potential problems of marrying into an institution. It looks decidedly better from the outside." We climbed into the cart. "And, yes, Davis, I knew I wasn't marrying a nun, if that's where you're going with this."

My temperature went up ten degrees. "Not at all."

"What I didn't know was how the family worked."

My head jerked back uncomfortably as we shot down the path. I accidentally screamed. He slowed down.

"For all practical purposes," he said, "everything that happens in the Casimiro casinos is on the up-and-up, because the first rule of gaming is don't cross the Gaming Commission. Without a gaming license, you're out of business."

The cart came to a sudden and unexpected stop, and I grabbed for the teeny dash. Note to self: don't ever get in a car with the boss.

"But that's not to say an audit of all other aspects of the corporation would pass the sniff test," he said. "The Casimiros don't keep forty attorneys and seventy accountants on the payroll for no reason. Now the family itself, that's a different story."

One I wanted to hear.

"Help me look for my ball," he said, wandering off.

He told me he'd worked his way through school, something I already knew, and that, truth be told, he'd married for the wrong reasons, something I'd already lived.

"Salvatore," he said, "my father-in-law, raised four entitled, self-indulgent, spoiled brats, who never lifted a finger except to call for a maid. And when Bianca set her sights on me for a weekend, her father pushed us toward a more lasting arrangement, because he already knew I would roll up my sleeves and work where his jet-setting sons wouldn't. So the incentives were there for both of us."

He looked at me. "For taking his daughter off the streets and out of the headlines, I received a million tax-free dollars, a position in a Fortune 500 company that was otherwise decades out of my reach, and ten percent of the division he put me to work in. I'm not sure what all Bianca's package included, but there's no doubt in my mind she was encouraged as well. Honestly, Davis, at the time there wasn't a good reason to *not* marry Bianca and millions of reasons to do it. I was working a ninety-hour week, and I have no idea what she was up to those early years; I barely saw her. Thomas, our son, surprised us both. If it hadn't been for him, I'm not sure what might have happened."

It was several minutes before either of us spoke.

"Yes, Davis, he is my son."

I could have died.

"And you need to know that if I divorce Bianca, I'll lose my job, and most likely custody of my son."

"Is that in a prenup?" I asked.

"No," he said. "That's common sense."

A nice guy like Mr. Sanders spilling his guts to an almost total stranger suddenly made all sorts of sense too. He needed some discretion. I was his discretion. Which meant the rest of his team, or somebody on it, wasn't his discretion. File away for later.

"There was a showdown several years ago," he picked up his own trail, "when Thomas was just a baby. I never saw it coming, because when I wasn't behind my desk or on the casino floor, I was with my son. I remember Bianca had been in Italy for months, and Salvatore called me to his office to inform me that not only had he fired all three of his sons, he'd changed his will to preclude them and cut out their enormous allowances."

"Your wife's too?"

"Yes," he said. "They handled it admirably, as you can well imagine."

"What did they do?"

"They turned to their mother," he said, "and that lasted a few years. But eventually, my three brothers-in-law went to work for different vendors that service the Casimiro casinos."

"Like Total Gaming Corporation?"

He turned to me. "Exactly."

I sucked in icy air. "When did you realize Bianca was

supplementing her income in your casino?"

"I didn't," he said. "Natalie was the one who caught it."

We shared a long minute of listening to the wind whistle.

"Do you trust Natalie?"

"I couldn't do my job without her."

Not what I asked. "What's your goal, Mr. Sanders? How do you want this to end?"

He turned to me. "I want you to tell me my wife isn't responsible for anyone's death."

I might not be able to grant that wish. I wanted to ask him if he loved her, because I couldn't get a feel for where this was coming from—his heart, ego, or wallet—but I couldn't get the words out.

"I've known about the game for a while now," he said, "and I can honestly say that if it weren't for the dead bodies piling up, I'd be happy to look the other way."

He wasn't worried about the money.

"And Bianca's going to do exactly what she wants to do."

Okay, not his ego.

"It's my son, Davis."

Ah. The heart.

"He can't have a murderess for a mother."

Was Mr. Sanders asking me to dig deeper or cover up?

I wandered to a sunny spot while he did more of the golf thing, and we didn't speak again until after we drove up and down even *more* brown hills. I needed a Dramamine.

"Do you know Morgan George, Mr. Sanders?"

"Morgan George." He tried it on. "Morgan George," he repeated. "I'm not sure if I recognize the name, or if it's so common that I feel like I should," he said. "Tell me who Morgan George is."

"It's Morgan George, Jr., actually. You were at UNLV at the same time he was."

Mr. Sanders shrugged one shoulder. "That doesn't mean a thing," he said. "Big place."

I twisted around in the seat. "He went on to work for Total Gaming, and he wrote the software for Double Whammy Deuces

Wild."

Mr. Sanders looked off into the distance, a look of recognition playing across his face. "A black man," he said.

"Yes."

"I do know who he is," Mr. Sanders said. "Make that was."

"Did you meet him at school?"

Mr. Sanders shook his head.

"Work?"

"No."

I waited while Mr. Sanders did more golf: surveying, posturing, adjusting the visor he wore. He smacked the ball through the air, then watched, apparently pleased with where it plopped.

He caught my eye. "I came home from work one day and he was there. With my wife." He tossed the club he was holding into the air and caught it in the middle on the way down. "Six weeks later, the guy was dead."

I steeled myself, then asked, "Is your wife sleeping with my ex-husband?"

"I believe so."

SEVENTEEN

A day of golf, an afternoon of digging through archived news and obituaries on the internet. A pleasant and productive phone call to the police department in Atlantic City pretending I was a reporter. Another call, playing the role of genealogist, with a nice woman at the *Las Vegas Sun*. The longest call to Total Gaming Technology's twenty-four-hour troubleshooting hotline, assuming the persona of a really dumb slot machine tech, and with the most patient human on Earth. A final phone exchange, impersonal and netting me exactly nothing, with my mother.

An evening with a peanut butter and banana sandwich, two almost-frozen Natural Lights, and a big box I exhumed from the back of Bradley Cole's closet. In it: handwritten letters dating back three decades, photographs, airline ticket stubs, loose change, high school ring, buttons in teeny plastic bags, cuff links, more than twenty birthday cards from his mother, receipts for extended warranties on car things, and two old condoms. (I knew they were old because for one, they were crunchy. For two, I've never seen the brand behind the cashier in a checkout line.)

One last phone call to Natalie to weasel my way into yet another department of the Bellissimo I had no business being in. Two and a half hours of sleep.

The alarm screamed dark and early. I stumbled to the front door to retrieve the package waiting on the welcome mat. It contained the most heinous outfit yet, much worse than the housekeeping uniform. I tugged it on in the bedroom, the copier blocking the only mirror, because I didn't care a thing about seeing my reflection. Natalie sent a short, dark wig and wire-rimmed eyeglasses to complete the look. I didn't bother with makeup. I whined a lot during the process of getting dressed.

I'd arranged for George to shuttle me back and forth for my latest assignment, more to keep the lines of communication open between us than anything else, but when I climbed in the backseat of his cab at six in the dark morning and he started snickering at my costume, I decided I really didn't have a thing to say to him other than, "Shut up, George."

He turned around to face forward, but I could still see his shoulders rising and falling with mirth. "You're never going to catch a man dressed like that."

"Who says I'm trying to catch a man?"

He pulled onto Beach Boulevard, turning right toward the Bellissimo, several miles away, but more visible against the backdrop of the dark pre-dawn than I'd ever seen it during the day. I'd ridden away from work under the glow of the moon dozens of times, but never to. There had to be a million Bellissimo lights blinking against the black sky, and I was about to see the switch that turned them on. To catch a glimpse of the switch, I wore head-to-toe navy-blue canvas Dickies and boots that called themselves Wolverines. I could barely move. The boots weighed seven pounds each. My headgear was a white hardhat.

"What time are you supposed to be there?" George asked.

"Seven."

"Where is it you need to go before?" He glanced at the clock on the dash. "You having your picture made?" He laughed at his own joke.

"Very funny." I set the hardhat aside so I could pick at the ugly pants. "I was thinking we'd get a donut."

"Come again?" He caught my eye in the rearview mirror.

"A donut, George. A cup of coffee and a donut."

After a long argument, which I won, I stayed in the car while George's lazy self went into the Krispy Kreme Doughnuts, doing a brisk business, considering the ridiculous hour, where he stood in line for three chocolate-glazed and a bucket of coffee. A neon sign announcing hot donuts cast a blinking red glow on me.

When George returned, he drove a block east to a darkened fast-food restaurant, parked just left of a streetlight, then twisted in his seat so he could either watch me eat, or have another laugh at my expense. When I saw the set of his jaw, though, I knew the fun and games were over.

"You're not going to like it, George," I said through thick chocolate.

"I already hate it."

I explained my theory to him: Bianca Casimiro had made a deal with his son to write backdoor software for a video poker game. "Double Whammy," I said through chocolate.

"What kind of backdoor?" George asked.

"Where there'd be a key of sorts, George, where the game could be won at will."

"And he did this? My son rigged this game?"

"It looks like it."

I leaned heavily on the fact there was no evidence that led me to believe his son had out-and-out complied, or even profited in any way. It felt more like Morgan had been forced or coerced. I purposely left out the part about Mr. Sanders catching his wife with George's son. Because Mr. Sanders hadn't said what he caught them doing. Just that he'd caught them.

Afterward, it was so quiet in the car, I could hear the steam coming off my coffee. I'd explained my theory as kindly, respectfully, and gently as I could, and this in spite of how George was laughing at me fifteen minutes earlier, but his heavy heart sucked all the air out of the car anyway, and I had to crack a window to breathe.

After several moments of silence, I wondered if George had fallen asleep.

Finally, he asked, "What else?"

"She knew how to win it," I said of Bianca, "but it's a two-man job, so she lined up a pawn."

"Talk to the pawn," George said.

"I can't. He's dead."

"How did he die?"

"His neck was snapped."

"Ah," George said. "Same killer. A large man with a martial arts background. And that means my son's death wasn't premeditated."

I agreed. Killers had their ticks, and this one went for the neck. Breaking a neck left very little in the way of evidence. Whoever murdered these men hadn't thought out his first kill, or he wouldn't have made such a mess. He cleaned up his act before his next victim met his maker. "I'm sure you're right, George." Unbelievably, the coffee still hadn't cooled enough to drink, but that didn't keep me from trying, and I got a scorched tongue for my efforts.

"I can think of two who might fit the bill," he said, "those big guys you work with. Got a pick between 'em?"

"I honestly don't know, George. I don't want to stick my foot out and trip the bald one, unlike the other one," I said, "the one with the big teeth. Every time I'm in the same room with the teeth one, I want to poke his eye out with a fork, but the truth is I don't have anything on either of them."

"Have you looked?"

"Briefly." Well, my father looked briefly. "I should nose around."

"Good idea," George said. "Rifle through their desks."

Their offices scared me. *They* scared me.

"George?"

"Hmm?"

"You know how sometimes you really don't know who has the hate?"

I beat down the evil that jumped in my throat, and I'm sure George was doing the same. We shared a secret, me and George. The only way to keep going—left foot, right foot, inhale, exhale— was knowing the greater purpose. To stop evil. If we gave up, we'd leave a hole. Then someone would fall in it.

"There's another shill in there now," I choked out. "He's playing the game for them, whoever them is, and last I heard he was still alive. I don't know what's coming, George. I guess he's next if someone doesn't stop them."

"Your ex," George said.

My mouth dropped open. "Who? What?"

He started the car. "I wasn't born yesterday."

The new day finished dawning as we drove to the Bellissimo in silence, other than the music of me slurping coffee.

When we arrived, he turned to me. "Morgan fixed the machine's brain so it would pay out," he said. "What did the other person do?"

"He was an electrician."

"How do you know that?"

"It's right on the internet, in his obituary."

"What do you think electricity has to do with it?"

"I think the Whammy game loses power for a split second," I said, "long enough to reset. I think a power surge triggers the win. When the jackpot hits, it's within an hour of a power surge."

"How do you know this?" George asked.

"Surveillance video."

"Ah." Then, "How in the world," his black eyes bore into mine, "does someone tamper with the power in a casino?"

It wasn't all the power, just the Whammys, but then wasn't the time for details or I'd be late. I took a deep breath and let it out slowly. "I'm about to find out."

Fifteen minutes later, a very large man dressed just like me pushed through double doors to the reception room, where I waited alone. "Sandy?" He glanced between a clipboard and me.

I looked around for Sandy too. Then I jumped up and shot out my hand. "Yes," I said. "Sandy McCormick."

"You're from accounting? Going to take a look around?"

"That's right."

"Well." He tipped his hard hat. "Welcome to Electrical Engineering. Follow me and I'll give you the ten-cent tour."

* * *

I trailed behind him to another world, a scary world. Every piece of equipment was the size of a school bus. Half were on end, rising two stories into the air. Catwalks were built above everything, and scores of people dressed in the navy blue Dickies uniform crawled all over the place. Wide walkways between the machines were marked by red-painted paths, and emergency cut-off switches were scattered along the walls. The noise was deafening. My guide added to it by screaming.

"On any given day, the Bellissimo load requirement is thirty-five megawatts, but we're built out to fifty-five. That's enough juice for a whole city. Hell," he laughed, "we *are* a whole city. Now over here, we've got thirteen-point-two kilovolt feeders coming in off three different substations. See those?"

I followed his hand and nodded, but I had no idea what I was looking for, or at, and he might as well have been speaking Russian.

"We've got six steel rooms here bolted together," he yelled. "This is just the first, the largest, and built on exterior walls for the head room. Follow me and we'll go downstairs and take a look at the conduit."

I trudged along, hoping a conduit wasn't an animal. As promised, we took a look at the miles of conduit—not animal at all—and every navy-blue uniformed electrician took a look at me. From there we walked a mile through a tunnel before climbing eerily silent steps. He swiped a card hanging from a chain around his neck, and glass doors slid open to the noise again.

"Do you know where you are?" he yelled.

"I don't have a clue," I yelled back.

"You're below the casino. The vault is over there." He pointed. "And the main banking center is that way." He swung his arm in the opposite direction, clearing my hard hat by a mile.

The room, as large as a theater, without a splinter of natural light, had rectangular metal silver cabinets, each the size of a one-car garage, spaced along the walls with six huddled together in the middle of the concrete floor. Coming out of the cabinets were thousands of colorful ropes made of wire climbing up walls and steel poles to disappear into the ceiling. The fronts of the metal boxes had blinking panels.

"Every switch in here is on a single feeder with emergency generator backup," my guide yelled. "It leads to a threesome."

Finally, a term I was familiar with.

"We're on thirteen breakers in this room, each on a twenty-five kilovolt automatic transfer. Every outgoing feeder ties straight into one of the main sources, then they merge. So if we have an outage here," he pointed to one of the garages, "its neighbor," he pointed to another, "picks it up."

"How often does that happen?" I asked. "An outage."

"We shoot for never," he said, "but you know the old saying, shit happens?"

I did.

"Well, it happens here too."

"Does it ever happen with slot machines?"

"Slot machines are the green cables," he said. "And they don't necessarily work like a light fixture, or say an oven in one of the restaurants. They're piggybacked," he looked at me, "backed up twice," he explained. "Because if they go down, it has to be reported to the Gaming Commission."

Them again.

"But it happens," he said. "We had an incident a couple of months ago where a lady somehow dropped a tiny earring, not any bigger than a minute, on the bill feeder, then sent a five-dollar bill through that caught the earring, and a whole bank of machines went black."

"Really?" I couldn't see Eddie Crawford wearing earrings.

"There was liquor involved."

Of course there was. "What happened?"

"Backup kicked in," he said. "The other slot machines tied in with the one that went down barely blinked, they didn't even stay down long enough to lose data. The players kept playing while maintenance dug the fried earring out of the downed machine and the casino people did a week's worth of paperwork over a little gold hoop." He glanced at his wristwatch, then at the next door.

"Wait." I grabbed for his arm. "Can a player unplug a slot machine, then plug it back in?"

He looked at me like I'd lost my mind. "No. Ninety-eight percent of the machines have outlets underneath, through the cabinets and the floor. I think someone would notice a player moving a machine and a cabinet to get to the outlet."

"What about the other two percent?"

He adjusted his hat. "Sometimes on the progressive slot machines there's an exposed floor switch tying the marquee to the bank of machines, but it's not like a light switch, clearly marked off and on. It's a recessed floor button no bigger than a pencil eraser. A player wouldn't know what to look for. There isn't anyone out there who'd know what to look for unless they were the one who'd installed it."

Oh, hallelujah.

"Now follow me through here," he said, "and I'll show you our babies."

"Babies?" I had to break into a run to keep up with him.

"We have our own fuel cells," he yelled over his shoulder. "They feed right into the central boiler room. Watch out," he swiped his card again, "it's hot in here."

* * *

"Same time tomorrow?" George asked me.

"No." I pulled off the hardhat and the black wig came with it. I scratched my whole head. George watched me in the mirror out of the corner of his eye, and he looked just this side of frightened. I looked, I was sure, better than I felt.

The guided tour had lasted several more miles, then I had to sit in a glass-walled office and flip through hundreds of pages of overtime sheets as if I cared what was on them. Every once in a while, I'd jot a note. Mostly *Davis loves Bradley*. Nervous electrical engineers who didn't want to lose their overtime pay filed by regularly, smiling if they caught my eye. I went to the kitchenette twice for coffee, and got hit on by electricians both times. That would be my first and last trip to Electrical Engineering. I wasn't going there again. No way.

My tour guide, whose name I finally caught after we reached the offices and everyone we walked past gave him a back-pat and a shout-out, Dale Boy, poked his head in the door at noon.

"I'm outta here, young lady."

"Thanks for your time, Dale Boy."

He looked offended. "It's just Dale."

"Dale."

At three that afternoon, I closed up shop. I cut through the second level of the employee parking garage to get to the other side of the state of Mississippi where George was and fell into the backseat. "Take me home, George." I leaned my head back and kept my eyes closed until the car stopped.

"What'd they do to you?" George asked. "Beat you up?"

"I walked ten miles in these concrete boots," I said, "and then sat under florescent lights for the next twenty hours."

"Girl, you need to toughen up."

"Says the man who naps in a car all day."

"I put my time in, thank you."

"Speaking of putting in your time, George, let me ask you something." I was talking to the floorboard, because I didn't intend to walk another step in these leather slabs. I fought with the hooks and laces, and noticed, while tugging on the tongue, that my boots were actually Wolverine *pups*. I was wearing little boy boots. No wonder my feet hurt.

"Say what?"

I raised my head. "Assuming you've thought about this today, what's your theory on why they haven't been caught?"

His mouth twisted. "Time, for one thing."

"Time?"

"Yeah," he said. "So much time between big wins."

"What else?" I asked.

"Geography," he said.

"Geography?"

"Yeah," George said. "It's a popular game. You can find it in most casinos, and they have. They've won big money in Vegas, Atlantic City, and now Biloxi."

"No one's connecting the dots," I said.

George turned to look me in the eye. "Seems to me her husband has her number."

And you, George. You have her number too.

Me? I wasn't so sure.

*   *   *

I passed out in the blue uniform and sleep, glorious sleep, ruled my world for the next several hours. When I rolled over in Bradley's bed and looked at the clock, it was just after seven. Perfect. I stripped out of the uniform, grabbed the Wolverine puppies, marched out the front door, down the hall to the garbage chute, and sent the uniform flying. The boots thudded down the metal tube. I turned, in my pink underwear, to find Bradley's next-door neighbor in his open doorway holding Hefty bags in each hand. His mouth dropped so far open I could see his dental history. I covered what I could, hugged the wall, and scooted past him; he google-eyed me the whole way. I kept jiggling Bradley's doorknob long after I knew I'd locked myself out. I heard the neighbor's Hefty bags thud to the floor.

A humiliating hour later, I removed the price tags from a platinum-colored silk top, $340, skinny white jeans, $480, and pulled Tory Burch wedges out of their raspberry and tangerine box, $570. I took a blow dryer to my $500 hair, applied $200 of MAC makeup, then armed with a chocolate-brown leather Fendi hobo, locked Bradley Cole's door. That time, keys in hand.

I loved the casino part of my job.

Fifteen minutes later, I unlocked Bradley's door. I'd forgotten the sky-blue contacts.

Twenty minutes after that, I walked past the waterfall where Hollywood was waiting. "Welcome back, Miss Dunlow."

I loved the Bellissimo.

* * *

I hated the Bellissimo.

I blew through forty thousand dollars of house money without winning a penny in less than an hour. Almost eighty losing hands in a row at five hundred dollars each. It happens. It wasn't even my money, but time stood still, nothing mattered, and my world was reduced to me, a large sweet-tea martini with a floating curl of lemon zest, and one stupid machine.

Double Whammy Dammit.

I was so frustrated half an hour in that I started backtalking the slot machine when it dealt me worthless cards. "Are you kidding me? You're kidding me, right? Seriously?"

Hollywood, hovering in the background, looked nervous.

Note to self: learn how to play this game.

Ten minutes, or I should say another ten thousand dollars later, had I known how to trigger the win, I'd have done it then and there. Not that I'd have known what to do next. The jackpot was up to $1,292,560. I could hear Natalie now: "You weren't supposed to win it."

Of one thing I was certain: it wasn't nearly as much fun when I wasn't winning, it was downright miserable when I couldn't do anything but lose. I could only imagine how players who were stuffing their own money into the machines felt. If I'd lost that much of my own money in that short a period of time, I'd have been in the floor, curled up in a ball, and crying my eyes out. Maybe then, I'd see the stupid electrical switch I was looking for. If I didn't find it soon, I'd be forced to watch surveillance video of my sorry ex-ex-husband. The question was, would I live through hours of watching Eddie?

Doubtful.

In the end, I sat there in a daze, staring at the machine that had so thoroughly betrayed me.

"Would you like me to extend your marker, Miss Dunlow?" Hollywood kept his distance when he whispered the suggestion.

I turned to him. "Honestly, I don't know what to do." I surrendered with both hands. "I don't understand how I can play this hard and not win a penny."

He looked sympathetic, but he didn't say anything.

"What do people do when they lose everything?" I asked.

"They go home."

Right. Win or go home.

"Maybe try a different machine," he suggested.

"With what?"

"Casino Credit will extend your marker by ten percent with just a phone call."

That would be another four thousand dollars. Eight hands. Natalie might have something to say about it, but I could deal with her later. "Okay," I said. "Do it."

Hollywood took a step backward. "I'll be right back," he said. "Why don't you choose another machine?"

He was my best friend, my confidant, my advisor. We were in this together. "Should I? I mean, I've lost so much to this one. Don't you think it will hit soon?"

He gave me a gratuitous smile. "That's up to you, Miss Dunlow."

No, I was on my own. A place I knew well.

It took longer to get the four thousand than it did to lose it. Ten minutes for Hollywood to return with it, five to give it to Whammy.

I went home.

Well, Bradley Cole's home.

EIGHTEEN

It was Sunday, and I woke up with a gambling hangover, which wasn't anything like waking up after losing a Jägermeister pong tournament, because that felt so much better. A gambling hangover was when you woke up with a lonely quarter left to your name, if that, wondering what in the world went wrong with your game. I snarled at the Whammys in the dining room on my way to coffee.

It was a glorious late-February morning. Signs of spring were everywhere, and by my third cup, I'd convinced myself *I* hadn't lost forty-four thousand dollars, Marci Dunlow had. *I* didn't have to figure out how to pay it back, *she* did. *I* didn't have the worst luck of anyone ever, that was her. As my gambling hangover cleared, a sharp stab of loneliness took its place, a sentiment I didn't entertain often, and I decided I'd better get to work before I got any lonelier and did something stupid, like drive home.

Sunday was the one day when things were quiet within Corporate Bellissimo, which made it the best day of the week to snoop around and learn more about my coworkers. What I wouldn't give to snoop around Natalie's office, but she'd hand me my head on a platter if I did. She'd know, too, because she knew everything, and because there were ninety-seven security cameras in her office. Seriously. Every two inches.

Mr. Sanders was in New Hampshire, returning the next day, not that I even wanted to snoop through his office. I had a good handle on him, and I already knew what was in there. Cinnamon candy.

No Hair and/or Teeth's secrets would yield answers to a few of my burning questions, but I didn't have access. No Hair, I assumed, was enjoying the day being happily married. Teeth was on property, and I fully intended to avoid him.

I pulled the belt of Bradley Cole's robe tighter and stepped onto the lanai with my Bat phone. I speed dialed No Hair.

"This had better be good."

"Hey. It's me, Davis."

"I know who it is."

"I need a little something-something," I said.

"It's my day off."

"What?"

"It's my day off. I've already had to go in once. Call Paul."

No Hair hung up on me, so I called him right back.

"*What?*" he demanded.

"Why'd you have to go in?"

"Who wants to know?"

"Me."

"None of your business. Call Paul."

"I did. I tried to call him." Which wasn't exactly true.

"I talked to him fifteen minutes ago," No Hair said. "You probably can't reach him because he was on his way to the thirtieth floor."

The thirtieth floor? My mind jumped back to my housekeeping days. I mentally located the thirtieth floor. "That's the Elvis floor," I said. "What's he doing there?"

I heard No Hair suck in a big breath and let it out slowly. "That's not the Elvis floor, Davis. That's the Sanders' residence. She's due in tonight, so he's sweeping the residence."

"He's sweeping?" I laughed.

"Technical surveillance counter measures, Davis. He's sweeping for bugs."

Ah.

"And why is it he can't answer the phone and sweep at the same time?" I asked.

"Cell phones are blocked on thirty, Davis. If you need him, you can find him, as you say, on the Elvis floor."

"What if she's there?"

"If I thought she was anywhere close, I wouldn't suggest you go."

"Exactly when will she be back?"

"Can we talk about this later?"

He told me how to get into his and Teeth's office (the very thing I wanted to do), and where, once in, to locate an elevator key that would allow me access to the thirtieth-floor elevator. "Don't touch a thing. Get the card and get out of my office. Stay out of my desk. Open the one drawer, get the passkey, then get out as fast as you can. Don't go into Paul's office at all."

Whatever.

"The elevator on thirty opens into a reception area where there'll be a security guard," No Hair said. "Don't mess with him. I'll let him know you're coming. I'll tell him you're a house-decorator person. Look like one."

"A what?"

"A curtain person. A sofa person. A knick-knack person," he said. "Take a tape measure with you."

"What am I supposed to do with it?"

"Measure a wall. Talk about countertops or something. You only need to get past that one desk. You can do it."

"You don't think Paul will want me to help him sweep, do you?"

"No, Davis," No Hair said. "I'm assuming you're not trained on the equipment."

"Who isn't trained on a broom?"

"We all know you are, but we're not talking about flying."

No Hair, after calling me a witch, hung up on me again. I opened the refrigerator door and put the phone where the eggs went. I wasn't calling No Hair back to ask for anything. Ever again.

* * *

At that juncture, I had a healthy collection of options to hide the blonde, all on belt hooks in Bradley Cole's closet. I fingered through and chose the one that had come home with me from the hospital after my finned-fish accident. It was closest to my natural hair color, so at least when I caught my reflection in closing elevator doors, I wouldn't wonder who it was only to realize I was looking at myself. I had no intention of running into anyone, so I dressed in Lucky straight-leg jeans, a mint-green cashmere pullover, and short caramel UGG boots. Looking a little too much like myself, I went ahead and put contacts in, aiming for blue, but accidentally grabbing Bianca green.

Before I left, I jotted Bradley Cole a note: "Bradley—have to run to work for a bit. Back soon. XXXOOO, Davis."

I drove the Bug to work, took note of George's absence, parked in the empty vendor lot, tiptoed past dark offices, took the stairs down two flights, walked four miles uphill in the snow, crossed a desert, and finally I was pressing the keypad outside Teeth and No Hair's cave. Catching my breath from the hike, I wondered again why their offices were so far from everything else, void of natural light, and what in the world that smell was.

I couldn't locate a light switch to save my life, so using the penlight on my keychain, I batted my way to No Hair's door, stepped in his cubicle, and settled in behind his desk. The air was almost too thick to breathe. He needed potpourri, a very large fan, and lamps.

It took no time at all to hack his computer. He'd given me the codes to the door and his desk: four, five, six, seven, and five, six, seven, eight. Getting to the welcome screen of his computer was, naturally, six, seven, eight, nine. (He should know better. If I stumbled across an ATM card in his desk, I could drain his bank accounts.) The elevator pass was right where he'd said it would be.

Now that I had the glow of the computer monitor to work by, I snooped through the rest of his desk, finding nothing all that interesting, except for the fact that the lower right desk drawer was locked. Ah-ha. No Hair's secrets. I dug around for a key but didn't find one. I'd have picked the lock but didn't want to take the time.

It took forever to pull up the surveillance video of Eddie the Ass winning the big money, and as soon as I did, I minimized it. I had other things to see first; I needed to know what had gone down before the win.

The facial-recognition software wasn't altogether user friendly, or I wasn't very good at it, because I couldn't find film of Eddie Crawford and Bianca Casimiro Sanders together. After three searches, I decided that was because there wasn't any. I gave him no credit, because they didn't pass out judiciousness in Pine Apple. Had it been up to him, there would be an XXX movie of them. Coming soon to a theater near you. I had to assume either she was an expert at avoiding the cameras, or the evidence of them together had been deleted from the system for the obvious reason: her husband signed the paychecks.

There was another possibility, but it was a stretch: maybe there was no footage of them together because The Affair was part of the scam. Maybe they were just business partners—not bed buddies. She was no saint, by her own husband's admission, and yes, random women did fall into Eddie's bed. Often. Likewise, Eddie was a smooth talker. And there was no denying Eddie looked good. Eddie would probably be a good-looking sixty-year-old, but I still couldn't see it. Bianca Sanders was way too far out of Eddie Crawford's league. Bianca Sanders was out of her own league.

I searched them separately and retrieved enough footage to keep me glued to the screen for the next six weeks. I needed a break from Eddie, in general, and on the computer, so I loaded Bianca, fast-forwarding through miles of feed that went back years. The creepiest part was that looking at her was like looking in a mirror. There was, between us, almost a ten-year age difference, but for whatever reason, probably a Botoxish reason, we didn't look a day apart.

Oh, for our bank balances to be twins.

She *never* smiled. She had a dead set to her jaw and her resting face was one of rage. She wore oversized sunglasses indoors and out, rain or shine, so I wasn't treated to her steely stare but a few times. She didn't walk so much as she marched, and she was impatient, not pushing an elevator button once, but angrily trying to poke it through the panel. She slammed doors, she chewed food in a circular motion, she pressed against her bejeweled knuckles when forced to pretend she was listening to someone speak, and she smoked long skinny cigarettes when she played the Double Whammys in Private Gaming. She shook her finger in people's faces—the spa staff, housekeepers, her son's nanny, and several times in the video histories, her husband's.

She dressed impeccably, and almost always in head-to-toe black. She could open a store with her jewelry. She could open a mall with her luggage and fur coats. I counted six different animal pelts on her just last month. She was in town only four days yet managed to wear six different furs. Cruella.

The film had date and time stamps, and all told, it looked like Bianca spent an average of three to four weeks a year in Biloxi. Clips of her from June of last year (furless) jumped straight to sightings in October (swathed in fur). Where was this woman when she wasn't here? There wasn't one scrap of evidence she'd been within ten feet of her son in any venue on the property other than, assumedly, their private residence, which wasn't a viewing option.

Disturbingly enough, there was one constant: when she arrived or departed, which was almost all she did, somewhere in the grainy background was my driver, George.

Zooming in on the bank of machines that had broken my heart the night before, I queued them for sunrise on the day of Eddie's win, and almost fell asleep watching nothing. For the first three hours of tape, it was like staring at a still life, even though I had the video running at warp speed. Between ten and eleven, a handful of people passed the machines, mostly Bellissimo employees, then nothing until three o'clock, when Hollywood strolled by. I rewound and watched an attendant cleaning the fronts of the machines at three thirty that afternoon, but he didn't do anything that could have triggered the jackpot, unless polishing away fingerprints that weren't there did the trick. Not one of the people who had been near the machines that day had taken out the batteries, pulled a plug, or whipped out a ray gun and zapped them. Then, at 4:25 that afternoon, Eddie took a break. Before I could switch cameras to see where he might have gone, at 4:27, Bianca Casimiro Sanders waltzed in. I almost fell out of No Hair's chair. I knew she was in on it, but I never expected to see the elusive Mrs. Sanders at the scene of the crime.

She sat down at the fourth machine. I could see the small LCD display with the scrolling progressive total above the machine in the background. She ignored Hollywood, who looked nervous on the small screen, stiff and fidgety, without a clue as to what to do with his hands. She removed her dark glasses, hooking them in the already-plunging neckline of her black sweater, then looked straight into the camera. I jerked away from the screen and yelped out loud. The glint reflecting off her icy green eyes was trained directly at me, and it was a full-out threat: *Watch this and you'll be sorry.*

A waitress walked up with a tall drink, passing it to her, and when Bianca went to set it down, she missed. I watched the tape seven or eight times, slowing it to a crawl, and watched, frame by frame from every angle, as she intentionally dumped the drink between video poker machines four and five.

Employees rushed to her aid from all points. The screen was so full of attempts to keep her dry, with so many knees and elbows flying in every direction possible, their collective life missions redirected at sparing Bianca Casimiro Sanders any contact with moisture. Once the cleanup was complete, the waitress stepped back into the frame with a replacement drink, this one going straight to Bianca's dermal-filler-enhanced lips.

So much went on in such a short period of time that the first four times I watched it, I missed the LCD display and the slot machine lights blinking. When I finally caught it, the flash was so fast I couldn't even get a time on it. They went down, then powered back up in a split-second, just like Dale Boy said they would. Had I not known exactly what I was looking for, there was no doubt I'd've missed it. Just like my video poker buddies, sisters Mary and Maxine, told me. "The whole game goes black for a second," Maxine had said, "then it pulls right back up. It's real quick."

It was then that I connected the dots. I already knew the lower-stakes version of this game, the one Mr. Sanders and Natalie sent me to my first day on the job, was rigged too. It paid in the $8,000 neighborhood every three weeks to a good-looking man named Eddie. But good-looking Eddie was depositing less than a quarter of the win into his checking account, and he wasn't winning alone. It took two people. Who else did Mary and Maxine tell me was there every time the game hit?

Say it ain't so.

Was Teeth doing more than watching Eddie win the lower-stakes game? Was he actually in on the con? Was the high-stakes team Bianca and Eddie, and the low-stakes team *Teeth* and Eddie?

I don't know how long I sat there before I pushed the play button and started the video feed again.

Bianca Casimiro Sanders stood. Six Bellissimo employees, including Hollywood, cleared a path for her. She walked away without ever playing. She was there eight minutes, just long enough to dump a drink. Two minutes later, Eddie Crawford returned.

Showtime.

I split the screen into quads and watched him win from four different vantage points. I was glad I'd skipped breakfast.

He chose a machine, ninth in the row of ten, fed it two thousand dollars in hundreds, then began playing, betting only one credit. No one seemed to pay a bit of attention to him, the staff, I bet, still reeling after the soggy encounter with the boss's wife.

On his sixth spin, Eddie was dealt a straight, winning twenty-five credits, at which point he doubled his bet to two credits. Ten hands later he lined up eights, and the four of a kind paid him forty credits, then he began playing the maximum bet, five credits. After a dozen hands, he glanced at his watch. I zoomed in on it. A Cartier. With diamonds instead of numbers That good-for-nothing lowlife excuse for a human being.

The watch was probably worth what he owed me.

After another three hands, he admired his diamonds again, at length, as if he were counting. I checked the time, since he seemed to be so interested in it. He'd been playing almost thirty minutes; it had been thirty-seven minutes since the game had reset itself after its cocktail.

Next, nothing I could see about the game prompting it, he dropped back down to a one-credit bet. He hit nothing: he won nothing. He ran his palms down the length of his thighs. His shoulders rose as he took a deep breath, and he very deliberately placed a two-credit bet, poking the machine's buttons slowly, because, as I knew firsthand, counting wasn't easy for him. (I was still mad about the watch.) He collapsed against the chair back and his left hand rose to rub his forehead, a familiar (and unwelcome) Eddie tick that made me cringe. He rubbed his hands together, like *here we go*, and pushed the bet-one-credit button three times for his next hand. He was dealt two fours, he held them, but wasn't dealt another four on his second draw, losing the hand. I wasn't the least bit surprised when he placed a four-credit bet next, was dealt a soup hand (a little bit of everything), losing again.

"And we have a winner," I announced to No Hair's dark empty office, as my ex-ex-husband placed a full-credit bet, but not with the bet-max button. He pressed the bet-one-credit button five times in a row, then pressed deal.

Ding, ding, ding—Royal Flush.

I turned away from the computer and let Eddie celebrate in private.

I didn't celebrate so much, even though I had good reason. X = B the first time for a one-credit bet, all the way to X = B the fifth time, for a five-credit bet. But only after Whammy reset after powering down for a split second, and only when the credits were rolled up individually. And that was how it was done.

Now what? I scratched at the itchy wig.

I cleared the cache and hard drive of No Hair's computer for the time I'd been on it, then shut it down, plunging myself into total darkness. I batted for and found my purse when I heard something beep. My head jerked up in the darkness.

I heard three more beeps. Someone was coding the exterior door.

I hit the deck, aiming for the space under No Hair's desk, just as the door to the reception area burst open. I banged my head on the edge of his desk on the way down, saw stars, huddled into a tight ball, and stopped breathing altogether.

"Shhh! Be quiet! Did you hear something?"

It was my twin.

"No. Wait. Maybe. Why? What did you hear?"

It was my ex-ex.

Bianca: "I know I heard something."

Me: *You didn't hear anything. Don't come in here.*

Bianca: "Never mind. Hurry, Edward."

Me: *Edward?*

Eddie the Ass: "Which office?"

Me: *Not this one! Not this one! Not this one!*

A slice of bright cut across the carpeted floor of No Hair's office as they thankfully entered Teeth's. There was just enough ambient light under the desk for something to catch it, something shiny. I squinted, then quietly reached for it. It was a two-inch stretch of clear packing tape, and underneath it, a key. It could wait. I pressed myself farther into the recess under the desk, staring at the key, my chin on my drawn knees, my arms wrapped tightly around them.

The drawers of Teeth's desk were being opened and closed, and I couldn't make out the details of their conversation, other than they were irritated, in a hurry, and clearly looking for something.

Teeth was in on it. For sure.

Just then, one of the cell phones in my bag began buzzing. I mistook it for an earthquake and almost had a stroke. Thankfully, I had it muted. It stopped vibrating for a half a second, then immediately began again.

Bianca: "It's not here, Edward. I, for one, am leaving."

Me: *Yes, leave.*

Eddie the Ass: "But he said it would be here."

Me: *It what?*

Bianca: "Let me walk you through this, Edward."

Me: *Edward?*

Bianca: "The drawer isn't locked. If the drawer isn't locked, we don't need a key. Furthermore, Edward, the unlocked drawer is empty."

I stared at the key just inches from my nose. I stared at the locked drawer just inches from my elbow.

Eddie the Genius, after a pause to process: "Oh."

Me: *Yeah, Bianca, get used to that.*

Everything went pitch black as the door to Teeth's office slammed shut. I jumped and hit my head *again*.

Bianca: "There it is again."

Edward the Ass: "What?"

Me: *Nothing. Go.*

The exterior door opened, then closed, effectively plunging me back into total, and thankfully solitary, silent darkness.

For hours, which might have actually been minutes, I did nothing but pant, hand over heart to keep it in my chest. I was close to calming down when the phone in my purse buzzed again sending shock waves back through me. I couldn't move, I couldn't breathe, and I wondered how many years of my life had been frightened away.

I reached up and pulled off the wig and let out the breath I'd been holding, still under the desk in the dark. I freed the key from beneath the tape, then crawled out, banging my head on the way up just like on the way down.

I rubbed my head, then sank into No Hair's chair.

I placed the key on the desk. I dug in my purse and located my own keys, then used my penlight to take a look at what all I'd managed to leave Bradley's condo with. I had my Marci Dunlow identification, my super-secret cell phone, and nine dollars. The three calls I'd missed were from home: the station (my dad), home (my mother), and the Front Porch (Meredith). I knew what that was—a family feud—and it would have to wait.

I entered the code for No Hair's desk again. With a stab of guilt, I tossed my cell phone in the middle drawer, knowing my mother would give me down the road for being out of reach, but I had bigger fish to fry. I tried to stuff the wig in with the phone, but it wouldn't fit. Now I had a good reason to open the mystery drawer. (Like I needed one.) I slid the little key off the desk and stabbed at the small lock, opened the drawer and found a Glock.

It was a beauty. A Glock 27 .40 caliber with a standard nine mag. I wasn't about to touch it, but that was only until I caught a glimpse of what was underneath. I angled the penlight, and there they were, three bright blue Bellissimo casino chips. The one I could see clearly was a $5,000 chip. Was it my birthday? A Glock .27 and $15,000?

Was I looking at what Bianca and Edward had been after?

All of a sudden, I knew exactly what to do, and I'd have to touch the gun to do it. Emotion, or temporary insanity, took over, pushing logic aside.

The next ten minutes of my life were a blur. I touched the gun, with the intent to move it so I could get to the $15,000, but old habits die hard. I felt the grip, and the next thing I knew I had the gun up. I dropped into a Weaver stance with the Glock trained on an imaginary bad guy across the dark room. Then I accidentally blew a new door into No Hair's otherwise solid wall.

The same scene could unfold a hundred times, and ninety-nine of them, I'd still assume no one would leave a loaded gun in a desk drawer without the safety on.

When the ringing in my ears stopped, I could hear myself panting, and my vision was limited to flashing red ghost globes from the muzzle flash. I would have happily tossed the gun through the nice new hole in the wall, like getting rid of a lit grenade, but knowing the safety wasn't on, if I threw it I'd probably shoot myself in the process, so I found enough wherewithal to gently lay it down on the desk, watching my own hand shake like a ninety-year-old's. I backed away until I bumped into the back wall. I slid down it. I sat there, heart racing, waiting in the dark for someone to come shoot *me*. I could smell gunfire.

I had no idea how much time passed before I began entertaining the idea that no one heard the shot, no one was coming to get me, and my best move was to put as much distance between myself and No Hair's office as possible.

I pulled myself up, rationalizing leaving the scene of my own unlawful-discharge-of-a-firearm crime. So the gun had misfired. It shouldn't have had a round in the chamber, and it certainly should have had the safety on. I picked it up again, my hands still trembling, clicked on the safety, and popped out the clip. Then I wanted away from it. I put the gun and the clip where I found them, trading for the three casino chips, then closed and locked the drawer. I swallowed the little key.

(No, I didn't.)

I ran, not bothering to lock up after myself, considering the new entrance and all, then took the straightest path I could to the casino. Once there, I aimed my sights on the closest bar.

"Whiskey."

"Well?"

"Well, what?" I asked. "I need whiskey. Please."

The guy rolled his eyes and poured.

I tossed it back.

Edward wouldn't win a million dollars today if Marci Dunlow got there first. (Early birds, worms, and such.) Then Bianca Sanders wouldn't kill him, which was only fair. She could get in line behind me. I was there first.

* * *

I got in line. Knowing the video poker machines wouldn't take the blue tokens and fortified with whiskey, I made my way to the casino banking center. I was in good company; the bank was packed.

There were five cashiers behind a tall marble counter with gold bars up to the ceiling. Which was probably why they called the area behind the bars the cashier's cage. The seven lines leading to the cashiers were four or five people deep, and no one seemed to be in any manner of a hurry, neither the bankers nor the bankees. I could've used another whiskey, but I took deep measured yoga breaths instead, or maybe they were deep measured Lamaze breaths, knowing I had to calm down if I intended to finish what I'd started.

It was my first visit to the banking center. Beside me, at the back of the line, was a kiosk of pamphlets advising gamblers to save themselves from the evil addiction. If they were standing in line waiting for more money to gamble with, wasn't it already too late? I picked up one and skimmed it, in yet another attempt to distract myself from what I'd done, and I'd summarize the gambler warning this way: if you can't be reasonable about how much you lose, you don't get to come back. So be reasonable. I moved up a spot, beside an antibacterial hand sanitizer dispenser. I cupped a hand under it and kept it there for several squirts. After all, I'd just fired a weapon. Which was when it occurred to me I hadn't wiped down the gun.

Not good.

In fact, bad. So bad.

Trying to decide if I should retrace my steps to No Hair's office and wipe my prints off the gun, imagining a crew of Bellissimo suits already there examining the hole I'd blasted in the wall, the man in front of me stepped away. It was my turn.

Once at the desk, I quickly discovered the reason for the bars: stacks of banded cash and racks of casino chips were everywhere. I placed the three blue chips on the counter between me and the cashier. "Can I cash these in?"

"Of course." She smiled. "Whoa! Congratulations!"

She spread out the three chips, displaying them for the cameras, then scooped them up and tapped them twice against the counter. Her cash drawer popped open. She turned the chips over, pausing for the briefest of seconds, just long enough to catch my attention.

"I'll be right back." She backed away, smiling, and took the $15,000 in casino chips with her.

Before I could imagine where she'd possibly gone or why I was as nervous as a thirteen-year-old at cheerleading tryouts, she was back with a man at her side. She smiled, he smiled, I smiled, we all smiled.

"Do you have a player's card?" he asked.

"Yes!" I dug it out.

"ID?" he asked.

I pulled that out too. I was passing this test with flying colors.

A small plastic disk appeared. The cashier opened it. "We need a thumbprint and index finger for anything over ten thousand," she said.

Which sounded reasonable to me. And no risk, because my prints led exactly nowhere.

The man and woman exchanged a rapid-fire non-verbal communication of some sort, and I had a feeling they were about to tell me that for whatever reasons, they weren't cashing the chips for me, when he nodded, giving her the go-ahead.

She dropped a healthy stack of money into an automatic bill counter, depressed a button, and cash started flying.

Before the man stepped away he asked, "Where will you be playing, Miss Dunlow?"

I pointed in the wrong direction, but they, not to mention what happened before I met them, had me flustered. "Behind the waterfall."

Finally, the cashier placed three banded stacks of $5,000 in front of me. I scooped. I smiled. I backed away with the cash.

"Hey!" a lady I plowed into protested.

"Sorry."

I quick-stepped to Private Gaming.

NINETEEN

It happened so fast.

A different tuxedoed young man was doing the honors at the entrance to Private Gaming, Hollywood's weekend counterpart, I guessed, and the new one more Broadway than Hollywood. He took one look at me, almost fell over, reached up and pressed his hidden earpiece, where apparently someone behind the curtain informed him that I was *not* Bianca Sanders, and then they probably told him to get it together.

"Good afternoon, Miss Dunlow," he said breathlessly, his face Christmas red.

"I'll need a bottle of water and a Bloody Mary," I breezed by him, "extra olives."

"Certainly."

I wished what I was about to do could wait until Monday, when I could run everything by Natalie and ask for (her blessing) backup, but to quote Mr. Sanders, the iron was hot. It couldn't wait. I wouldn't have been able to call her anyway, because my cell phone was in No Hair's desk. I could've used a house phone, but that wouldn't do any good, because the only help available was Teeth, who was almost certainly in on the scam with Bianca and Edward. I had no backup. And If I hadn't found the chips, I wouldn't be there at all, because I'd tapped out Marci Dunlow's line of credit the night before, a situation that couldn't be corrected without, again, Natalie. Finding the chips was almost a sign, and if I didn't heed it, backup or no backup, Bianca Sanders and Edward the Ass Crawford would win the big money on the Whammy game. Again. And since one of the elements was obviously timing, with thirty-seven minutes passing between Bianca glitching the power and Cartier Eddie winning, I had to get going. I was in a now-or-never situation. If I could win it, first of all, it'd be fun, and second of all, Eddie wouldn't.

I sat at the fourth machine and said, "Here goes nothing."

A waitress arrived with my drinks. I thanked her, then shooed her away with one of my many hundred-dollar bills. I knocked back half of the Bloody Mary, finally had something for breakfast that wasn't alcoholic (two olives), then reached for the water. I twisted off the lid, perched the bottle on the edge of the machine, then elbowed it.

"Uh-oh," I said aloud.

I let about half of the water loose before righting the bottle, hoping it would be enough to find the little button, and apparently it was, because almost immediately the video poker machines winked at me. I downed the rest of the Bloody Mary, hoping vodka and whiskey weren't a bad combination, and hoping no one in surveillance got winked at too. I noted the time, I tried to breathe, and the peppery tomato juice burned through me, causing me to hallucinate about Pine Apple. For the first time since I'd left, I missed home.

I traded the fourth Whammy seat for ninth, the machine Eddie won on. I pulled a half inch of hundreds from one of the money stacks, loaded them into the hopper one by one, then let the music of the game calm me down. It had been eight minutes.

The next twenty minutes flew by. I actually won back a little of the money I'd lost the night before (whammy *this* you crazy game), the whole time watching the clock.

Broadway was a squirmer. He left me alone for the first fifteen minutes I was there, thank goodness, because he might have taken issue with me dousing the carpet, but more and more, it felt like he was hovering.

"Where is everyone?" I asked him on one of his many trips by.

"What's that?"

"Where did everyone go?" I asked.

He shrugged, his eyes dancing all over the room. "It's Sunday afternoon, you know. Not much going on."

"You must be expecting something." I poked at the screen, holding two tens.

"How's that?"

"The two men at the entrance." I tipped my head.

When I'd arrived, there was the usual tuxedoed greeter. The next time I looked up there were two large suits, one dark gray, the other dark blue, flanking the waterfall. They looked almost menacing from behind, and they were definitely packing, one a leftie, his shoulder-holster bulge on the wrong side. I assumed they were Bianca's Welcome Wagon, and what seeing them said to me was *hurry*.

"Extra security," Broadway said. "We have VIPs in the building."

Ah.

Turning back to the machine, checking the time, I was almost too numb from earlier events to be the least bit excited when I began the sequence of play that would hit the jackpot. I just wanted it over with and out of there.

With the one-credit and two-credit bets behind me, my stomach near the floor, I reached to place the three-credit bet as someone invaded my space from the left. A large hairy hand flew in front of my face and slapped the Whammy screen. With his other arm crooked, he pushed against my chest, separating me from the game. I didn't hear or see the two suits behind me, the ones who'd been at the entrance, until they unceremoniously jerked me out of my chair.

*   *   *

My world was reduced to three solid walls, one wall of tinted glass, a steel door, a long table, and four metal chairs. I'd been there before, with the Duprees, the brother/sister safe-cracking team, but on the other side of the glass.

At first, the only thing I could come up with was I'd been yanked off Whammy so I wouldn't win it before Bianca and Eddie had the chance, but as more and more time passed, I began imagining worse.

What worse, though? I hadn't done anything.

Except blow out a wall.

Which didn't warrant a holding cell.

I was left alone in the room with my hands cuffed behind my back to stew about it for long stretches. A woman who wouldn't speak to me carted me off to an adjacent restroom that smelled like sick at regular intervals, and four different times the guy who'd smacked my poker game with his furry paw came in and asked me my name.

"Marci Dunlow."

"How about any aliases? A middle name? Maiden name?"

"Discretion," I answered.

"Marci *Discretion* Dunlow?" He slapped the table with his open palm, and we both jumped, me and the table. "This will go so much easier if you cooperate, Marci *Discretion* Dunlow."

For the first three hours, I felt stronger about cooperating with the man who signed my paychecks than I did the furry one. It was the one directive I'd received from Richard Sanders, and it would take the fourth hour of leaving me in the room alone to decide that the only way out was to tell them my name. By then, I'd convinced myself Richard Sanders had never imagined this scenario when he'd insisted that I remain anonymous.

Or was he behind it all? Was this a test?

I might have been losing my marbles.

I devoted a small portion of my miserable time in the room coming to the decision that I absolutely had to start getting along better with my mother, if for no other reason than how happy it would make my father, and that distracted me. When I wasn't distracting myself with Pine Apple thoughts, I could only think about how caged-animal I felt. Things itched that I couldn't scratch—my ears, my nose, an ankle. At one point I was convinced a stray eyelash was underneath one of the tinted contact lenses, and there wasn't a thing I could do about it but try to blink it away.

My emotions flew between rage, stone-cold fear, and disbelief. Any second, I expected someone to rush in and apologize for the mix-up, but any second didn't come. At the end of the fourth hour, my chin on my chest, weary to the point of exhaustion, Furry Paws was back, and he brought friends. Three suits filed in behind him, and one of them mercifully uncuffed me.

A new face took the seat across from me. "I don't know what to call you," he said.

"Marci Dunlow."

He leaned in. "We both know you're not Marci Dunlow. We need your *name*, young lady."

We waited an indeterminable amount of time for me to cave. There was no air in the room, and the only sound was the scrape of a chair. I got the words out in a whisper, but they all heard me.

"It's Way." I rubbed my wrists. "Davis Way. My name is Davis Way, and I work here."

The one closest to the door stepped out. The other three and I listened to each other breathe until he returned.

"That's not anyone's name who works here," he announced, letting the door slam behind him. "I don't think that's anyone's name at all." He was the most menacing of the four, a gray-haired Fed-looking guy. He resumed his post against the closed door. "So this is how you want it to go?"

"I don't want any of this. You asked my name, I told you."

There was silent communication between the men, a throat clearing, a cough, a few long sighs, and some whimpering, but that was me.

"Okay," the one directly in front of me said. "So be it." He introduced himself, saying he and the gray-haired man were with the Gaming Commission, which threw me, and that the other two, including Furry Paws, were detectives with the Biloxi Police Department.

"What's your name?" Gaming Commission One, sitting directly

across from me, asked.

"Davis Way," I said.

"Try again," Biloxi Detective One said.

"My name is Davis Way. Call Natalie Middleton, and she'll verify it. Call her," I begged. "I'm on the Bellissimo security team."

"Young lady." Gaming Commission One tapped his fingertips together. "Three shifts of security have been brought in, along with every department head we could round up." He tipped his head toward the tinted-glass wall. "Not one of them could identify you. No one had ever heard of Marci Dunlow. I can run this new alias by them, but I have a feeling they don't know Davis Way either."

"Okay." I tried to breathe. "The only person here today who can identify me is Teeth. And his real name is either Jeremy or Paul, Coven or—" I couldn't come up with it "—something else."

"Paul Bergman," Gaming Commission Two supplied, "and we brought him in first."

What? Terror grabbed me about the neck and strangled the very life out of me. I tried my best to process the information: Teeth threw me under the bus. No more wondering whose side he was on.

"Young lady," Gaming Commission One said, "I don't know how to phrase this delicately, so I'll just put it out there."

He waited until I looked directly at him.

"Your appearance has startled everyone." And he didn't mean it in a good way. "Are you possibly under psychiatric care?"

"Excuse me?"

A photograph of Bianca Casimiro Sanders appeared on the table, and by all accounts, it was a shocking resemblance, even to me.

"Think about it," he said.

He was giving me the option of playing the Crazy Card, but instead, I played my Ace. "Call Richard Sanders," I said. "He'll explain."

"Well," Biloxi Detective Two laughed sarcastically, "it's not a very good time to call Mr. Sanders, now is it?"

"Right." I nodded for dear life. "He went to see his son, but he'll be back any minute."

"He's in surgery," Detective Two was in my face, "and you'd better hope he makes it."

"*What*?" It came out on a huge woof of air.

They all stared at me.

"Is he okay?"

Gaming Commission One settled back in his chair. "Why don't you tell us? Is he okay? While you're at it, tell us your name."

"It's Way! Davis Way!" I insisted. "And how would I know if he's okay or not?" My jaw dropped as his implication hit home. I scanned the other accusatory faces. "Surely you don't think I shot Mr. Sanders! I was in the casino! You people dragged me out of the casino! I didn't *shoot* anyone!"

Gaming Commission One leaned in. "I never said he was shot."

My lungs collapsed.

"We'll get to that in a minute. For now, let's talk about the counterfeit chips."

It went downhill from there.

* * *

They left me alone for the next hour, then burst back in. I have no idea what I did during that time, other than watch the clock tick and pray.

"Miss—"

"Way. It's Davis Way." I'd said it a million times.

Gaming Commission One reached up and scratched an ear, sighing deeply.

"One more time," he said. "We have Davis Way's prints, and they're not yours."

"There's a reason for that! Please! Contact my father, he'll explain everything!"

"We're trying. We've had to send agents to Pine Apple, because no one there will answer a phone."

That struck a fresh new terror in my heart.

"We did get through to the last number you gave us," he glanced at a slip of paper, "Mel and Bea Crawford, and when we asked if they knew a Davis Way, they disconnected, and the line has been unavailable since."

Oh, someone save me.

"And you're not Marci Dunlow, either," he said, "because she doesn't exist. Who are you? This is your last chance, and if you don't give me your name, I'm booking you as Jane Doe. With all you have ahead of you, trust me, you don't want to go in the system Jane Doe."

I had no idea what time it was, but I felt like I'd been there for days. I was cold, starving, and at times I'd cried so hard, I think I was dehydrated. At that point, I was truly willing to tell them anything—where and when I lost my virginity, where and when Bradley Cole lost his (I'd read the details in a letter from his high school sweetheart when she tried to start things up again after seeing him at their ten-year reunion), or even about the time I'd locked up my old nemesis Danielle Sparks for a whole weekend out of meanness.

I'd spilled all the beans, told them everything, yet not one of them believed me, and there was no one to back me up.

I took one last huge breath. "What is it, exactly, that you're charging me with?" I asked. "I've told you who I am, why I'm here, and where I got the casino chips. If someone who looks like me shot Mr. Sanders, you need to talk to his wife. I work here, and I'm a former police officer."

I searched the faces for any traces of consideration and found none.

The Gaming Commission representative who'd been manning the door the entire time crossed the room slowly, bent over, and put the tip of his nose almost up against mine. "One last chance," he said. "Why did you shoot Richard Sanders?"

"I didn't."

"Where did you get them?"

"Get *what*?"

"The counterfeit chips."

(Those chips were counterfeit?) "Jeremy Coven's desk. Call him."

"Jeremy Co*vey* is unavailable."

"Ask George Morgan."

"There is no George Morgan."

"Morgan George!" I shouted. "Morgan George!"

"Who's deceased!"

"What about Mary and Maxine? The little old ladies in the casino?"

"We've looked ten times. There are no little old ladies."

Was it still Sunday? The Lord's Day? It must have been.

"Do you see a pattern here?" He stood, towering over me. "There is no Marci Dunlow, no Davis Way, no little old ladies, no George Morgan, no Morgan George. There is no cab. We finally heard back from Bradley Cole, and he said he thought his renter was a woman named Anna Merriweather, who, by the way, DOESN'T EXIST!"

By then an expert at sudden-onset crying in front of total strangers, tears dropped off my chin that I didn't know were coming.

"You have the opportunity to help yourself if you'll tell me who you are and where you got the counterfeit chips."

"From Jeremy Co*vey*'s desk."

"Before or after you shot Richard Sanders?"

"I. Didn't. Shoot. Richard. Sanders."

"Do you think we're idiots, Miss Doe?"

"At this point, I do. And stop calling me Jane Doe."

The man shook his head in a tsk-tsk way and motioned someone in at the same time. The door cracked open, and a female police officer entered.

"Stand up," my interrogator demanded.

I couldn't. There was no way my legs were going to hold me. She took two steps and helped me, by jerking my shoulder out of its socket, wrenching me upright.

"Jane Doe, you're under arrest—" Jane's Miranda Rights followed.

I launched into a panicked screaming blubber. "My father! Why won't you call my father?"

Gaming Commission Two looked straight at me as I was being cuffed. "The chief of police in Pine Apple," he said, "who you claim is your father, has had a massive heart attack, and that, apparently, has made the whole town unavailable."

The room began spinning around me. I heard a woman's piercing scream, then everything went black.

TWENTY

It might have been hours, it could have been days later, when I woke up cuffed and shackled to a hospital bed. My left side was cuff-free but connected to a hospital apparatus. I was alone in the room, but saw an officer stationed outside of the door.

I turned, as best as I could maneuver, toward the wall.

"Daddy." I said the word, but no sound came out.

There was no clock, the television screen was dark, and nothing was within my reach, not even a sip of water. My inclination was to scream, but I stifled that into the thin pillow. I stared at the wall, putting the pieces of the nightmare together, and I stayed that way, frozen, until a nurse, accompanied by a female police officer, entered the room.

"Oh." The nurse stopped short of the bed, the officer almost piling into her. "You're awake."

The officer turned away and spoke into her headset.

"Do you have any information about my father?" I begged her.

A look of confusion slid down her face, and she began flipping through the chart she was holding, as if the answer might be in there. "Your father?" she asked.

The officer's raspy voice filled the room. "No chitchat." She opened the door and stuck her head out to speak to the other officer, as the nurse adjusted the IV in my left arm, then strapped a blood pressure cuff around the bicep of my right.

The nurse had a kind face, a gentle touch, and an ample midsection along with ample everything else. She hugged my arm into her warm middle while she pumped the bulb of the blood-pressure gauge.

I looked up at her, and tears slid from my eyes. "Please find out if my father's okay," I whispered. "His name is Samuel Way, from Pine Apple, Alabama. He's had a heart attack."

"Hey!" the officer's voice cut through the sanitized air. "Shut up, Doe."

The nurse barely closed an eyelid, winking at me, and gave the quickest of nods. "You don't look like you could hurt a flea." Her lips didn't move as she whispered it.

"How long have I been here?" I whispered. "What day is it?"

"It's Sunday night," she said, again without moving her lips. "You've been here several hours."

I never saw her again.

Half an hour later a different nurse accompanied by two female officers burst into the room. There was nothing warm or fuzzy about the new nurse. She'd been in the room three seconds before she jerked the needle out of my arm, while the officer freed me from my cuffs and shackles from the other side of the bed. The second officer leaned against the wall looking bored. The words Mississippi Department of Corrections were embroidered on her uniform.

The first one said, "You have one minute in the bathroom." She tossed me two orange squares of folded cotton. "Leave the door open."

I was shackled to a wheelchair, but only as far as the front door. After that, I was jerked upright and dragged to the van that carted me off to the police station to be booked.

Bright lights were trained on me from every direction, and I ducked them as best I could. I was shouted at from all directions. "Why'd you do it?" a particularly loud voice cut through the din. "Why did you shoot Richard Sanders?"

* * *

An hour into the booking process I became numb and stopped fighting them. I was too stunned and too afraid. The fear factor had nothing to do with what was happening to me, I was afraid for my father. I stared at my cuffed hands in my lap without blinking. The clock on the wall struck midnight.

"Your name?"

"Davis Way."

The woman tapped a pencil against the desk. She quickly scanned the room—several other female officers were in various stages of booking several other female offenders—then leaned in. "This will go so much easier for you," she almost whispered, "if you'll tell me your name."

I felt a sliver of hope. She was a few years younger than me, probably fresh out of Officer Training, and probably not yet totally jaded. "Four, zero, seven. Six, one. Six, seven, eight, two," I said. "Look up my Social."

"I can't do that," she whispered.

"You can. It's right there on the screen."

"I'm not supposed to," she said, visually sweeping the room again.

Instead of grabbing for her pencil, which would have had her grabbing for her piece, I asked if I could write it down for her. "Look it up. You'll see I spent years on the job in Pine Apple, Alabama. Now I work undercover for the Bellissimo, and the list of reasons you can't find me in the system is ridiculously long."

She bent over the clipboard in front of her and pretended to write. With her head ducked she said, "Why won't anyone there back you up?"

"Apparently they're busy." My head was bowed too. "The president was shot." I covered my face with my hands, so anyone looking might think I was crying, and it being a room filled with all sorts of emotion, mostly rage, hopefully they'd be bored with me and instead watch the drunk twenty yards away who kept spilling out of her chair.

"I think my father had a heart attack," I said to my booking officer, "but they very well could be lying to me."

"Why would someone lie about a heart attack?" the officer's

eyes darted.

"To gauge my reaction," I said. "To see if I'm who I say I am. Would you please, *please* make a phone call for me?" I begged with my eyes.

She sniffed. She shuffled things around on her desk. "One," she whispered. "Only one." She reached for a yellow sticky note, just about when the drunk passed out cold, pitched into the lap of the officer trying to book her, then wet her pants. The officer screamed and spilled the drunk onto the floor.

My officer ignored it. "And only if this is a real Social Security number."

This kind gesture was absolutely more than I could take, at which point I did bawl like a baby.

"Get a hold of yourself," she spoke through clenched teeth. "Let's go." She stood.

We had to step around the puddle of comatose drunk.

My booking officer, Raines, her badge read, took me through the fingerprinting process. "You want me to call a lawyer, right?" she whispered while rolling my left thumb. "If you're with the casino," she spoke without moving her lips, "call one of theirs."

"No," I whispered back. "I need you to call my sister. Find out about my father, and tell her I've been sent to—" my mind raced "—Dubai."

She looked at me as if I were crazy. "If I were you," she whispered, "I'd call a lawyer."

She didn't offer any additional advice while she completed another ten minutes of paperwork, then led me to yet another holding cell.

"What's this?" I asked, as bars clanked closed to separate us.

"We need a gunpowder residue test."

A what? It took a second for her words to sink in, and when they did, I must have fallen into my own puddle on the concrete floor, because I was only aware of hard, cold concrete. Voices broke through the fog. My officer. A man. "Get her on the cot," the man said. "You can still GSR her. Then cart her back to the hospital."

* * *

Having failed the gunpowder residue test, they carted me to the prison infirmary instead. The next day, I was dumped into General Population, better known as the Drunk Tank.

The words "bond hearing" weren't spoken to me, but the words "bang, bang, Bianca" were, always in passing, always with snickers, and never directly to me. Apparently I was somewhat of a prison celebrity. I was pointed to, gawked at, and gossiped about relentlessly. I picked a spot on a green metal bench, a spot on the wall to stare at, and sat there for two days and nights while prostitutes and DUIs around me were either bonded out or processed.

Sometime during the third day, I was called to the desk.

"Doe!" the overweight and cranky officer in attendance yelled across the room. "Jane Doe!"

I picked up my heavy head and the room warbled around me.

"Jane Doe!"

I'd had so many names in the past two months that I no longer recognized any of them.

"Last call," the guard said, waving a piece of paper in the air. "Personal message for Jane Doe."

I jumped up and almost fell down. "It's me," I called out, reaching for the wall. I made my way to the desk.

"You're Jane Doe?" I'd seen this woman from across the room, but hadn't been close enough to notice she was balding. You could see every bit of her scalp through her thin hair.

I stood there, holding the edge of her desk for support.

"You're the one who won't eat," she said.

"I guess."

"Don't blame you," she said. "You've got a message here from the officer who booked you. Maybe you'll know what it's about." She pushed her glasses up the wide bridge of her nose. "Triple bypass."

* * *

From there, I spent two more days staring at the infirmary walls, then I was processed and assigned to B Block as Jane Doe, pretrial.

Pretrial status was prison purgatory, and there was no way out of it until someone within the system took an interest in the case. Being at the center of the biggest story since Hurricane Katrina, it was hard to guess if the momentum would speed things along or slow them to a crawl. I could be pretrial for a week; I could be pretrial for a decade.

My cellmates were both of Hispanic descent, and clearly didn't want a new roomie. They spoke nothing but Spanish above, below, and through me, but would speak choppy English to anyone else. Even though it was relayed to me in overdrive Spanish, I got the message the minute I was shoved into the cell: don't touch their things, don't breathe their air, don't make eye contact.

I crawled into the space they designated as mine, my size coming in handy, because they didn't give me much, a skinny top bunk and that was it. I curled into a ball, my back to the cold wall, and tried to cry, but I was too scared. I didn't know if my father was dead or alive, and no one from the Bellissimo had come to save me.

The charges against me were multiple fraudulent acts, felony theft, criminal conspiracy, computer trespassing, receiving stolen property, and criminal impersonation. The homicide charges were pending, and I could only guess that was because Richard Sanders was pending. I was told I'd be assigned an attorney as soon as I identified myself.

"Officer Butrum." I asked every guard every day. "When can I speak to an attorney?"

"You'll have to get with your counselor on that."

"I haven't been assigned a counselor!"

"You will be." He sucked his teeth. "Sooner or later."

Phone calls in prison were a joke. For one, you had to have

money to use the phone, and I didn't have a dime. No one knew I was an inmate, so no one deposited money in my account. For another, the two pay phones in the prison cafeteria were under the jurisdiction of two white-haired lifers, the female versions of Teeth and No Hair. They decided who used the phones, for how long, and in what order. I wasn't on the list. And lastly, who would I call? I had nothing to do but go over and over what had happened in my mind, blindly and numbly walking the perimeter of the fenced-in prison yard where those of us who didn't have prison jobs were dumped for four-hour stretches twice a day, rain or shine.

If my father survived the surgery, he was recovering. Not knowing where I was would certainly be less stress on him than knowing. I wouldn't call home. I couldn't contact anyone at the Bellissimo, because there wasn't even a chance the switchboard took prison calls, and I didn't know anyone's direct number; they'd all been programmed into my cell phones. If I could get through, Natalie would be the call I'd make, but according to a one-paragraph announcement in the business section of a three-day-old *Biloxi Sun Herald* that had blown up against the fence in the yard, the Bellissimo was busy welcoming Evelyn Gardner, interim assistant to the interim President and CEO, Salito Casimiro. The quick announcement made no mention of Mr. Sanders, Jane Doe, the shooting, or his condition; I only knew Natalie and Mr. Sanders weren't at their desks. For all I knew, No Hair was gone too. Teeth? I couldn't care less.

I was truly on my own.

* * *

Not soon enough, I was assigned a counselor. His name was Dick Crowder, and he was the most beautiful thing I'd seen in almost two weeks. He had a comb-over plastered onto the back half of his oversized freckled head, watery, buggy eyes, small, misshapen, brown teeth, and his polyester pants were hiked up so high, they were closing in on his man breasts. He had stick-thin twigs for legs and the smallest feet I'd ever seen on a man. He had a nasally, Jersey accent, and he wouldn't make eye contact when he was speaking; he looked off and up to the right.

"Miss Doe," he said to the calendar on the wall, "the wheels of justice are turning slowly for you, and for that I apologize." He shifted in his chair and switched focal points to something else lofty. "First," he said, "I'll ask how you're doing."

I nodded with my whole body, so grateful for his tone, his genuinely apologetic attitude, and to be sitting in a real chair away from my cellmates. Taking a deep breath, I measured my words, my desire being to have at least one decent relationship within these miles of razor wire.

"Mr. Crowder, my father has had a heart attack, and a subsequent triple bypass. If you could get me any information about his condition, I'd be forever grateful."

His eyes rolled along the squares of ceiling tiles, back and forth. "I'll see what I can do." He pushed a piece of paper and a pencil my way. "But under the circumstances, I will only be able to identify the inquiry as coming from incarcerated Jane Doe. Whoever you're writing down will most likely not be willing to release any information."

I scribbled down the name of the hospital I was born in and my family had frequented through the years. Stabler Memorial, in Greenville, Alabama, was a twenty-minute drive from Pine Apple if you needed a flu shot, but an eight-minute drive if you needed anything else and had a vehicle with sirens and a lightbar. I slid the information to Mr. Crowder.

"What else?" he asked.

"I need to know Richard Sanders' status."

"That I can't help you with."

I didn't think so.

"You have a lot of marks against you, Miss Doe," he said.

I maneuvered this way and that in the chair, trying to get in his line of vision, which wasn't going to happen without wings.

"Pretrial drags on, as you're finding out firsthand, not to

mention what a high profile case yours is."

I felt like standing and waving. *Over here!*

He flipped through my file, then looked back to the calendar. "Let's start with the basics," he said. "What's your name?"

"Davis Way. D-A-V-I-S. W-A-Y."

He sniffed. "Have you come up with any way for us to verify it?"

"I've given out my personal information to everyone I've seen, Mr. Crowder, and I'll be happy to do it again."

He stared at the calendar. "Unless you have something new, we can move on."

My shoulders slumped a little more. If that were possible.

"Okay, moving on. Is there anything you need that you don't have?"

That was a loaded question, but I knew what he meant. "I could use some things from the commissary, Mr. Crowder, and something that fits better." Three of me could have fit into my prison jumpsuit. "But what I need more than anything is a lawyer."

"Now there again, I can't help you with that."

And for some reason, he locked his gaze on the opposite wall, zeroing in on a framed eight-by-ten of the Governor. For the rest of our conversation he looked to his boss for reinforcement.

"We can assume," he said to the Governor, "that the District Attorney is dragging his feet on assigning someone until the formal charges are made on the homicide issue."

"*Homicide?*" I jumped up. "Has Mr. Sanders died?"

"I didn't say that," Mr. Crowder said to the Governor, "and have a seat."

I sat, using the chair arms to lower myself.

"What I was saying was, there aren't enough pro bono attorneys to go around. You won't be assigned one before you're charged." He held up a finger, then proceeded to clear his lungs in a way that made me glad I hadn't eaten in weeks. Under normal circumstances, I'd have offered him a tissue, or a bucket, but these were anything but normal circumstances.

"Don't be in any hurry," he choked out. "As soon as they charge you on the homicide issue, you'll be moved down the hill."

Up the hill housed the petty criminals—Class C felonies and better. The ax murderers were down. I'd seen the small collection of maximum-security buildings while walking the yard, and never imagined myself there. How had things gotten that far? And where would it go from there if Mr. Sanders died? Chatter within the prison walls was just as ambiguous as my new counselor. Inmates continuously sneered and leered both "Bang, bang, Bianca! Shot him *dead!*" which meant Mr. Sanders hadn't survived the shooting. With equal airtime, my fellow inmates hissed things like, "Boss man's coming after you, Bianca," which meant he was still alive. I didn't acknowledge either; I kept to my corner.

"Miss Doe?"

I tried to breathe.

"I'll inquire about an attorney for you," he said, "because at least you can get started on this other business." He was apparently familiar with the long list of charges against me, although he was still talking to the Governor. He let out a whistle. "Until then," he pushed another piece of paper my way, "you can put up to three names on your visitor list and tell me what you need from the commissary. I'll see what I can do." He tore his gaze off the photo to look at his watch.

I'd already given at least fifty mental miles of pacing the perimeter of the yard to what names I would put on my visitor list. The other zillion miles of pacing, I tried to figure out why Bianca would want to kill her husband. I wrote down one name and pushed the paper toward him.

"That's it?"

I nodded.

"And what can I help you with from the commissary?"

"I need a bar of soap," I said. Why the prison passed out toothbrushes, toothpaste, and shampoo, but made you purchase a bar of soap was beyond me. "And some writing paper, envelopes, something to write with, and stamps."

He scratched his bald head, displacing the long strands

plastered from ear to ear. Realizing this, he began patting his hair back into place. His fingernails were dirty.

"Have you not made any friends?" he asked. "It would seem some of the other women would help you with sundries."

"I know better than to make friends in here, Mr. Crowder."

"So you've been incarcerated before?"

I slapped my head. "No! I'm a former police officer!"

Sure you are, his face said. "You know," he glanced at his watch again, "it would help so much if you'd give us your name. Really, Miss Doe, how much worse can it get? Are you concerned about extradition to another state?"

I pressed my lips together tightly and begged the sudden tears to stay in my head.

"Think about it, Miss Doe. Unless you're facing homicide charges somewhere else, you'd be so much better off just telling us."

"My name is Davis Way." I reeled off my Social. I opened my mouth to spout off more, but he held his hands up in a halt motion.

"Give me the name of an immediate family member who can verify your identity," he said, "in person. Show up with a birth certificate and baby pictures, and I'll call them." After several minutes of complete silence, while silent tears made tracks down my face as he memorized the pattern on the Governor's tie, he tapped his pen and said, "I didn't think so."

He pushed back from his desk and pulled open the middle drawer. He passed me two sheets of blank paper and one stamped envelope. "This is all I can do. You'll have to purchase more or get with a fellow inmate and work something out."

I reached for them and found my voice. "Thank you, Mr. Crowder."

"Good luck, Doe. I'll see you next week."

I hoped not.

* * *

I had one shot. It took me until lights out, huddled in my corner, to write the letter. I wanted, more than anything, to use my resources to contact my sister, but that would do more harm than good. If I didn't devote a good portion of my waking hours imagining my father's recovery—the crisp, pale sheets on my parent's bed, a Robert Parker thriller on the nightstand, the afternoon sun streaming through the plantation shutters and cutting lines across the foot of the bed—I wouldn't be able to breathe. I would not divert attention from his healing by turning the spotlight on myself. Besides, I could hear my mother now: "Of course she's in jail. Where else would she be when he really needs her? No, Meredith, don't you lift a finger. She got herself in there, let her get herself out."

Of my small Bellissimo crew, I felt certain at least one of them knew exactly where I was and exactly why, and they wanted things the way they were. Contacting the wrong one could spell conviction for me. And George. How do you address a letter to a man using an alias who lived in a cab? I didn't have an attorney to contact, so that left me with one rotten option.

Eddie, Mel, and Bea,

I swear to you, all three, on all that is holy and unholy, if you do not respond to this letter immediately I will make the rest of your lives a living breathing hell. I need out of this prison, and I need out NOW, and if one of you doesn't get to Biloxi and get me out, your chicken-fried chicken-liver Thursdays are OVER. I will burn that place to the ground with the three of you chained to the fryer. Breathe a word of this to my family, and you'll be so sorry.

I'll see you <u>tomorrow.</u>

Bring a lawyer.

Davis

I had no way to erase it, and less than a quarter of an inch of ink showing through the rubbery prison pen casing, so I used the rest of that sheet of paper to draft the letter that I sealed and turned in at mail call.

Eddie,

You only know the second half of how to win the money. I know the first.

Another thing I know is that you only receive a cut, and if you'll help me, not only will I forgive and forget about the money you owe me, I will let you walk away with every penny of what you win. There's a one-week window on this, so you'd better not spend too much time thinking about it. To get the money, Eddie, you're going to have to get me out of jail. I'm in prison, in Biloxi, and I need an attorney who can get me bonded out. Call that guy in Montgomery who gets you out of your DUIs and get him to give you the name of the best criminal defense attorney in the state of Mississippi.

I desperately need to know about my father, Eddie.

And please please put a twenty in my prison account. They've got me in as Jane Doe, Block B, Harrison County Women's Correction. Get a lawyer who can get me bonded, get a bondsman, and do it NOW.

You've been waiting on your big break all your life, Eddie, and this is it. A million dollars to do with what you want. All you have to do is get me out of here.

Don't write me back about any of this. They can't read what I write to you, but if you write me back, the prison system will read it first. Don't write, just show up. Don't mention any of this to anyone in my family or the deal is OFF, and bring food, anything, four loaded cheeseburgers, whatever, when you show up.

You will no longer owe me, Eddie. Instead, I will owe you.

Davis

I sat back and waited. To pass the time, I played video poker in my head. On the third morning after sending it, I held my breath every time a guard's footstep fell outside my cell, thinking they were coming to tell me I'd been bonded out.

On day seven, my increasing panic turned to despair. I'd mailed the letter to his parents' house, knowing Eddie was here in Biloxi, but also knowing his nosy mother would get in touch with him to tell him he had a letter from a prison in Mississippi to be opened by him only, and as nosy as he was, he'd hustle home and read it.

Enough time had passed for all of that to happen, yet it hadn't. In the seven days since I'd mailed the letter, I'd eaten one slice of stale bread and sipped no more than two ounces of murky water that had floaties.

On day eleven, my worst fears were realized. "Jane Doe" was one of the first names announced at mail call. Eddie had written me back to tell me to kiss his ass, but in fact, it was even worse. The letter was from his mother, and it wasn't an original. It was a copy.

To whom it may concern, because I don't really believe it's you, Davis, but if it is, I couldn't care less about whatever kind of mess you've gotten yourself into, and for the life of me, I can't figure out why you'd try to drag my son into it. Haven't you done enough? I would think, with all your family is going through, that you'd be thinking about something else other than the money you SAY Eddie owes you. You were <u>married</u>. It was his money too. Get over it. If you think getting him to steal for you is the right way to get yourself out of trouble, then you have bigger problems than we ever imagined.

Not that it's any of your business, but we haven't heard a word from our son in months. One more thing, whoever you are, don't write me back. You know what they say—you make your bed, you lie in it.

Bea Crawford

I should have sent the first letter.

The people in charge read the letter a hundred times before I did, and the District Attorney read between the lines and decided "financial gain" was the motive he'd been seeking, and what a stretch, with Bea's letter his only evidence.

Well, that, and they knew I'd fired a weapon on the night in question.

I knew the system well enough to know that bringing formal charges against me meant my future held a lot more of the same. I would sit there and rot in pretrial status while the steam built up on their airtight case of greed, a smoking gun, and an obsession with Richard Sanders that led to me impersonating his wife, then shooting him. They'd assign me the sorriest lawyer they could find, someone who couldn't get his own mother out of a speeding ticket, and in a year when this thing finally went to trial, I wouldn't have a chance in hell against a jury of my peers.

Three days after receiving Bea's letter, I was charged with the attempted homicide of Richard Sanders, plus a laundry list of other charges. The worst was Bea's snipe about what my family was going through. The only ray of light was that Richard Sanders must be alive.

* * *

Interestingly enough, Mississippi doesn't require your physical presence to accuse you of taking a kill shot at an unarmed pillar of the community. I was heavily escorted to a room on the second floor of the prison's administrative building and shoved into a metal chair with a video camera and television in front of me. The camera was on a tripod, and the television was on a rolly cart. Attempted homicide charges against Jane Doe were handed down via video conferencing.

I kept one eye on the television, watching the pre-hearing activities inside the courtroom, while one of my captors barked instructions and threats. I made cooperating gestures and noises. From what I could see inside the courtroom, the judge, already on the bench, along with the bailiff, suits, and court clerks, looked bored. They were having coffee, private conversations, and passing around yawns. Someone must have been interested, though, because intermittent strobes of light bounced around the room and off their faces. Soon enough, there was order in the court, and my director gave the three-finger countdown.

"My name is Davis Way," I shouted. "Help me, Judge!"

The video camera light went from green to red, and the guard with his finger on the trigger looked at me in disgust. "Did we not just go over this?"

I squeezed my eyes shut and rocked back and forth.

"Do you think you can keep it together?" he asked.

I nodded with my whole body. At least I had my name out there. Surely it would be repeated a thousand times today. Surely someone somewhere would start digging.

The camera guard gave me a threatening look, and three others pulled out stun guns. The electronics whirred to life again, the judge's long face filling the screen.

"No more outbursts," he warned.

I shook my head vigorously, agreeing. I was stunned enough.

"You're in a lot of trouble, young lady."

Again, I agreed.

"Answer yes or no only to the following question," he warned. "Do you have an attorney?"

"No."

The judge complained to his audience at length about chicken-shit corporate crackpots who wouldn't know a career-making pro bono if it walked up and bit them, then turned his attention back to me. "You'll be assigned a public defender forthwith," he said.

The charges against me were read. I was given the option of postponing my response until some poor soul was roped into representing me. I declined.

"Not guilty."

"Held without bail."

The screen went dead.

* * *

The next day they transported me down the hill to live with the ax murderers. I was processed and shoved into a two-bunk cell with a convicted felon.

As it turned out, my new roommate liked me even less than my old roommates. She eyed me for two seconds, then yelled, "You!" Her steel gaze turned to the guards. "No way! Get her out!" She came at me swinging, and she must have connected, because I woke up in the infirmary again, completely confused, with a needle in my arm.

I'd immediately recognized the face of the girl who'd put me there, as it had happened, but couldn't place her before I saw stars. Sometime during my infirmary respite, my subconscious put a name to the irate face. Heidi Dupree, the Casino Marketing assistant who, along with her brother, had been cleaning out room safes. And she could've been my ticket out, because she could verify my identity enough to make someone listen, except for the fact that I never saw her again. That and she hated my guts.

Rising on an elbow, I counted eight empty infirmary beds in the room I was becoming increasingly familiar with.

"Morning." The only other patient, a tremendously pregnant prisoner, greeted me.

"Do you know what day it is?"

"Nope," she said. She was peeling an orange, the citrus scent bursting through the small room. It was the first edible thing I'd been close to in weeks and had one of my ankles not been shackled to the metal frame of the bed, I'd have pounced on the pregnant woman and confiscated it.

"Doe! Nice of you to join us." A jolly prison physician suddenly filled the room, interrupting my plans to drag the bed with me to steal the pregnant woman's food. "I was coming in to give you some wake up juice, and you saved me the trouble. And the state a thousand dollars." He chuckled at himself, then dropped the syringe he'd been holding into the pocket of his white coat. He appeared to be well past retirement age. He was grossly overweight, sweating profusely, and his eyes were so glazed over, it could be he helped himself to treats from the prison pharmacy cabinet every ten minutes.

"I've got some advice for you, Doe." He licked his pale, cracked lips. "Your fasting program is going to kill you. You might like it better here in the infirmary, but you're going to end up in a body bag if you don't start eating."

I thought of the mound of colorless mush prisoners were served twice a day, accompanied by a paper cup of a transparent purple liquid, and knew I'd stick with the fasting no matter how many times I ended up there.

"Big day for you, Doe, you're moving," he announced. "So up and at 'em. Your infirmary vacation is over. You're headed to solitary."

"What? Why?" I tried to sit all the way up, but the room spun around me. "I haven't done anything."

"You're in here because of a fight, right?"

"I'd hardly call it a fight!"

"Whatever," the doctor said. "The State doesn't consult with me on the rules or the room assignments."

A female guard appeared at the end of the narrow bed and began separating me from it.

"You have fifteen minutes to clean yourself up." The doctor nodded toward the adjacent infirmary facilities as he none-too-gently yanked the needle out of my arm. "You have a visitor downstairs. Your counselor's giving you fifteen minutes of visitation before the transfer."

I almost passed out again at the thought of a visitor. No one could show up and ask to see you in prison; they had to be on your list unless they were clergy. I had a list—a short short list that was a long long shot. Chances were a Bible thumper was waiting patiently in the visitation room to save my degenerate soul. Well, he'd do. And if he believed me, he might save my incarcerated butt.

The shower was wonderful, private (if your definition of private was no curtain or door and a guard watching), and the infirmary toiletries were almost up to EconoLodge standards. The female guard passed me what would be my new uniform: granny panties, a sports bra laundered within an inch of its life, hospital-type scrubs in a pale blue color, and slip-on plastic shoes. After the shower and the merciful time with a real toothbrush and a real squeeze of Crest, I fingered my wet hair, dressed, and honestly felt as good as I had the first time I'd worn a Natalie outfit. Thankfully someone finally knew I was here.

* * *

I spotted him right away, alone at a cafeteria-style table in a corner. Wasting a full one-fifteenth of my time, I found a wall to hold me up and drank him in. I made my way across the room on wobbly legs and fell into the chair opposite him. We stared at each other for another precious minute, him scanning my face, looking for anything familiar.

"Bradley Cole." I could hardly breathe. "Thank you for coming."

"I got your note," he said, his cautious eyes smiling.

What note?

"The one you left on the fridge. That you had to go to work, and you'd be right back."

I closed my eyes to squeeze in the humiliation. I opened them one at a time, and he looked, more than anything else, amused.

"I would have called," he said, "but my phone was in the refrigerator."

I crawled under the table.

(No, I didn't.)

"How did you find me?" I asked.

"You left a lot of clues." He pushed up the sleeves of my favorite green sweater of his. "To tell you the truth, I can hardly move around the clues. I hope you don't mind, but I moved your copier to a storage unit."

In spite of everything, and for the first time in weeks, I smiled. Then laughed. "My lease said no pets. It didn't say anything about office equipment."

He nodded slowly. "True."

"So the copier led you straight to me?"

"Not exactly."

Bradley Cole laced his fingers, and his clasped hands were dangerously close to mine on the table between us.

"I found more than a few sets of identification, a hundred wigs, several Bellissimo uniforms, and two destroyed slot machines. I pieced it together with the six o'clock news, and," he surrendered, "here I am."

"Here you are." I whispered the words.

My joy, my gratitude, and my thankfulness overwhelmed me. It didn't help that he was such a perfectly gorgeous man, more so in person than any photograph began to capture.

"And you've gotten messages," he said.

"Messages?"

He nodded. "I found an envelope that someone slid under the front door, and someone else threw a rock with a note on the lanai."

"Did you bring them?"

"I didn't bring the rock."

That did it. If I wasn't completely in love with Bradley Cole before, I certainly was after.

"The guards wouldn't let me through with the notes."

"Tell me you read them," I said.

"I did," he answered, "not being nosy, more like seriously trying to figure out who you were and where you'd taken off to."

I nodded.

"You must really like Pop Tarts."

For the second time since my incarceration, I laughed. Glorious laughter. Maybe I would try prison food; this man made me want to stay alive long enough to get out.

There was so much commotion in the large room—kids everywhere—that no one kept a clock on me, and I spent twenty-eight minutes with Bradley Cole, who was decidedly more impressive in person than in spirit. Too soon, though, a guard shouted, "Doe. Time's up."

If Bradley Cole and I marry and have ten kids, I will tell them the story of how we met as often as my mother tells the one about me ruining her life: "Daddy came to see Mommy at the prison. We had a big table all to ourselves in a room full of people. And nine months later, you were born."

He was Robin Hood. He was Officer John McClane. Bradley Cole was Dudley Do-Right, and I was Nell, tied to the tracks.

The first thing we talked about was my father. Bradley promised me he'd know my father's status within the hour, and he'd get news to me as quickly as the prison system would allow.

I was without words. I kept my lips pressed tightly together and gripped the seat of the chair I sat in with both hands to keep myself from tackling Bradley Cole and smothering him with love and gratitude.

"Now let's talk about your situation."

My father's health was my situation.

"Richard Sanders," he said.

And there was that.

"Is he going to make it?" I held my breath.

"Absolutely," Bradley Cole said.

I exhaled and patted my chest.

"He took the shot above the ear, through and through," Bradley said. "It hit his optical nerves and a retinal artery."

I covered my eyes with my hands.

"It looked," he said, "being a headshot, a lot worse than it really was, which led to a ridiculous amount of sensationalized media, and he was taken by helicopter to the Shreveport Cranial Trauma Center for a seven-hour surgery, which in turn made the story even bigger. The media had him fighting for his life, when he was in fact," Bradley said, "fighting for his *eye*."

"The surgery, was it successful? Did they save his eye? And what about his hair?"

"His what?" Bradley asked.

"Never mind." I waved. "Can he see?"

Bradley shook his head. "No word on that yet, but it's only the one eye. Worst-case, he's lost vision in one eye."

"Are you reading all this in the paper?"

"No." Bradley shifted in his seat, and I got a whiff of his sandalwood soap I loved to shower with. Make that used to love to shower with. I wondered, for a split-second, if the prison would let him bring me some. Then I thought of razor blades and bars of soap, and decided they wouldn't.

"I'm getting it at work," he said.

"The soap?" I asked.

Bradley blinked several times.

"The messages." I switched gears quickly. "What did they say?" The weeks of famine must have brought out my inner idiot. I forced myself to ignore how shockingly handsome Bradley Cole was in person, and to snap back into the here (prison), now (attempted homicide charges), and why (would he be here to help me?).

"Right," Handsome said, "the messages."

"I don't understand why anyone would've left messages at the condo. They *have* to know I'm here." I held my hands out like a Price Is Right model, displaying the magnificence of the Mississippi prison system. "Yet no one has made the first attempt to help me."

"From what I understand," he said, "mine is the only name on your visitor list. How do you know they haven't tried?"

"Until I can figure out how I got here," I said, "the wrong person coming to see me would do more harm than good."

"Do you know who the wrong person is?" he asked.

"I have a guess," I said, "but it's a frightening one. Other than that, I'm pretty sure Mr. Sanders' wife is in it up to her eyeballs."

He processed the information, then he closed what little space there was between us. His green eyes had a gold tint, which played perfectly off his five-o'clock shadow, golden as well. "What *is* your name?"

"It's Davis," I said. "Davis Way."

"I like it." Bradley Cole sat back. "Davis Way," he tried it on. "Nice." And then he smiled, honestly, a first-date smile. I felt it, I swear, all the way from my dyed-blonde hair to my new slip-on plastic shoes.

"Why are you back in Biloxi, Bradley? I thought you were out of town until June."

"I had a long weekend," he said, "so I came back to evict you."

"*What*?"

"Davis." He threw his hands in the air. "My phone rings off the hook about you. I've taken calls from neighbors," he ticked the list off on his fingers, "from the building super, and then a few weeks ago about forty calls asking me about Marci somebody, and none of the calls were particularly nice."

"Well, your neighbors aren't exactly nice either, Bradley. And neither is your dry-cleaning guy."

With a wide smile across his handsome face, he came across the table again, making my heart pound again. "Did you send my mother a hundred tulips on her birthday and sign the card from me?"

I could feel myself turning several shades of red.

"How in the world did you know it was my mother's birthday?"

Oh, dear.

In the twenty-eight minutes we spent together, he never asked if I shot Richard Sanders.

* * *

One thing I found in Solitary I hadn't found anywhere else in the prison system was a human.

Her name was Fantasy Erb: five foot eleven, thirty-one years old, mother of three boys, and she should have been a runway model in New York, not a prison guard, or CO as they were called, Corrections Officer, in Mississippi. She worked the day shift, and the only way I knew that in my timeless world was because she delivered the first of my two food trays, the one that had the boiled egg (green yolk) beside the mound of gruel instead of the later-in-the-day side of gray mushy stuff, which might have been mutated cauliflower or potato, beside the mound of gruel.

Fantasy was the one who told me why I'd been placed in solitary.

"They didn't have anywhere else to put you, girl. We're built out for twelve hundred guests, and we're busting at the seams with twice that."

"That's a relief."

"Depends on how you look at it," she said. "Mississippi's not so relieved."

"It's most likely the casinos," I offered. "Cash brings out the criminal in otherwise law-abiding citizens."

Fantasy's eyes narrowed.

"I didn't mean me!"

She took a retreating step, as if to separate herself from her new homicidal ward. She turned to walk away, her keys clanging, then stopped, spun, and took two long strides back to my cell. She looked left and right. "I will say this," she kept her voice soft, "if you listen to local chatter, there's a whole lot of confusion as to what happened at the Bellissimo."

"I didn't shoot him."

"Of course not."

Right. Everyone in prison was innocent.

"No, seriously," Fantasy said, "you seem harmless, and I'm not just saying that because you're two feet tall. Believe me, girl, I know the difference."

She looked like she was about to stroll away, and I had to keep her there, if for nothing else than civil conversation. "How long have you worked here?"

"Too long," she said. "I've climbed up the pay ladder to the point of being stuck. I can't go anywhere else and make this money," she said. "And I've got a kid with bone-plate problems that would be a pre-existing anywhere else. So here I am. Stuck."

I knew exactly how she felt.

She locked a laser beam on me. "And I won't do anything that might get me unstuck."

I heard her—boundaries. Or in that case, bars. So instead of asking her to pass me her Sig Sauer P238, I asked about my father. I'd see her again before Bradley Cole would cut through the solitary-confinement red tape.

I couldn't sleep that night, waiting for Fantasy's shift to start.

"I'm so sorry, girl," she said. "My boys had homework coming out their ears last night, and the only thing I can tell you is that there isn't anything bad on the internet. The only story I could find told what you already knew: he had a heart attack and a triple bypass."

* * *

Thanks to Fantasy, I began eating again.

"Tell them you're diabetic."

"But I'm not," I said.

"So? Everyone in here lies. Tell them you are, and until your next physical when they figure out you aren't, which could be when pigs fly, you'll get fresh fruits and vegetables instead of mystery casserole."

From that day on, I had a banana, a small container of fat-free peanut butter, and a slice of wheat toast for breakfast. My second meal was almost always tomato soup, five stale crackers, and an apple or an orange. Starvation problem solved, and more than that, she sneaked me food.

"Up and at 'em, Doe. Inspection."

She came in, flipped my mattress, pretended to frisk me, shined a light down the sink drain, and when she left I had a glorious cornbread muffin, warm, swimming in butter, and a Dr Pepper over crushed ice. I almost cried.

She snuck me to the shower too, and even allowed me a small slice of privacy, in the room with me, but with her back turned. I was allowed two showers a week; she got me out of there every day. "What are you doing scratching that head, Doe? Get up. We're going to the showers."

She brought me a second set of prison digs, and between the

cotton top and drawstring pants was a zipped plastic bag, sandwich size, with a tablespoon of thick liquid green stuff in it. "Wash the one you're wearing in the sink," she said, "then spread it out under your mattress to dry."

When I wasn't eating, showering, washing prison clothes, worrying about my father, or planning my jailbreak, I thought about Bradley Cole.

My history with men was pathetic. The stuff of nightmares. Four years passed between my life-altering encounter with Mr. World Cultures Teacher and the next time I worked up the nerve. When I did it was a three-night stand, which everyone knows doesn't even count. Then another year passed before I dated a Biology major, Geoff, for six boring months, immediately followed by a two-night stand (again, didn't count) with the coxswain on the UAB rowing team (he smelled funny), then the long, tumultuous decade of debauchery with (do I have to say it out loud?) Eddie the Ass. That's it. Sum total. None of which had prepared me for Bradley Cole. Just like all the photographs hadn't prepared me for the 3-D version.

For example, his hair wasn't dark blond, like in the pictures. Bradley Cole's hair was gold. Fourteen subtle shades of gold, including sunshine, candlelight, and honey. It was neat, short, very lawyerly, and looked soft. His green eyes weren't just green; they were green flecked with gold, and they were like the rest of Bradley Cole: warm, engaging, and brilliant. The man glowed. (Maybe that was me glowing.) Past all the glow, he was six feet tall with an athletic body, the tapering kind, that said baseball. (Bradley Cole's body said Varsity Pitcher Throws Perfect Game No-Hitter Shutout in State Championship.)

I couldn't stop thinking about his hands.

Sadly, my only true point of male-good-looks reference was Eddie the Ass. He was the physical man-bar in my life, and, admittedly, he was pretty. Bradley Cole wasn't pretty—he was all the way handsome. It took me days to figure out what was missing in Bradley Cole. Eddie the Ass had *something* Bradley Cole didn't. I finally put my finger on it: the Sleaze Factor.

* * *

Day six of solitary dawned to the music of Fantasy rolling a cart down the hall. I sat up, feeling the metal supports beneath the wafer-thin pad pretending it was a mattress, to see, first thing in the morning, the not-Fantasy guard, Jerry. "You got a package from your attorney, Doe."

My bare feet hit the cold floor.

I had an attorney?

A shock of blonde hair fell into my face, while it all registered. I was a blonde, I was in prison, and Jerry was in charge of me. And more than that, the glowing Bradley Cole was an attorney.

Jerry used a handheld device, trained a beam, and the window in the gate that made up the fourth wall of my cell slid open, at the same time a rubber support protruded, the exact shape of the food trays, but instead of a bowl of soup, Jerry tossed in books. One slid to the floor, and seeing what I could call a personal possession, I dove for it.

One afternoon I'd stretched out on the bed and taken mental inventory of everything I owned, both in Biloxi and at home. It was a crazy long list. Everything from an antique typewriter I'd swiped from Meredith's shop, a Dutch Doll quilt Grandmother Way had hand-stitched, to Burberry rain boots I'd only worn once. In prison, I was cut off from everything, the things that mattered and things that didn't, and the three books being mine—they mattered—I didn't want anything to happen to them.

From my knees, clutching the fallen book to my chest, I looked up for Jerry to thank him, but he'd closed the window and moved on, back to the desk chair he used as a La-Z-Boy.

I spread the books out and sat on the cold floor with them. I picked them up, one by one, hugging them, inhaling them, then running my fingers over all their surfaces. I turned each one over, gently shook them, and of course nothing fell out. I lined them up by size.

The smallest was *Sit Still and Wait for It* by Sasha Jones. I could have fit it in my back pocket had I had one. The next was a previously well-loved paperback romance, *The Missing Secretary* by Lilly Jasmine. Lastly, largest, and the bestseller as far as I was concerned, *A Bypass Surgery Survivor's Guide to a Long and Healthy Life* by P. Derrick Ameston.

I didn't wake up screaming that night.

TWENTY-ONE

Bradley Cole warned me he wouldn't be back until he had news, but he'd failed to warn me that with hope, which he'd given me, it would be a long wait.

Receiving the best news ever, that my father was recovering, didn't provide the relief I thought it would. Initially, of course, it did; I cried, danced, laughed, and relived every moment of my childhood. I fell to my knees and assured God I'd keep all the prison promises I'd made, and after an entire day of that, I collapsed in relief. The biggest relief? No more endless hours of imaging my father without life or my life without my father.

But I had to fill the hours with something, and as they dragged on, his healing actually served to make my situation worse: I had to get out of there and get to Daddy before someone else did. I had to get out of there before Daddy put two and two together and came up with trouble. I had to dig myself out before Daddy was forced to. If my father learned of my predicament, he'd have a heart attack.

I got that Bradley Cole wanted me to *Sit Still and Wait for It.* Regardless, after another day, I began pacing my four-by-six cell, and read *The Missing Secretary* twice, the good parts more times than that.

I replayed the twenty-eight minutes with Bradley a million times, picking it to pieces, and tried to make sense of the book titles. Where in the world was Natalie? I used Fantasy as a sounding board when she had time, but she was more interested in the Bradley Cole angle than anything else. "Girl," Fantasy said. "You've got it bad for him."

"He's pretty wonderful." I looked at her. "And I miss his clothes."

The rock on the lanai had to have been George, and the accompanying message asked more questions than it answered. The note around the rock had three words, written in block letters and underlined twice: IT WASN'T HER.

It wasn't her? Her who? Bianca?

"Why would he throw a rock on the lanai?" Bradley had asked.

"So he wouldn't be recorded by the condo's security cameras walking a note in," I answered. "George's story is a long one, and he operates completely under the radar."

"He's the cab driver who parks at the VIP entrance, right?" Bradley asked. "Where the shooting took place?"

I nodded.

"Then he saw the whole thing. All we have to do is track him down."

"No." I shook my head. "He only knows who it wasn't. If he knew who it was, he'd have said."

"I'll find him," Bradley promised.

"That will never happen," I said. "George is so long gone it's as if he was never even here."

The note under the door had been from No Hair. Bradley paraphrased it for me: No Hair said my situation was my own fault for snooping around in his desk. While he knew of my predicament, there wasn't a lot he could do about it, seeing as I'd left a trail.

"The note said you left your *hair* in his office and that she walked right to it. He doesn't say who 'she' is or what 'it' is. Do you know, Davis," Bradley asked, "who 'she' is, what it means by 'you left your hair,' or how you left a trail?"

I couldn't answer because my life was flashing before my eyes.

"The note said he was with Richard Sanders." Bradley's voice was far away. "But it didn't say where."

I couldn't respond because the world's worst news was sinking in.

"Davis?" Bradley waved a hand in my face. "Can you fill me in?"

"Sorry." I shook the cobwebs out. "George is saying Bianca didn't shoot her husband, and No Hair's saying I forgot my wig, and my prints were on the gun."

Bradley Cole could not have been more confused. (Not that I wasn't.) "No what?" he asked. "No hair, did you say? I don't understand the hair issue."

I couldn't explain because I was too busy thinking about lethal injections.

"What gun, Davis? You shot a gun that day? Your prints are on what gun?"

"Doe!" a guard interrupted. "Time's up."

Bradley Cole reached out and placed his strong, warm hands on top of mine. The room spun around at his touch.

"Don't worry," he'd said. "I'll get to the bottom of this. Don't worry, Davis."

Seven ridiculously long days and nights had passed since our meeting, with no word from him other than the books. There were times I wondered if I'd dreamed it.

"Stop worrying," Fantasy said. "He'll be back."

The words had no sooner left her lips when, on my eighth day of solitary confinement, the intercom in my room squealed. "Doe. Your lawyer's here. Transport in ten."

"See?" Fantasy said. "I told you."

* * *

With Bradley Cole my attorney of record, I could meet with him anytime, and we didn't have to do it in the crowded visitation room. Although, honestly, I'd have done it with him anywhere: crowd, no crowd, judges, videographers, zoo animals, I didn't care.

We were allowed thirty minutes in a private room: all glass walls, guards on every corner, and speakers that could be turned on should the penal system think I was spouting off geographical coordinates to the bodies I'd buried.

Bradley could bring his brief case, any documents related to my defense, and his cell phone, although no signal made it in or out of the bunker. He had to leave his keys, weapons, and any street drugs for resale he might be sneaking me at the door.

That day he wore a white button-down oxford shirt under a blue sweater and khaki pants. His shoes were the Italian loafers that, at my last sighting, were on his closet floor between my (Meredith's) Tory Burch peep-toes and Michael Kors black leather clogs.

I was wearing blue prison scrubs.

Honestly, we gooed at each other for the first little bit like he was there to pick me up for the prom. I wondered if I might be imagining it. Maybe it was just me doing all the gooing.

"How are you holding up, Davis?"

I nodded, smiling. "I'm better," I said. "Better."

"You got the books," he said.

"I did. I love them all. Although there's not much to *Sit Still and Wait for It*," I said. "I read it at night to fall asleep."

He laughed. "I haven't read it. But if you want to write a review with a sleep-inducing warning, I'll post it for you."

Things got real serious real quick. "He's okay?"

Bradley's voice was soft. "He's fine, Davis. He's doing fine. He's making a great recovery."

I squeezed my eyes closed, swallowed hard, and tried not to blubber.

"I picked up the phone to call a dozen times," he said, "and couldn't figure out what to say or how to say it. So I got in the car and drove to scenic Pine Apple, Alabama."

He reached for his cell phone, pushed buttons, and passed it to me. Our hands touched, and a guard banged on the window with his baton.

I scrolled through the underwater photos, underwater because I began crying as soon as I saw the first image of my father, wearing gray wool pants and a yellow V-neck sweater, strolling the rows of Mother's winter garden beside my parents' home, my mother and sister at his elbows, my niece several steps ahead.

"Sorry I couldn't get closer."

"Oh, Bradley, please don't apologize." I rearranged the tears so they were all over my face instead of two boring rivers. There were more than twenty images, and in all of them Daddy looked so thin, and so scary pale, but he was alive, smiling in several shots, and seemingly not too much less of himself after the heart attack and surgery. I fell against the chair back, exhaling the breath I'd been holding for so long with the proof in my hands. I clutched the evidence against my chest, and Bradley looked a little nervous for his phone, or maybe jealous, because most days, today being one of them, I skipped the threadbare sports bra. It itched.

I could live the rest of my life with Fantasy as my only friend, Bradley as my only link to the outside world, prison scrubs my entire wardrobe, and the prison walls my only view, as long as my father was okay.

Finally, I passed his phone back to him, our hands meeting again, and mouthed two words I'd uttered a million times, but never before from the rock bottom of my heart. "Thank you."

He waited patiently until I was ready for more, and when he thought I was, he landed an envelope on the table between us. Meredith's handwriting jumped off it.

"Oh, no." I stared.

Davis,

What the hell? You've pulled some stunts in your day, but this one takes the cake.

Daddy's going to be fine.

I got a crazy phone call telling me you were in Asia, or Africa, I can't even remember it was all so scary-horrible-chaos those first days, but I do remember this—I didn't believe a word of it. Once we got Daddy home and I turned on a television, I knew exactly where you were. I left poor Mother alone with our very ill father, buckled Riley in the car, and drove to the prison only to sit there—with my CHILD—for TEN HOURS, DAVIS, to be told over and over again that you weren't there, and that I couldn't see the

Jane Doe they were holding on the casino shooting.

What the hell, Davis?

No, Mother and Daddy don't know, although Daddy's on the right track, and he'll know soon. You had a grace period as your father was TOO SICK to even worry about you, but that's over, and he's snooping around. Yes, as always, I'm trying to cover for you, making up phantom phone calls and even sending Get Well cards.

Seriously, Davis.

After reading it several times, I turned it over so Meredith would stop screaming at me. "Where did you get this?"

"I'd been in Pine Apple ten minutes when she walked up to me and said we needed to talk."

"No!" It felt like high school, when Meredith caught me smoking a cigarette and I had to wash the dinner dishes on her nights for a month. No telling what her silence would cost for this.

Bradley nodded. "I thought I was being sneaky."

"Yeah." I sighed. "She was raised by a police chief."

"Your hometown's really small."

"It is," I agreed.

"I liked her store," he said.

It didn't seem to me that Bradley Cole would be wasting time making small talk about the Front Porch if there wasn't something else about his meeting Meredith that he didn't want to tell me.

"What else?"

"Nothing."

I crossed my arms and waited.

"She said for me to tell you she wasn't an idiot," he said, "and that your ex-husband is nowhere to be found."

"And?" I asked.

He took his time. "She said the whole town thinks you've run off with him."

We sat quietly for a beat.

"So?" Bradley took a tread-lightly breath. "You and your ex?"

I wondered if he was asking regarding my current state of affairs, or life in general. It didn't matter; the answer was the same.

"Honestly, Bradley," I said. "I'd rather be here, in prison, than anywhere with my ex-husband."

"Okay, Davis." He shifted in his seat. "Time to tell me the whole story."

I did the best I could.

"You realize," he said at the end, "I'm not a criminal lawyer."

"Perfect," I said. "I'm not a criminal."

I didn't leave anything out.

He listened intently, made notes but asked no questions. In the end, he had only one comment: "You do look exactly like her."

TWENTY-TWO

On my fifty-sixth day of incarceration, Teeth washed up in the St. Bernard Bay, ninety miles west of the Bellissimo. His dentist identified the body over the phone. It didn't take long to find the cause of death, because the bullet wedged so tightly in the base of his skull that even the ocean hadn't managed to free it had come from the gun with my prints on it. At the time, it was Metairie, Louisiana's problem, but it was only a matter of paperwork before it would be mine.

The object of my dreams—and truly, I meant it, I'd dreamed about him from the first night I climbed into his bed—had said he had good news and bad news.

"Which do you want first?"

Thinking there might be bad news about my father, I asked for it.

He told me about Teeth.

"No!" I was incredulous. "That's not bad news! It's the straw that will nail my broke-back camel's coffin!"

"No," Bradley Cole was calm, "it's not."

"I'm going to be charged with his murder! This is devastating!" I was pacing and panicked. "I didn't really like Teeth all that much, and there's no doubt he had something to do with the Whammy con, but I didn't wish him dead either. And I sure didn't kill him."

"Please sit down, Davis." He patted the chair beside him.

He reached for and found my hand underneath the table, which gave me all manner of new sensations to add to the electric-chair sensations I was already having.

With his free hand, he pushed paper in front of me. It was the ballistics report from Richard Sanders' shooting. I used my teeth to turn the pages so I wouldn't have to let go of Bradley's hand.

(No, I didn't.)

After looking at the report from every possible angle, I turned to him. "Am I reading this right?"

Bradley Cole nodded. "You are."

According to the ballistics report, the bullet that hit Richard Sanders had whizzed above his ear back to front. Shreveport Cranial Trauma Center agreed: entry posterior, exit anterior. He and Bianca had been face-to-face, and Bellissimo surveillance backed it up with forty-four zillion stills. The shot had come from the bushes behind him, not the wife in front of him. Bianca had squeezed off a round, and they recovered the casing, but the estimated trajectory indicated she had been aiming for someone in Hot Springs, Arkansas—not her husband. Taking a hard look at what had really happened, it was amazing the shot that did hit Richard Sanders didn't go through him, then into Bianca.

If Bianca didn't shoot him, who did?

"How did you get this?" I asked.

"I've got people," Bradley Cole said, and with his words, I reached up and ran a hand through my blonde hair. Him having people made me think of Natalie booking me an appointment with the hair person—Shreveport. Or maybe it was Spokane. Bradley had people. Natalie had people. Why didn't I have people?

I suppose I had a strange look on my face, because Bradley studied me intently, then asked, "Where in the world are you going with this, Davis?"

I looked at him. "I was thinking about my hair."

Bradley nodded slowly. "Of course."

Things got very quiet, and very personal.

"You are amazing, Davis," he whispered, our heads close.

"So are you, Bradley," I whispered back.

Honestly, I couldn't feel my nose. Or my toes. Or much in between. It took forever to get back on track, because, as my

Granny Dee used to say, love is a many splendored thing, and I was completely splendored by him. Eventually, though, the prison clock ticking, the subject of Teeth's big dead body landed between us, shoving all the would-be romance aside.

"They'll still charge me with it," I said, my heart rate having finally returned to normal range. "They have my prints."

"Even if, Davis, it's in another state, so there's a small window of opportunity."

"Opportunity for what?"

"That's the best news." He had the most dazzling smile. "I think I can get you released before a charge is made on the Louisiana murder."

It made no sense. "How?"

"I'll file a motion to dismiss the attempted homicide charges in Mississippi based on the ballistics report."

We stared at the report on the table that clearly exonerated Bianca, which was to say the report that clearly exonerated me.

"That will never happen," I said. "It will take six weeks of crime scene reconstruction in court for them to drop the charges. By then, I'll be knee-deep in the Teeth deal."

"Maybe," he said. "Maybe not. But we won't ask for the moon."

"We'll ask for a star?"

"A bail star," he said.

I had stars in my eyes.

"Let's use this—" he tapped the ballistics report "—to get you out of here so you can go home."

"Home? I don't even have a home. Even if they release me, they're not going to let me cross a state line."

"Let's take this one step at a time," he said. "First step, bail."

It would be nice to get sprung from the slammer. I needed to get to Sacramento the Stylist again, and fast, because my red hair was peeking out.

* * *

Six days later, Bradley squeezed my hand under the table. "Are you ready, Davis?" he whispered.

I said yes with my eyes, which were burning from all the sunshine pouring through the windows of the courtroom.

"I need you to be really ready," he whispered, "for anything."

"What do you mean?" I whispered back. Something about his really-ready energy set off a few dozen of my alarms, but they could barely be distinguished from the hundreds of other earsplitting alarms going off inside me.

The bailiff started his speech, the judge took his seat, and the packed room of gawkers, media, and who knows who else grew quiet.

I raised my right hand and agreed to be truthful.

I sat down; Bradley stood up.

He asked that the court grant me bail. The whole time he was doing the legal mumbo jumbo, I was tugging on his jacket; he kept swatting my hand away. Wasn't my hearing about dropping the attempted homicide charges? Then bail?

"We need to know who your client is, Mr. Cole," the judge said. "I'm not releasing someone whose name I don't even know. Not even with this." The judge waved what had to be the ballistics report through the air. "Not even for an hour. Not even in your custody."

Bradley cleared his throat. "The defense calls Chief Samuel Way to the stand, your honor."

My head spun around like a crazy woman's. "Daddy!" I screamed it a million times as my father made his way down the aisle.

The judge banged his gavel.

The cameras clicked unmercifully.

"Hello, Sweet Pea." His smile was wide. He reached for me as he passed and our fingertips met. Meredith was beside him. She hissed at me.

After much ado, I was released until the trial to begin in three weeks, but under house arrest at the address listed on my last paycheck: Bradley Cole's. And even better, in Bradley Cole's custody. At that moment, and, well, lots of other moments if I were being truthful, which I'd sworn on a Bible I'd be, there was no custody I'd've rather been in.

"You'd better not put a toe out the door, young lady."

"Yes, sir."

They had to keep me close, because they were waiting on Louisiana to finish crossing their Ts and dotting their Is, then charge me with real-live murder instead of the lame attempted.

The same long-faced judge had the same parting words for me. "You're in a lot of trouble, young lady."

* * *

We put the ankle monitor on Meredith, and she was none too happy about it. We switched it at Bradley's over steaming bowls of gumbo from Mary Mahoney's, crusty French bread, and, before it was over, three bottles of red wine.

"You can't tamper with it." Meredith initially shrugged it off. "The alarm will go off the minute you touch it."

My father reached behind Meredith's ear and pulled out an ankle monitor key.

I clapped my hand over my mouth and laughed at Daddy's magic.

Meredith did not.

"If you can unlock it," she argued, "just leave it on the table. Why do I have to wear it?"

"Because it tracks movement, for one thing," Bradley said, "and it will expect you to do more than lie perfectly still around the clock. And you have to answer the check-in calls every two hours." He gave a nod to the newest intrusion to his home, the speaker unit near the front door. "You have to be Davis when they call."

Meredith tossed a crust of bread in her empty bowl, then

grabbed the wine bottle. "I have a child, you know." She glared at me.

"Riley's fine with Mother." Our father patted her hand. "You need to help your sister, Meredith, or she'll end up in the pokey for something she didn't do."

"How do you know she didn't do it, Daddy?"

"Meredith!" I yelled.

I came out of the shower, which I'd taken behind closed doors for a nice change, wearing my own hair—thank you, Miss Clairol— and ran smack dab into Bradley Cole.

He stared at me for a long moment, getting his first good look at the real me, and then said, "My robe's a little big on you, Red."

Thirty minutes later, I was stretched out on the carpet alarmingly close to Bradley, who was in a nearby chair. I had a real pillow under my head, a real blanket covering me, my real-live father just a hug away, and all that after having a real meal. To top it off, I had a real good wine buzz going.

We let Daddy have the bed. Even though it was barely eight o'clock, the strain of his first big outing since surgery had taken its toll, and he'd need to get a good night's sleep before the drive back to Pine Apple.

"I get the sofa." Meredith smirked at me.

"I don't care if I sleep on the kitchen floor," I said, so relieved to not be tucking myself into a cold cot behind steel bars.

We all looked to Bradley. It was, after all, his home. "I'll go to work and get a room."

"Are you sure?" I asked him as my head found the pillow again.

I don't remember a thing after that, a snatch of conversation, or even saying goodnight to my father. I did nothing but sleep dreamlessly until the fire alarm went off.

I jolted upright, having no idea where I was, what the noise was, or what the flashing red light in the darkness meant until I heard a strange voice repeating my name from the intercom by the door. "Last call, Way."

"Get up, Davis." Meredith was somewhere near in the dark, and she was in no better mood than she'd been in earlier. "Answer the box."

"You do it! You're the one wearing the ankle bracelet."

A throw pillow caught me in the side of the head.

I raced to answer Harrison County Penal System's courtesy call.

Afterward, Meredith already fast asleep again, I drank in my free, dark, and quiet surroundings, which made me want a drink of water. I tiptoed to the kitchen, still hugging my blanket, so grateful for the luxury of drinking water close by. Bathrooms with doors. Socks. Food. Bradley's clothes to sleep in again. At the sink, I slipped the window up an inch to breathe the uncarcerated air.

It was a bright, clear, beautiful night. I could see fourteen billion stars. I turned, wrapping the blanket tighter, and quietly stepped out to the lanai, because I wanted a whole lot more of the free air, and I wanted to see the moon's promise twinkling across the water.

"It's beautiful, isn't it?" the dark wicker lanai sofa asked.

I barely heard him.

I turned slowly. "Are you not *freezing*?"

"I could use another blanket," he said.

"I just happen to have one."

I heard him scoot, making room for me.

"I thought you were going to the hotel."

"Changed my mind."

"My father's two feet away."

"Then be quiet," Bradley Cole said.

TWENTY-THREE

All trails led to Las Vegas, so we took off for there the next morning on a Gulfstream V with the words "Grand Palace Casino" splashed across both sides, nose to tail.

"Let me get this straight." Meredith was fit to be tied. "I sit here and answer the prison box while you go to Vegas on his private plane."

"It's not his, it's his company's. And it's not private-private, Meredith. There are two pilots and a flight attendant. Who serves drinks. Right, Bradley?"

Bradley agreed. "But we get the cabin to ourselves."

My father's eyebrows shot up.

"Lovely." Meredith's mouth was one thin line. "You kids have fun while I sit here." Meredith, tapping a foot, gave me the stink eye, then turned it on Bradley, then Daddy, then back on me.

"Keep the blonde wig close in case they show up to arrest me," I said.

"And what do I do then, Davis? Go to prison for you? A foot too tall and in a blonde wig?"

"If it gets to that," I suggested, "make sure they put you in solitary. There's a really nice CO there."

"This can't be happening."

I turned to Bradley. "Do you have a brother?"

"I think if I did, you'd already know. Why?"

"She needs a boyfriend."

Meredith crossed the room to kill me, when Daddy, from the middle of the sofa, snapped his fingers. She froze. We all turned to

Daddy, who we'd forgotten was in the room. He had my research in mountains everywhere: on the coffee table in front of him, on the cushions to his left and right, and in the floor at his feet. He looked so good, so whole. If I could ignore the pharmaceutical sampler platter he inhaled every few hours, or the way he favored his left leg, or that his right hand absentmindedly explored what had to be the raging scar beneath his cardigan sweater, I wouldn't know what he'd been through.

"What's the connection between the secretary, Natalie, and the deceased, Paul Bergman?"

"The connection?" I scratched the long brunette wig on my head. "None that I know of. Other than she's missing. And he was missing. Why?"

Daddy looked up. "They have a lot of history," he said. "Too much."

Bradley and I looked at each other, probably thinking the same thing: any minute, poor Natalie's body was going to turn up and poor me would be the number one suspect.

"We'd better hurry." Bradley hefted our bags.

* * *

"Gorgeous plane," I said.

"Yeah," he replied. "Only the best for high rollers."

"Right." Two long seconds elapsed. "Do you fly in it often?"

"Not often enough."

We admired the roomy cabin, outfitted like a luxury den with sofas, mahogany side tables, and swiveling leather recliners.

"Just every once in a while?" I asked.

"A lot lately."

I bobbed my head. Smiled.

"And this same run too," he added. "Biloxi, Vegas."

I smiled.

"Vegas, Biloxi." His voice trailed off.

I smiled.

"How about something to drink, Davis?"

"I'm good." I looked out the window at retreating Biloxi. "Thanks, though."

"You're welcome."

"Nice weather, huh?" I asked.

"Really mild for this time of year."

Three seconds crawled by.

"Your sister," he said. "She's a little irritated."

"Boy, I'll say." I tried to laugh, but it came out sideways.

We were naked over all of Louisiana and Texas.

We woke as the landing gear ground from below the leather recliner we were asleep in.

* * *

"This can't be right." We were in a Grand Palace limo.

Bradley was zipping. "Davis, there's not one single thing right about this."

"I wasn't speaking to issues of attorneys and clients and privileges," I said. "I meant this far from town. Why would they be here?" I asked, eyeing the wig stuffed in my purse that I would soon have to don. "Why wouldn't they be in Vegas at one of the Casimiro's casinos?"

"We don't know that Bianca and Eddie are here," Bradley said. "We only know that a Bellissimo credit card was swiped here."

We'd asked the driver to take us to Wild Bill's, a place neither of us had even heard of, closed the privacy screen, and I'm not sure what all happened next. When I looked up, we were forty miles west of Las Vegas proper near the California line in Primm, Nevada.

Bradley picked up a phone to talk to the driver half a block away. The limo was the size of a school bus, and we'd covered every inch of it.

"We need to find a restaurant or a strip mall to park behind." He looked out the window as he talked to the driver. "We're too conspicuous."

Bradley listened.

"Right. Wild Bill's. But don't pull up to the door."

We hiked through tall weeds across an empty lot, zigzagged across four lanes of traffic, then traded natural light and breathable air for casino clamor, stale smoke, and plus-sized waitresses, all on the elderly side, all wearing very skimpy uniforms.

"Wow," I said. "This place needs an image consultant."

Our hands were still hooked by pinkie fingers.

"Let's look around," Bradley suggested. "See what brought them here."

We covered the small casino floor quickly finding nothing out of the ordinary and were about to turn around and try it again when I looked down a long dark hall that led to the restrooms. "There."

"Where?"

It was a bank of Double Whammy Deuces Wild hundred-dollar progressives. There were nine video poker machines in a recessed hall on the way to the restrooms, exactly where everyone wanted to gamble. The tops of the machines were littered with diluted drinks, balled-up napkins, and empty glasses-slash-ashtrays. The second machine from the left was dark and had yellow out-of-order tape in an X across the screen.

Just then, a heavily bearded man exited the men's room, tugging on the dark blue jumpsuit he wore. His Wild Bill's identification hung from around his neck. He was cut through the middle by a tool belt so heavy with hardware that he sounded like Christmas. Bradley stopped him.

"Excuse me."

The guy turned. His eyes were so bloodshot they made mine hurt.

"When will this game be repaired?" Bradley threw a thumb.

"I just answered that same question." He smoothed his moustache with a greasy thumb and index finger. "These machines don't get played twice a year," he said, "and now two people asking." A two-way radio hidden somewhere between the jackhammers on his belt squawked. "There's a slot tech coming tomorrow. Says he is, anyway." Without another word, he jangled off.

Bradley and I looked at each other.

"Let's go snoop at the front desk," I said.

"Good idea."

Bradley slowly pushed a hundred-dollar bill toward the desk clerk. "No," he said, "I don't need a room, but I could use your help."

The woman smiled as she tucked the money in her vest pocket. "Whatcha need?"

"Just a little information about one of your guests."

She perched her fingers over the keyboard in front of her.

"Bianca Sanders," Bradley said.

Tap, tap, tap.

"I have a B. Sanders. Checked in Tuesday," the woman said.

Three days ago, and it took a little mental computation on my part to get there. In the past forty-eight hours, I'd been in jail, in court, a blonde, a redhead, reunited with my father, and my year-long dry spell had ended multiple times. If anyone asked me what time zone we were in, I'd probably answer July.

After a long pause, Bradley asked, "And?"

"That's all I know." The clerk crossed her arms and smiled.

Bradley pulled another hundred out of his wallet.

"And nothing," the woman said, without looking at the screen again. "No room service, no restaurant charges, no minibar, no movies, no phone fees, no casino play."

"What room number?" Bradley asked.

The woman seemed to be weighing the pros and cons of violating such a universal rule of hotelery. Bradley cracking leather again turned out to be in the pro column.

"Sixteen sixty," she said.

The housekeeper on the sixteenth floor, naturally, didn't speak a word of English, but lucky for us, Bradley had a seemingly endless supply of hundred-dollar bills, and he spoke Spanish.

"Mandarin Chinese too." He smiled.

"Wow." I was impressed. But then I was impressed with Bradley Cole before I knew he spoke Swahili and Spanish. I was impressed with Bradley Cole before I met him. I was so impressed with him just then, I could barely walk.

He and the housekeeper had a little chat: enchilada, Si Señor, Feliz Navidad. The translation was that the room hadn't been touched. Another hundred from Bradley's wallet, and then it was touched. By us.

"They're not here."

"How do you know?" Bradley asked.

"I just do," I said. "No one's been here."

His head was in the closet. "Someone's been here."

I took the two steps from the bathroom to the closet and looked in.

"I know that bag," I said.

It was a teal-blue canvas duffel with caramel leather trim.

I used a tissue from the box in the bathroom to unzip it, revealing a neatly folded stack of women's clothes, the perfume of which sent me staggering backward. The bed caught me. It all fell so neatly into place, it would have knocked me down had I not been there already.

"I see boots." Bradley was poking through the bag.

"Brown leather boots."

Bradley turned to me. "Yes."

"Size six."

"I don't know," he said. "Do you want me to look?"

"You don't need to."

* * *

Bradley had a huge corporation behind him, and that meant a residential suite at the Grand Palace overlooking the Las Vegas Strip. (Pretty from a distance, not so much up close.)

"Nice." I let myself fall spread eagle onto the bed and closed my eyes. "A far cry from Wild Bill's."

Bradley's gaze went from me, stretched across the bed, to the phone, blinking red on the desk. Then back to me. Then back to phone.

"Those calls are probably from Biloxi," he said, "and they're probably about you."

He was right. There were two, both from my sister.

Message One:

Davis, the people you worked with before you were a jailbird are looking for you. A man named Jeremy has called and said it was urgent, and a woman named Natalie called and said the same thing. They both want to know where you are.

Surely she didn't tell them.

Message Two:

I'm taking the phone off the hook. The man won't stop calling.

Just then, the phone rang. I screamed.

"Okay." Bradley was trying to calm me, log onto his laptop, and hold the phone between his ear and shoulder at the same time. "Got it. Thanks."

Every casino in town had Double Whammy Deuces Wild, but only three had banks of hundred-dollar progressives: Bellagio, Mandalay Bay, and Wynn. Very upper crust. Just her style.

* * *

Mandalay Bay was our last stop, and that was where she breezed by us, never batting an eye, because she certainly wasn't looking for Bradley, and she was the very reason I didn't look like myself.

It was almost four in the morning; we hadn't slept since we'd napped on the airplane. We were half, if not whole, drunk from hanging around the video poker machines at the first two casinos.

At Bellagio, it was a slot attendant we got chummy with, who told us no one had touched the machines in days.

"To tell you the truth," he said, "no one ever plays these."

At Wynn, it was a waitress. "I've been in these mothers eight hours." She showed us her gold shoes. "And no one's played these. In a few minutes, Candy will be here, and she can tell you if anyone played on her shift last night."

Another round of drinks, then Candy showed. Same gold shoes. Nope.

We weren't surprised, but look under every rock, you know?

There were two things wrong at both casinos: Bellagio only had five machines hooked to the progressive, Wynn had eight, and both had totals inching toward the two-and-a-half-million mark. No one had come anywhere near winning them in months, if not years.

"It has to be the right setup," I explained to Bradley. "Nine machines. Like at Wild Bill's."

"One last stop."

Mandalay Bay was at one end of the Strip, and even in a city famous for not distinguishing between night and day, Mandalay Bay seemed to know what time it was, because it was deserted. We couldn't even find a waitress for (one thing) coffee or for (another thing) information. What we did find were the Double Whammy Deuces Wild, in the right configuration. They were even spaced far enough apart to see the magic button between machines four and five.

"I can't see a thing," Bradley said, peering between the machines. "Must be the tequila."

It was official. We needed coffee. If there had been a warm body to pry information from at Mandalay Bay, we'd have netted nothing. Because we were too spent to pry.

"If I'd known this was coming, I'd have gotten more sleep in prison."

"If we don't hurry," Bradley said, "you'll get to go back and get a nice, long nap."

"Only if you go with me."

He smiled. "We could be cellmates."

The only coffee to be had at that hour was an escalator ride below the casino at a twenty-four-hour bistro. The sound of our footsteps echoed off the domed ceiling until we reached the end of an empty corridor lined with dark retail shops. The bistro was ghostly quiet, with one machine hissing steam, one employee asleep behind the pastry counter, and the rest of the room divided into sections of unoccupied seating.

"Let's take ten." Bradley held two smoking cups of coffee.

"Let's."

We sank into an armless sofa with a view of the corridor.

"Where does this tunnel go?" I blew across the top of my coffee.

"Four Seasons," he said.

"And they don't have Whammys."

"They don't have anything."

"Is it like your casino?" I asked. "Mostly tables?"

"Four Seasons doesn't have a casino at all," he said.

"Wait," I said. "Are we not still on the Strip?"

"We are," Bradley said. "Can you believe there's a hotel here without a casino?"

"I can't. Who stays there?"

"Celebrities," Bradley said, "high rollers who have markers all over town, and basically anyone else with a ton of money who wants to hide."

I let my head fall back. My view reduced to a thin line of the empty corridor.

"Davis," Bradley whispered, "don't fall asleep."

I shook myself awake, then had to rearrange the wig.

"We should have ordered espresso instead of coffee," he said. "It would kick in faster."

If I hadn't been so tired, I'd have laughed, because it was so Natalie—espresso—and before I could finish the thought, she appeared.

Natalie Middleton, wheeling a Louis Vuitton, was a smoky-glass storefront away, on her way to Four Seasons.

I thought I might be hallucinating until she stopped right in front of us, glanced at the bistro, took a quick peek at her watch, then changed her mind and kept going.

It was Natalie, all right.

Without taking my eyes off her, I grabbed at Bradley, aiming for his thigh.

His head was against the sofa back, his eyes closed. "Honestly, Davis, I'm not sure if I can."

* * *

I ran, my love interest/lawyer/landlord on my heels, but no Natalie. She'd disappeared into thin air.

"Davis," Bradley said, "you're so tired. Maybe you just thought you saw her."

"It was her."

There was nothing between the bistro and two huge gold doors that led to Four Seasons except a fire escape, and it was heavy on the dire warnings side.

"Don't do it, Davis. There's an alarm on that door that will wake people up in Dallas. She didn't go in there."

I slid down the cold wall to the floor and rested my head on my knees.

"Come on." Bradley held a hand out. "Let's see if we can find her at the hotel."

Bradley Cole could have had enough hundred-dollar bills in his wallet to wallpaper the front lobby, and there was still no getting any information out of the Four Seasons Customer Service Associate behind the desk. Or his boss. Or the night manager. Who passed me a house phone. On the other end of the line was Security, who said he'd be happy to let me speak to someone at Las Vegas Metro, and he had them on speed dial, at which point we decided to call it a night. We caught a cab and collapsed in the backseat for the four blocks back to Grand Palace, because neither of us could walk.

* * *

We'd been asleep no more than three minutes when I sensed something wrong, a presence of some sort. I sat straight up in the bed to find No Hair twenty feet away in a chair, staring at me. His tie was an eye exam chart. The big E was under the knot.

"Morning," he said. "Or noon, rather."

I was down to the sixth line of the eye exam when I had to squint to read it. R, D, F, C, Z, P. Without taking my eyes off the chart, I reached over and batted at Bradley to wake him up.

"Okay, Davis," he said to the pillow. "This I can do."

No Hair stood. "I ordered coffee. I'll be in the next room."

"No Hair." My first words of the day. "It's Natalie."

"I know."

TWENTY-FOUR

"When did you know?" I tied the belt of my Grand Palace robe tighter and settled in a chair across from No Hair.

"A few days ago," he said, "or a few years ago. I can't decide. You?"

"A long time ago," I said, "or yesterday. I can't decide either."

We locked brains.

"So Natalie and—" It was on the tip of my brain.

"Paul."

"Paul," the word tasted funny, "were behind everything."

No Hair nodded slowly. "And I doubt he's resting in peace."

"Which means Bianca hasn't killed anyone or had anyone killed."

"Bianca's many things," No Hair said, "but to my knowledge, she's not a killer."

"Was I set up to go to jail from the beginning?"

"You stumbled into jail on your own, Davis."

"Yeah." I added sarcasm. "That was all me."

"Hey," he snapped. "Your job was to figure out the game. For whatever reasons—" his eyes narrowed suspiciously "—you took it upon yourself to go rouge and win the game. Plus you blew out a wall in my office. You going to prison was no one's fault."

But my own, he didn't say.

"What's done is done," he said. "From here on out, it's damage control."

"Okay." I placed my coffee cup in the saucer. "What was Bianca's role? Where does she fit in?"

"Nowhere." He scratched his big bald head. "Other than Natalie constantly casting suspicion on Bianca to keep it off herself, it doesn't look like Bianca had a role."

"What about the money?"

"What money?" he asked.

"The game, No Hair. The Whammy game. Bianca made millions on the Whammy game. That's grand theft. That's a role."

"First of all." He pointed a finger at my nose. "My name is Jeremy Covey. You can call me Jeremy, or Mr. Covey, or Hey You. But stop with the no hair business."

"Listen, Hey You." I pointed back. "I grew up in a small town. I've met more people in four months than I've met in my entire life. It isn't easy keeping up with everyone's name."

"Try."

"I will, No Hair. I will."

He rolled his big bald head.

"Who came first?" I asked. "The chicken or the egg?"

"What?"

"Did Bianca start winning before Natalie started killing? Or did Natalie start killing before Bianca started winning? And what does Bianca do with the money? Doesn't she have enough already?"

"Which one of those questions do you want me to answer?" he asked.

"All of them."

He walked me through it. Bianca demanded her errand girl, Natalie, locate the electrician who wired the Double Whammy game, which piqued Natalie's interest. Natalie found and produced Eddie the Ass Crawford. Then Natalie and Teeth, for the good of the Bellissimo, decided to keep an eye on Bianca and Eddie, and when they started winning millions, for the good of themselves, wanted in. But they couldn't figure out how the game was won. They researched it back to the game's programmer, George's son, and wound up with a dead body on their hands. They recruited their own electrician, and quickly had a second body on their hands. At which point, Natalie brought me in. I would tell her how to win the game and either Bianca or I would go down for her crimes.

"So Natalie had two easy marks," I said. "Bianca and me."

"You were a means to an end, Davis." Bradley Cole, wrapped in a robe that matched mine but fit him better, his hair wet from the shower, stood in the doorway between the two rooms. "I doubt you were her target."

"Okay." I threw my hands in the air. "I won't take this personally."

The two men formally introduced themselves, handshakes and such.

"I like your tie, man."

"Thanks," No Hair said.

Bradley poured himself a cup of coffee, patted me on the head, then sat in a chair beside me. He asked, "How did she find Davis to begin with, Jeremy?"

(Who?)

"She found Davis when she found Eddie Crawford," No Hair said. "She jumped all over the look-alike thing, convinced us you knew him well enough and looked enough like her to shut them down."

"When all she really wanted was for someone to show her how the game was won," Bradley said.

"Correct," No Hair agreed, then turned to me. "I told you, you were a perfect storm for the job. You had the background, you had the know-how, you looked just like Bianca, and her partner was your ex-husband, for Pete's sake."

I've never understood the for-Pete's-sake thing. Wouldn't it be "for St. Peter's sake"?

"Natalie's only motive was money?" Bradley asked. "You don't think she tried to kill Richard Sanders?"

"That's certainly a possibility," No Hair said, "heat-of-the-moment, or maybe he touched her coffeepot one too many times. For all we know she was aiming for Bianca but hit Richard instead."

Totally conceivable.

"The only thing we know for certain," No Hair went on, "is that

Natalie wanted money, and for Davis to go down for her crimes, past and present. She realized it wasn't easy to set up someone with Bianca's resources, but having *two* Biancas gave her the perfect out, because you, Davis," his head whipped my way again, "turned out to be an excellent candidate for prison, and she knew it before the rest of us had even heard your name. If she could get you in the door, pin everything on you, get *you* in prison, she could walk away."

I was speechless.

"And you handed it to her on a platter."

I couldn't breathe.

"First and foremost," No Hair went on, "she knew you'd figure out how Bianca was winning the money, something she couldn't do herself, and couldn't get out of the programmer or the electricians."

"I'll tell you one thing." I looked at both men. "I wasn't being paid nearly enough for all this."

No Hair snorted.

"What happened that night?" I asked. "The night you let me go to prison."

No Hair shifted in his seat. Poor seat. "It was my day off," he said, "but I had to go in because we were having a counterfeit chip problem."

At that point, I tiptoed out.

(No, I didn't.)

"Why didn't you just call the police?" Bradley asked.

"Because it was Salito Casimiro."

Ah. Bianca's brother.

"I was on my way to lock the chips in my desk, and I smelled Natalie's perfume. I flattened myself against the wall and watched her leave a gun in Paul's desk."

How in the world No Hair flattened himself against a wall was beyond me.

"I should've taken the gun with me," No Hair said, "but I didn't want to break the chain of evidence, so I locked it and the counterfeit chips in my own desk, and we all know what happened next." He turned my way and thumped me on the head with his eyeballs. "When I told you to stay out of my desk, I meant it."

No Hair went on to fill in the blanks he could. Natalie, with eyes and ears everywhere, knew I'd gone to No Hair's office, knew I'd had the small gun accident, and watched me cash in the counterfeit chips. She saw her opportunity and jumped on it. She got the Sanders' ball rolling by telling Richard his wife was getting ready to kill another Whammy partner, then told Bianca that Richard was on to her. At the same time, she had Teeth pounding the nails in my coffin—erasing my alibi from the hard drive and calling in the casino dogs.

Several questions remained: When did Natalie sleep? (I might have been the only one wondering that.) When did Teeth bite the big one? And the most important question—where was Natalie now?

I looked away and whistled a little tune, "Taps," I think. Natalie Middleton covered all her bases. Tag, Davis, you're it. "Do we have *any* evidence against her?"

"Not an ounce," No Hair said. "Every millimeter of video has been erased, so we don't have her planting the gun. And the one camera that caught the shooting directly doesn't have Natalie in it for a split second. All you see is who everyone believes to be you, Davis, aiming, firing, and running."

"We have to catch her," I said.

"If she isn't already long gone," No Hair said. "She's hit the Whammy game twice this week, stockpiling to make her getaway, because she has a brand new fly in her ointment."

"What fly?" I asked.

"You." Bradley and No Hair said it at the same time.

I bent over double again.

"She didn't count on anyone coming to your rescue, Davis," No Hair said.

"Happy to help." Bradley reached over and gently pushed my hair out of my face. He smiled at me.

* * *

We ordered food while discussing where to go from there, because No Hair was ranting about famine and hypoglycemia. I couldn't have swallowed a bite of food if Natalie walked in, put a gun to my head, and demanded I eat. Bradley asked, "Not even a Pop Tart, Davis?"

When I'd been staring out the window at the Las Vegas Boulevard traffic long enough for Bradley and No Hair to think I might be contemplating jumping, No Hair spoke up.

"You're not going back to prison, Davis. We'll find her."

Her who? I needed both. I had to have Bianca to be cleared on the initial charges, and I had to have Natalie or I'd go down for Teeth's murder.

Before room service knocked on the door with food, Bradley's cell phone rang in the bedroom.

No Hair asked, "Is he speaking Spanish?"

"Yeah," I said. "He's amazing."

"We'd better get moving." Bradley appeared in the doorway, phone in hand. "She's at Wild Bill's."

No Hair rose from his seat. The seat looked so relieved. "She's there to get herself yet another casino payday."

Bradley's phone rang again. He looked at the caller ID, then at me. "It's Harrison County Department of Corrections."

TWENTY-FIVE

Another line on my resume: fugitive from the law.

Meredith slept through a check-in, and that was strike three. Her first strike was stepping over the threshold to reach the newspaper at the elevator.

("I swear it was not even two seconds.")

She missed yet another hello-prison call when she was in the shower.

("No one ever said, 'Don't take a shower.'")

Then the nap.

("I heard it, but I thought it was one of Riley's toys.")

They hauled her in only to find out she wasn't me.

("Jail people don't *listen*. I told them I wasn't you a million times.")

Bradley was also in trouble, but he lied to give us more time. "Look," he said. "My place has windows. She climbed out one while I was asleep."

Someone on the other end yelled at him.

"Have you seen her?" Bradley demanded. "She could slip through the peephole of my front door if she wanted to."

The person on the other end yelled at him more. He winked at me.

"That's exactly what I'm doing. Give me forty-eight hours."

I was listening and pulling on clothes at the same time. I eyed the wig.

Not a chance.

The limo ride to Wild Bill's wasn't nearly as much fun with No

Hair along. "Did it take this long to get there yesterday?" I asked.

For the most part, we rode in silence, each of us examining our own personal worst-case scenarios. Bradley, I'm sure, was in fear of being stripped of his license to practice law, I knew I was in more trouble with Harrison County, Mississippi than ever, and No Hair loudly lamented our leaving before room service arrived, putting him in grave danger of missing two meals in a row for the first time in his life, then starving to death in a limo.

We were all concerned about how it would go down when we were face-to-face with Natalie Middleton. There were three of us, one of her, and No Hair was packing.

Still.

When we weren't riding quietly with our individual demons, we were on our phones. I talked to Daddy and an enraged Meredith, Bradley to his boss and then one of the other attorneys he worked with, and No Hair caught Mr. Sanders up, who sent me greetings, apologies for my troubles, and assurances my job was safe (big whoop just then), and after, No Hair called Mrs. No Hair, which was borderline nauseating. He actually blew smacky kisses to her over the phone. Then he whispered sweet nothings, and I do mean nothings: "No, I love *you* more. No, you don't, I love *you* more. I don't want to hang up first. *You* hang up first. No, *you*." I rolled my eyes so far back in my head, I almost fell out of the limo. Bradley found it, as was his peaceful and accepting nature, quietly entertaining.

Soon enough, we were there. The driver stopped a block away.

"I'm not hiking through the woods," No Hair said.

"There are no woods in Nevada, No Hair."

"You really better watch yourself." His finger was in my face.

"Hey, kids," Bradley said, "be nice. Let's stay focused here."

The three of us looked at each other as we approached the entrance.

No Hair zeroed in on Bradley. "You're the only one she doesn't know," he said. "You go to the game. That'll get her, because she doesn't want anyone to accidentally win it before she does."

"No!" I grabbed Bradley's arm.

"What's she going to do?" No Hair asked. "Shoot him in the middle of the casino?"

"He's right," Bradley said.

I was a nervous wreck.

"We'll hold back," No Hair said to me, "so she won't see us."

"You think?"

He actually growled at me.

During this tête-à-tête, we'd crossed most of the casino floor.

"No worries," I said. "She's not going to see us." I took another step. "We're too late."

Every Whammy seat was empty.

"Maybe she's not down from her hotel room yet." No Hair looked around. "We'd better pull back so she doesn't see us."

"She's not going to see us because she's gone."

They both looked at me.

"Look at the total." I pointed to the LCD display above the nine machines.

The progressive jackpot was $500,403. Make that $500,408.

"It resets at half a million. She just won."

* * *

"No way."

"Davis," Bradley said, "come on."

"I'm not sitting in the same room with him, Bradley. Period."

"You married him twice. You can't sit in the same room with him once?"

We were in a large conference room at Grand Palace. Most of the chairs were occupied, and most of the occupants on their phones.

No Hair was devouring several pounds of raw cow, two heads of lettuce drowning in smelly lumpy white dressing with a pound of smelly lumpy white cheese on top, and a baked potato the size of my foot, another pound of cheese on it. He was washing it down with a gallon of milk.

"Milk?" I asked.

No Hair swallowed. "Calcium, Davis, vitamin D."

"When's the last time you had your cholesterol checked, No Hair?"

"Excuse me, guys." Bradley scooted my chair down the table with me in it, then put his, with him in it, between me and No Hair.

The General Manager of Las Vegas Grand Palace was there, accompanied by two note-taking staffers. Representatives from Four Seasons and the casino manager from Mandalay Bay were there. Four of Las Vegas' boys in blue were there, huddled in a corner, waiting to take me into custody for extradition to Mississippi. Three representatives from the Nevada Gaming Control Board had arrived. Bianca Sanders and Eddie Crawford were on their way from the Casimiro's Mother Ship, the Glitz Resort and Casino, half a mile away.

"The second he walks in and sees me, he'll make a run for it anyway," I said. "So." I waved *whatever*. "It doesn't matter."

An eavesdropping policeman spoke up. "Don't worry, ma'am. We won't let him get away."

After being told for two hours that Bianca Sanders was unavailable, then a tad under the weather, she was given a choice: come in and talk of your own free will or we're coming to get you, and you'll be wearing handcuffs while we talk. Word returned that she'd finally agreed, yet she didn't arrive for almost three additional hours.

When her limo finally pulled in and the entourage escorted up, the sun had set, and the details had been worked out, which was fine, because Bianca hadn't been invited to work out details anyway. She was there to have discharging a firearm in public, fleeing the scene, withholding information, and hindering an investigation explained to her. According to Mississippi, charges against me wouldn't be dropped until charges against her were filed. Eddie Crawford was just a wart on her ass—we had to look at him until she decided to cut him off.

State Gaming Boards shut down Double Whammy Deuces Wild progressives across the map starting in the northeast: Atlantic City, Detroit, and Philly, then Tunica, Biloxi, New Orleans, and Baton Rouge. There were two banks of Whammys in California; they'd been unplugged, along with the Wild Bill's machines, just for good measure. Bellagio's were roped off and dark, just like Wynn's.

The only game in town, coast to coast, was at Mandalay Bay.

Four plainclothes officers were in place.

One of the Four Seasons' representatives closed his phone and addressed the assembly. "There's still no sign of her. The last time her hotel door opened was at nine o'clock this morning when she left in one of our limos for Wild Bill's in Primm."

We all knew the rest of the story. She'd instructed the driver to wait for her, that she'd be no more than an hour, but she never returned to the limo.

Wild Bill's reviewed every inch of surveillance footage. One of the last images of Natalie Middleton was of her stepping into the main cage office to be paid her jackpot of more than $1.2 million dollars. She requested the payment in $50,000 cash and the balance in electronic transfer, which cost her a $5,000 cash tip, but would cost Wild Bill's a fortune when the Gaming Board finished with them over the no-no. She'd presented—of all things—Marci Dunlow's identification, but with her likeness, not mine, on an Arizona driver's license. (Note to self: find out if there really is a Marci Dunlow somewhere.)

There was no footage of her leaving the main cage office, but the cashier, two witnesses, and the casino manager all told the same story: Natalie/Marci asked for directions and was shown out a side door to the adjacent restrooms, where a camera clearly caught her pushing into the Ladies' Room, and from there, she disappeared. She never exited the restroom.

They continued poring over the footage, but it looked as if Natalie Middleton had simply evaporated.

Everyone turned to the three of us.

Well? Twenty faces asked.

Before we could offer an explanation or suggest any possibilities as to where Natalie had disappeared to, Bianca Casimiro Sanders busted in. While I was in the process of picking myself up off the floor, she was in the process of scanning the room. She found me.

"You only wish you looked like me."

No, I most certainly did not.

Then she said, "Your ex-husband is an idiot."

Now that I couldn't argue with.

TWENTY-SIX

Bianca Sanders was in Las Vegas for her father's seventieth birthday. The male passenger on the flight manifest (I'd hacked) was not Eddie Crawford, it was hers and Richard Sanders' thirteen-year-old son, Thomas. The Casimiro family had gathered in Vegas to celebrate a patriarchal birthday.

Or so she said.

She hadn't come to Vegas for a birthday party, she'd come to Vegas for a makeover party.

The Bianca Sanders who burst through the double doors was wearing Steven Tyler's mouth. It was as if someone had taken a bicycle-tire pump to her. Her engorged lips were snarled so far away from everything else on her face, we could see all of her gums. Her lips entered the room a full minute before she did, and as she began her tirade, spitting venom with every word, it soon became obvious that in addition to the lip business (as if that weren't enough), her facial features were completely frozen. She kept the same icy mask on with every word, be they "fluffy baby bunnies" or "I will slit your throat in your sleep."

Under the weather? The woman looked like she'd been thrown under a moving train.

"I've seen her this way before," No Hair said from behind his hand. "She'll go back to normal in a week or so."

In the end, Bianca very reluctantly agreed to return to Biloxi within twenty-four hours to face trumped-up felony charges that would be dismissed as soon as they were read, but the formalities were necessary for my release. No one doubted how little she thought of the program.

The room fell completely silent in her wake: jaws were slack, heads shook, liquor flowed freely.

One of the Grand Palace Vegas attorneys turned to Bradley. "I wonder if that's where your girl is," he said. "At a doctor's office, having her facial features rearranged."

It wasn't a bad idea, and we were fresh out of good ideas, so police details woke plastic surgeons all around town with Natalie's photograph, but the next morning as I was boarding the plane to return to prison in Mississippi, they still hadn't scared her up.

Natalie Middleton had vanished.

* * *

There were worse ways to travel, but still, five hours in the Casimiro jet with two U.S. Marshals—one mine and one Bianca's—was unsettling for me and the end of the world for her.

Her father, Salvatore Casimiro, offered me the ride, apparently not giving his science experiment of a daughter a choice in the matter. I certainly had another choice—Con Air—but I'd have to wait in a Vegas jail cell for days, if not weeks, to catch one of those chartered flights, then zigzag across the country in an air bus with felons being assigned and reassigned. Mississippi was adamant: Go to jail. Go directly to jail. Do not pass go. Do not collect $200. And, no, you aren't in the custody of your attorney any longer, in fact, we have a few choice words for him too.

Bianca washed down two Xanex with vodka, then retreated to the in-flight bedroom for the duration of the trip, her escort dozing at the door. I slept most of the way myself. When I woke, I panicked about going back to jail, and I missed Bradley Cole.

It took more than thirty hours to process me at the prison. If Bianca Sanders had been the least bit cooperative it might have only taken three. As it turned out, Bianca was supposed to spend most of her first forty-eight post-op hours on her back to keep the fresh toxins in her face from running amok. So every hour, on the hour, proceedings came to a complete stop while Bianca stretched out as a masseuse shuttled over from the Bellissimo manipulated her face. She whined, to everyone within earshot, she had no intention of ever brandishing a weapon again, because the aftermath of red tape was unbearable, the locale deplorable.

By the time I was finally released, Bradley had returned to Biloxi. He was waiting for me in the lobby. He stood, he put an arm around me, then led me out of a correctional institution for the second time since we'd met.

"Did you drive by, Bradley?"

"He's not there, Davis."

"Can you take me there?"

"Davis." Bradley stopped me in the dark parking lot. "He's not there. I asked the limo drivers if they'd seen him, and they haven't. In more than two weeks."

My heart hurt. I looked up and memorized every line of sweet Bradley's face. "Could you take me to the Bellissimo anyway?"

"Why?"

"I need sleep."

"Then let's take you home," he said.

"I can't go to Pine Apple, Bradley. I can't cross a state line until this is over."

"Davis," he said. "Your lease isn't up for another two months."

* * *

Richard Sanders returned to the Bellissimo with much fanfare. It was a new day. On his arm, his wife. Neither No Hair nor I said a word. A large part of our job was to look the other way. Bianca Casimiro Sanders summoned me her first morning back in Biloxi. She picked a really bad time to call.

"Don't answer it."

"I have to, Bradley. It's the Bat phone."

I stepped off the elevator onto the Elvis floor, then was escorted to Mrs. Sanders. She wore full makeup, perfect hair, a black silk robe, and black stiletto heels. At eight in the morning. At her feet were two furry rats, or maybe small dogs that looked like furry rats, both wearing black silk bows on their little heads. The urgent matter Bianca so rudely interrupted my morning for went like this: "You'll stand in for me at events. Ribbon-cuttings and such. That'll be all."

Mr. Sanders hired a new secretary who was just that—a secretary. She answered the phone, made appointments and coffee, and ushered people in and out. When five o'clock rolled around, she punched out. She didn't know Richard Sanders' blood type and she never would.

I got a raise and an office. No Hair was promoted; he was my new boss, and we were looking for a third, and possibly fourth, addition to our team. I tracked down Fantasy Erb from my behind-bars days—not that many days ago, actually—and No Hair agreed to interview her. She was savvy, strong, she knew how to follow rules and when to show mercy. I wanted her in quickly because there was something suspicious going on at Shimmy, the Bellissimo's ridiculously popular (and ridiculously loud) nightclub, involving almost-naked dancers, and I wanted no part of almost-naked dancing. In public, anyway.

Meanwhile, No Hair and I spent long days digging, poring, and searching for clues as to Natalie's whereabouts, but there were none to be found. It had been six days since she'd disappeared from the restroom in Primm, Nevada, and with each tick of the clock, the possibility of finding her diminished.

"She's in Jamaica," No Hair suggested. "Or St. Bart's. We'll never find her."

A bench warrant had been issued for the contents of Natalie's condo in New Orleans, and we were digging through the whole bunch of not-much-help retrieved from there. No other warrants had been issued, because the last thing we wanted to do was scare her away. Our only hope was that she'd slip up and surface, then we'd nail her.

I was hard at work when I felt No Hair staring at me, and not for the first time since we'd returned.

"What's eating at you, Davis?" he asked.

I had nothing to lose by saying it out loud. "George."

"The cab driver?"

PMS, or PMDD, or INSANITY took over, because it turned out I did have something to lose by saying it aloud—hydration. I started crying and I couldn't stop.

"Good grief." No Hair jumped up and began looking for something—a baseball bat, a tranquilizer gun, a box of Kleenex. "Get a grip, Davis." He stood two feet away from me and awkwardly patted my back. "There, there, now. Come on and stop leaking. What's the problem?" No Hair scanned the room, looking for backup, I imagine. "Has something happened to the old guy?"

"That's just it, No Hair." I used my sleeve. Then I used my other sleeve. "I think Natalie got him. He's absolutely nowhere. He's gone."

"I didn't realize you two were so close." Beads of sweat had popped out all over No Hair. He nervously tugged on Albert Einstein, who was on his tie. You'd think after twenty-two years of marriage, he'd have a little experience with females having smallish meltdowns. He stumbled around, then found a seat a comfortable distance from me. "He's probably right outside, sleeping in his cab."

"He is not," I barely said it aloud. "I check twice, sometimes ten times a day, and he's not there. She got him. The only one smarter than him is her. George had Natalie's number days before we did, he tried to take her down alone, and we'll never find his body." I took a deep shaky breath. "There'll never be justice for his son's death, and now there'll never be justice for his."

"You don't know that," No Hair said. "I'll tell you what. I'll help you find him as soon as the court business is over."

I sniffed. "You promise?"

No Hair tried to crack a smile. I recognized it as such because I'd seen him do it before, but the first few times I mistook it for food poisoning.

"So how's it going with you and the lawyer?" He cautiously

changed the subject.

I mopped my tears, sat back, and sighed/smiled.

"See?" No Hair asked. "I told you."

"You didn't tell me shit, No Hair."

"I wish you'd watch your language, Davis. Do you talk like that in front of him?"

* * *

The first of what would be many hearings was set for Monday morning, eight sharp, all parties be present or be in contempt. The proceedings were closed so the media would have as little information as possible, because wherever Natalie Middleton was, she was staying on top of things, of that we had no doubt. If just one reporter heard her name, it'd be over.

The State would drop all charges against me after I proved myself innocent in a court of law. That meant Bianca Sanders on the stand, testifying on my behalf.

The media was starving for any crumb of news. To compensate for what they didn't know, they filled the airways and information outlets with what they did know, which was amazingly little. The evening before, Bradley and I, having taken a break from watching the Wild Bill surveillance footage for the umpteenth time, were channel surfing and breezed by a still of a high school yearbook photograph of me in my majorette finery. I grabbed for the remote to make it go away.

"No!" Bradley held it a mile out of my reach. "I want to see."

Representatives from all sorts of government agencies had all sorts of business to discuss with Eddie Crawford, so naturally, he'd disappeared.

Fine by me.

Bianca Sanders told the authorities Edward was dead to her, and don't bring up his name again in her presence, which forced the rest of us to do all the Eddie explaining, including what we knew or didn't know of what might possibly be a Sanders' Open

Marriage policy.

"Were Bianca Sanders and your ex-husband having an affair?" a state gaming agent asked me.

"I don't know, and I don't want to know," I said.

"Don't you think her helping him siphon millions from the Double Whammy game is strong evidence of an extramarital affair?"

"Unfortunately, my ex-husband didn't profit from the Double Whammy game, so no. We believe Bianca Sanders, in her own misguided way, thought she was protecting her husband by participating in the Whammy con."

"Protect her husband from what?" the agent asked.

"Her brother."

"The counterfeiter?"

"Yes," I said. "We believe he was blackmailing Mrs. Sanders."

"You believe?"

"We're looking into it."

"Do you have any idea where he is?"

"The brother?" I asked.

"Your ex-husband."

"Pine Apple, Alabama."

He scribbled it down.

"No," I said. "Two words. Pine. Apple."

"You're kidding, right? That's hilarious. And what did you say your name was?"

* * *

We knew there'd be media coverage, but we had absolutely no idea there'd be a convention. Halfway down the courthouse steps and bunched in a semi-circle around the doors, reporters and cameras were twenty-deep, clearly very invested in something. Or someone.

"What in the world?" Bradley asked.

"I wish I had a hat," I said.

"Bianca must be holding a press conference."

We couldn't find an empty parking space for several blocks.

"Should we go in the back way?"

"No," Bradley said, his eyes on the media circus. "Let's see what the press is so interested in."

He took a step, then turned to see me rooted to the sidewalk.

"Come on, Davis. You have to do this." He held his hand out. "Whatever they ask, just say no comment."

I was afraid that as soon as one of them saw me we'd be trampled. A few at the back of the pack seemed to recognize me, but only glanced. No microphones were shoved my way.

Bradley and I shrugged.

"Maybe this will go easier than we thought," he said.

"What in the world are they all looking at?"

Natalie Middleton, wearing the same clothes she'd been in eleven days earlier, looked like she'd crawled to Biloxi on her hands and knees from Wild Bill's Casino in Primm, Nevada. She was chained to the massive courthouse doors. She was so thoroughly chained that upon being discovered, a welding crew had been called. That idea was scrapped after they all but fried her leg, so a second crew had been called in, that one with chainsaws. It would seem chainsaw crews didn't move with anywhere near the efficiency of news crews, because the only tools present were cameras.

The crowd, recognizing me, parted. Bradley and I stopped a few feet away.

Her left leg was tucked beneath her, propping her up. Her right arm, twisted behind her head, was chained to the bent leg pulley fashion, so if she moved one she risked injury to the other. She looked mighty uncomfortable. Her left arm was stretched above her head, chained to the brass handles of the massive courthouse doors, the opposite leg, the one that had a big red welding welt across her bare ankle, to a stone pillar.

She wasn't going anywhere.

Natalie and I shared a long cold look.

There were so many things I'd like to have said to her, but

changed my mind. Every path had its puddle. Natalie Middleton landed in hers face first, and she would drown in it. She knew it. She didn't need to hear it from me.

I stepped away, shielded my eyes against the sun, and began searching the street.

He was standing at parade rest beside his cab.

My hands flew to my heart.

He saluted me, then drove away.

DOUBLE DIP

Gretchen Archer

A Davis Way Crime Caper (#2)

Keep reading for a sneak preview of the next book in the series.

ONE

The Gulf Coast has two seasons: scorching and slot tournament.

It goes from one to the other in a matter of hours.

I grew up two hundred miles north of the coast in Pine Apple, Alabama, where I was a police officer for six years and where we had four seasons, the regular ones. I moved south to take a job on an undercover security team at the Bellissimo Resort and Casino in Biloxi, Mississippi, where there were only two temperatures: 120 degrees and 21 degrees. With the beach out the back door, it was easy to keep casino patrons happy during Season One, but to keep them happy and thawed during Season Two it took slot machine tournaments that began the day the Bellissimo pool was covered and didn't end until it was uncovered. The big sign said, "Pool Closed for Slot Tournament Season! See you in April! Good luck!"

My name is Davis Way. I'm almost thirty-three years old, almost five foot three, and my hair is almost red. I don't understand abrupt changes in weather, and I don't understand slot tournaments. I get tennis, golf, and ping-pong tournaments; they involve skill and strategy. Pushing the button on a slot machine and coming out the champion took no skill, no strategy, no pings or pongs. It took one thing—luck.

My immediate supervisor was a man named Jeremy Covey. He didn't have a hair on his head, not even an eyebrow or eyelash. Being terrible with names, I called him No Hair until I could remember Jeremy. By the time I remembered, it was always too late. It was No Hair Jeremy who first aimed those two words at me—slot and tournament—way back in the summer. (Last week.)

We were in our Friday afternoon sit-down with our boss,

Richard Sanders, President and CEO of the Bellissimo, in the back of a limo on our way to the airport. Mr. Sanders had an appointment on the other side of the globe and we were accompanying him, but only as far as his Gulfstream 650. The car pulled to a stop on the tarmac when No Hair casually changed my weekend plans.

"One more thing." No Hair looked at me. "Davis."

I didn't need one more thing. It had been a long week already. My partner, Fantasy, and I had pulled quadruples, working from sunup Monday until three seconds earlier at the casino's Plethora Buffet, of all places, waiting tables, of all things. The tips were pathetic. The head chef—who did no cheffing; he supervised large blocks of unidentifiable frozen food being lowered into big silver pans, unevenly top-coated with fake cheese, then baked to almost burnt—was plowing through $2,500 a week in snow crab legs, and snow crab legs weren't on the buffet menu. We caught him selling the nasty things—I'm finned-fish intolerant—out of the back of his Kia Cadenza in the parking lot of the U-Can-Pawn. The chef was running a crab con on the Bellissimo's dime.

No Hair called it a "classic double dip."

"Everyone in the whole place double dips, No Hair. Those buffet people will stick their forks in anything."

"I'm not talking about his table manners, Davis. I'm saying he's getting a paycheck and stealing from us at the same time."

Right.

Fantasy and I, when we finally caught up with double-dip man, spoke to him about how ill-advised his program was, then passed him to Biloxi Metro, me holding my nose the entire time. The red tape afterward had kept us from attending our regularly scheduled Friday meeting with the boss in his office, and we had one eye on the weekend when No Hair came up with the bright idea that we ride with Mr. Sanders to the airport. Which was fine—I was always up for a road trip—except Fantasy and I smelled like shark bait.

"You two sit over there." No Hair pointed to the little bitty bench almost in the front seat. Mr. Sanders, a football field away at the other end of the car, asked his driver, a man named Crisp, to crank up the air and crack his windows.

Richard Sanders, in addition to signing everyone's paycheck, was married to the casino owner's daughter. She was a handful. He, on the other hand, was a great boss, a nice guy, an honest man, and extra handsome. He was on the cover of *Forbes* magazine a few months earlier. "Gulf Coast's Golden Boy Gambles It All on Macau."

Mr. Sanders thanked us for solving the crab caper, then told us he'd see us on Skype the next Friday, the Friday after that, and the Friday after that, because he would be on the other side of the world for that many Fridays.

"If negotiations go well, I'll be back for the big tournament." He inventoried a leather portfolio full of personal electronic devices between his shoes, then looked up. "You three keep things to a dull roar while I'm away."

Of course, we nodded. Will do.

We pulled into the private jet airport and an electric gate slid open. The limo was a foot from the airplane when No Hair piped up with his "one more thing."

"You're going to help us kick off slot tournament season this weekend, Davis." He passed me a skinny folder. "Fantasy," he turned to my skinny partner, who'd been my Corrections Officer in prison (long long story), "you'll be backing her up. Stay close."

"Wait," I said. "I can't work this weekend."

The trunk of the limo popped open as Mr. Sanders gathered his iThings. He had a leg out the door. "Is there a problem, Davis?"

"No, sir." I showed him my teeth.

"I'll see you all in a few weeks," he said. "Hold down the fort."

I let Mr. Sanders get a foot from the limo before I pounced. "No Hair!"

"Don't start with me, Davis."

It would take two of me to make up one of No Hair's legs, so I generally didn't start with him. "I have a moving truck coming tomorrow," I said. "I haven't packed a single thing."

"Work it out." He helped himself to Mr. Sanders' recently vacated seat, rocking the whole limo in the process. "I know it's last minute, but it can't be helped. Something caught my eye, and you need to play in the tournament."

"What?"

"The slot tournament," he said. "You're playing in it."

"No," I said. "What caught your eye?"

"A little old lady. There's a seventy-four-year-old woman registered for every slot tournament from now till summer," he said, "and her home address is a church in Alabama."

"Is she a priest?" Fantasy stretched her legs. Which were twice the length of mine. And above her long legs, she was stunningly pretty. Fantasy had ink-black hair she'd recently cut into a pixie, skin the color of a hazelnut caffè latte, and sky-blue eyes. "Who lives at a church in Alabama?"

"Exactly," No Hair said. "I want to know who lives at a church in Alabama." He turned on me. "I want to know her every move. I want to know who she makes eye contact with. How many cats she has. I want to know her shoe size."

"Why do you want to know her shoe size?"

"You get my drift, Davis."

I got his drift.

"Step on it, Crisp," No Hair said. "I've got to get home to the missus." He burrowed in, closed his eyes, and played possum until we were back at the Bellissimo. Crisp slid to a stop behind No Hair's car in the executive parking lot. "See you Monday, ladies."

I turned to Fantasy in a panic.

She patted my knee. "You can do this."

"I don't even know what a slot tournament is." My Bellissimo undercover adventures, to date, hadn't included a slot tournament. I'd scrubbed shower stalls, dealt Texas Hold 'Em, and decorated wedding cupcakes, but I hadn't been anywhere near a slot tournament.

"It's self-explanatory," she said. "A group of people play slot machines at the same time. The highest score wins. Here." She held out a hand for the folder. "Let me see."

I passed it to her.

She flipped through. "You don't even have to be there until

nine tomorrow morning." She held up a DMV portrait of a Senior Citizen. "And you need to find this lady and ask her how many cats she has."

That lady was everyone's grandmother: deep laugh lines, wire-rimmed eyeglasses, embellished cardigan sweater. (Shasta daisies.)

"And then what?" I wondered aloud. "Shoot her?"

"Get her shoe size." Fantasy passed the folder back to me. "Surely, it won't take shooting her to find out what size shoes she wears. Go home. Sleep on it. Figure it out in the morning."

Crisp let us out at our parking lot, the peasant parking lot, four miles away from everything else in the world.

"Come with me to the office so I can find something to wear," I said. "I don't want to come to work any earlier than I have to tomorrow."

"Gladly." She fanned her face. "I need to change clothes."

Fantasy was an excellent partner. She was up for anything, fearless, and didn't take prisoners. Probably from being a prison guard for seven years. In addition to her job skills, she always had my back, mediated between me and No Hair, and provided valuable family and relationship counseling, two things I found myself in occasional need of. We made a good team: Davis Way and Fantasy Erb, Bellissimo Super Secret Spies. With names no one caught the first go-around.

We swiped ourselves into the building, then took separate paths to our workspace, which was located below the casino and sea level. Fantasy and I operated as far under the radar as possible. We kept low profiles so we could infiltrate various departments within the Bellissimo without being recognized, and spent just as much time posing as casino patrons, so we traveled the property independently and often incognito, heads ducked and hugging the walls. Working in stealth mode required us to have offices that were impossible to get to. Like Hawaii. But once there, worth it. Just like Hawaii. We made our way there.

(Our offices, not Hawaii.)

We met up at an unmarked door between Shakes, an ice cream parlor, and Gamer, a kid casino, in a no-traffic corner of the mezzanine above the main lobby of the hotel. From there, we followed a cold, dark, scary service hall, then used a keypad to enter a door that led to an elevator hidden on a dark wall. If someone were to stumble onto our space, they'd stumble right back out as fast as they could. If someone were looking for our space, they wouldn't be able to find it with a tour guide, a GPS, and a bluetick coonhound. If someone went to all the trouble of following us to our space, then managed to hack the keypad, they wouldn't be able to activate the elevator. Elevator operation was facial recognition only, and the elevator only recognized these faces: mine, Fantasy's, No Hair's, Mr. Sanders', and by default, Mrs. Sanders'. It was all very covert, very high tech, and very *Get Smart*.

We saw the blood as soon as the elevator doors parted.

Fantasy went right. I went left.

"Clear."

"Clear."

We backed into the elevator dodging a smeared trail of drying blood that led to a puddle in the corner. Roll call. Of the five people who had access to our elevator, we knew we weren't bleeding. No Hair had just left the property, and Mr. Sanders had just left the hemisphere. That left the wife, Bianca Sanders.

"What in the world?" Fantasy closed her eyes and let the back of her head hit the elevator wall.

On a huge sigh, I swiped, the elevator doors closed, and down we went. "I guess we're about to find out."

The elevator doors opened to more blood.

We followed the trail down the hall to our office. Fantasy had her gun drawn and signaled the countdown. On one, we blasted through. At first, we thought our offices were on fire. Bianca Sanders was stretched out on one of the sofas, and from the haze of smoke filling the room, she must have been chain smoking her long skinny cigarettes three at a time for the past hour. Her face was a ten on a grayscale of eight. Her left foot was wrapped in a bloody towel, and there was blood all over our nice gold sofa.

Fantasy batted through the smoke. "What's going *on* here?"

Bianca Sanders dropped her lit cigarette in the general

direction of the drinking glass she was using for an ashtray, missed, and announced, "I've been shot," before passing out, then tumbling off the sofa onto our nice, clean carpet.

I ran. Locked myself in the bathroom. It was all too much: the trunk full of snow crab legs, sitting the wrong way in the limo, the blood, the smoke, Bianca's bloody foot, because I was pretty sure I was pregnant.

PINE APPLE DELICIOUSNESS
From the Kitchens of Bellissimo Players Club Members

Pine Apple Escape
By Christine James

1 ounce Malibu rum
1 ounce banana liqueur
1 ounce Midori melon liqueur
3 to 4 ounces pineapple juice
Small splash of grenadine
Splash of sweet and sour mix

Add all ingredients in a tall glass filled with ice. Stir. Put a straw in it. Put your feet up.

Pine Apple Margaritas
By Linda Erickson

3 cups pineapple juice
1 1/2 to 1 3/4 cups orange juice
2 ounces fresh lime juice
1 cup triple sec
1 cup tequila
Ice
Salt for rim of glass
Fresh pineapple and lime slices

Mix fruit juices, triple sec, and tequila together until well combined. Rub rim of glass with a lime slice and dip in salt. Serve over ice and garnish with pineapple and lime slices. Makes 2 quarts.

Pine Apple Casserole
By Marilyn Starkey

2 (20 ounce) cans chunk pineapple, drained, 1/4 cup juice reserved
1/2 cup sugar
6 tablespoons flour
2 cups grated cheddar cheese
1 sleeve Ritz crackers
1 stick butter, melted

Combine sugar, flour, and cheese. Mix in pineapple chunks and reserved juice. Pour into casserole dish. In a separate bowl, crush the Ritz crackers, then add the melted butter. Stir well. Spread the cracker mixture evenly over the pineapple mixture. Bake at 350 degrees for 30 minutes.

Pine Apple Delight
By Amy Weaver

1 box of Pistachio instant pudding mix
2 cups of miniature marshmallows
1 large can crushed pineapple
1 (8 ounce) whipped topping
1 (4 ounce) chopped pecans

Toss pudding mix and marshmallows in a large bowl. Stir in the crushed pineapple. Add whipped topping and mix all ingredients thoroughly. Sprinkle pecans on top. Cover and chill overnight.

Pine Apple Cashew Chicken
By Tonette Joyce

2 tablespoons sesame oil
2 teaspoons ground ginger
1 tablespoon fresh garlic
Salt and pepper
2 pounds boneless chicken breasts cut into 2-inch strips
1 (20 ounce) can pineapple pieces in juice
2 ribs celery, chopped
1 large onion, chopped
1/4 cup chives
1 large sweet pepper (any color), chopped
2 tablespoons sweet and sour sauce
1 tablespoon rice wine vinegar
1 teaspoon corn starch
1 cup cashews
Asian 5-Spice, optional for extra "heat"

Prepare rice, rice noodles, vermicelli, or couscous. Drain pineapple and reserve juice. Add oil to pan with the ginger, garlic, salt, and pepper. Add chicken, brown quickly, then remove from pan and set aside. Add sweet and sour sauce, celery, onion, bell pepper, chives, and drained pineapple to pan, fry until slightly browned. Stir in rice vinegar. Mix the corn starch with the reserved pineapple juice and add to pan. Add browned chicken and simmer until cooked thoroughly. Fold in cashews just before serving over the rice, noodles, pasta, or couscous. For a spicier dish, add Asian 5-Spice to taste.

Grilled Pine Apple Wedges with Rum Sauce
By Cynthia Blain

Large whole ripe golden pineapple, washed, dried, cut (leave tops on) into four vertical quarters, then cored
2 to 3 limes, sliced
1 1/2 cups light or dark brown sugar
1 teaspoon ground ginger or ground cinnamon
1 stick butter, melted
1/4 to 1/2 cup white or gold rum
Maraschino cherries, halved (optional)
Fresh mint sprigs for garnish (optional)

Cut 6-8 vertical slits in each pineapple wedge, inserting a slice of lime in each. Place prepared pineapple wedges in individual heavy-duty foil packets. Mix all sauce ingredients and pour over each wedge equally. Add cherries. Wrap each wedge, sealing foil tightly. Place foil packets seam up on a hot grill and cook for 15-20 minutes, turning for even cooking. Can be eaten from individual foil packets or transferred to a serving dish. (Don't forget the sauce!) Serve with ice cream or sweetened whipped cream if desired. Garnish with sprig of mint. Serves four.

Spectacular Pine Apple Pie
By Lisa Hudson

1 (20 ounce) can crushed pineapple, drained
1 (14 ounce) can sweetened condensed milk
1 (8 ounce) whipped topping
1/2 cup chopped pecans
1 large lemon or 1/4 cup lemon juice
1 graham cracker pie crust

In a large bowl, mix sweetened condensed milk and whipped topping. Add drained pineapple. Add pecans and lemon juice. Gently fold. Pour into pie shell. Garnish as desired with crushed pineapple and chopped pecans. Freeze for a minimum of two hours prior to serving.

Pine Apple Pudding
By Melanie Edwards

1 egg
1/2 cup sugar
1 cup milk
2 tablespoons plain flour
2 tablespoons butter
1 can crushed pineapple, drained
1/2 pint whipping cream (whipped)
Graham cracker crumbs
Chopped pecans

Mix egg, sugar, milk, flour, and butter. Cook until thick. Add pineapple. Cool. Layer crumbs, custard, nuts, whipped cream. Refrigerate leftovers.

Pine Apple Poke Cake
By Shannon McCarty

1 yellow cake mix
1 package Dream Whip
1 large box instant vanilla pudding
1 (16 ounce) can crushed pineapple
1 cup sugar
1 (16 ounce) whipped topping

Bake cake as directed on Dream Whip box for Dream Cake. While cake is baking, in a saucepan, mix undrained pineapple and sugar and cook over medium heat until sugar is dissolved. While cake is still hot, poke holes with a straw, then pour pineapple and sugar mixture on top. Mix pudding according to package directions and pour over top of cake. Allow pudding to set, cake to cool, then frost with whipped topping.

Gretchen Archer

Gretchen Archer is a Tennessee housewife who began writing when her daughters, seeking higher educations, ran off and left her. She lives on Lookout Mountain with her husband, son, and a Yorkie named Bently. *Double Whammy* is her first Davis Way crime caper. You can visit her at www.gretchenarcher.com.

Made in the
USA
Monee, IL